For Carol,

Anne, Paul, and James

THE MABINOGI
AND OTHER
MEDIEVAL WELSH TALES

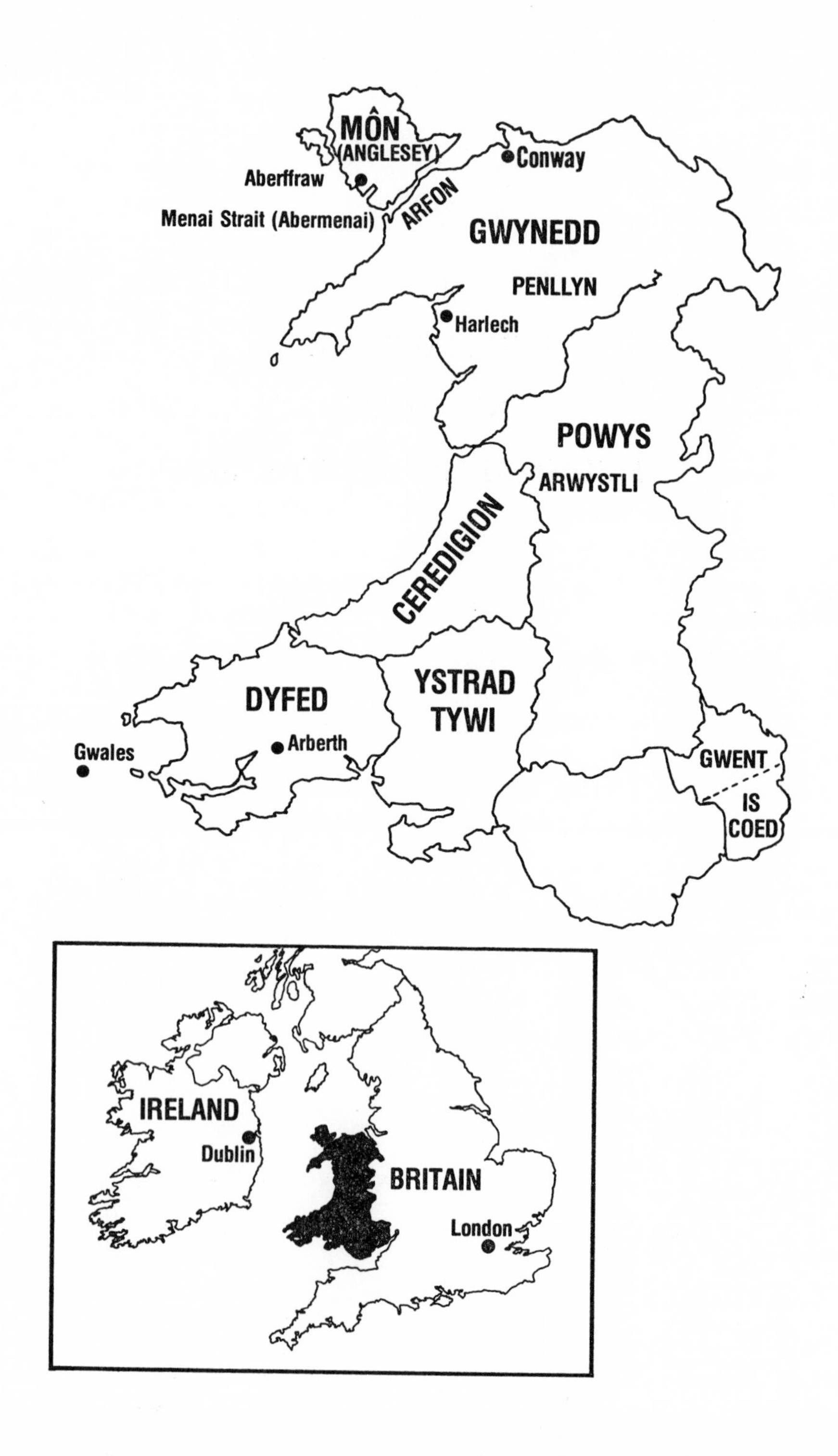

MÔN
(ANGLESEY)
Aberffraw
Menai Strait (Abermenai)
ARFON
Conway
GWYNEDD
PENLLYN
Harlech
POWYS
ARWYSTLI
CEREDIGION
DYFED
YSTRAD
TYWI
Gwales
Arberth
GWENT
IS
COED
IRELAND
Dublin
BRITAIN
London

The Mabinogi and other Medieval Welsh Tales

Translated,
with an Introduction,
by

PATRICK K. FORD

UNIVERSITY OF CALIFORNIA PRESS
BERKELEY LOS ANGELES LONDON
1977

University of California Press
Berkeley and Los Angeles, California

University of California Press, Ltd.
London, England

Library of Congress Catalog Card Number: 76–3885

Printed in the United States of America

Contents

Preface

The earliest important translation of the *mabinogi* into English was that by Lady Charlotte Guest. It is a graceful and romantic rendition, which was well suited to the tastes of her mid-nineteenth-century audiences. Its value for modern students of early Welsh literature is that it has been the only available English translation of the important Taliesin saga. More recently, we have had the rigorously accurate and literal translation of Thomas Jones and Gwyn Jones. It lacks the Taliesin material, but is remarkably faithful to the texts it translates; it remains a valuable English version of the *mabinogi* proper and other medieval Welsh tales. The present collection is not intended to supersede the Jones and Jones *The Maginogion*, but to offer a version that, while preserving the style and meaning of the original, is less archaic in tone; it seeks further to offer English readers the first translation of the Taliesin material in over a hundred years, in an authentic and accurate version.

The *mabinogi* and the other tales are rich sources of Celtic mythological tradition, but they are not less impressive for their literary virtuosity. The translation attempts to reflect faithfully both these qualities, and I have endeavored above all to provide a version that would be readable by university-level students in courses in mythology and medieval literature as well as by the general public. My primary concern is with medieval expressions of native mythological themes, and the selection of texts translated here reflects that concern. The three Arthurian romances, usually grouped with the *mabinogi* but here omitted, are excellent examples of medieval Welsh storytelling, but whatever their mythological underpinnings, they are undeniably romances. "The Dream of Rhonabwy" and "The Dream of Maxen Wledig" fall into yet another class that reflects a much more conscious literary activity, and have also been excluded.

The present translation, like that of the Joneses, is based chiefly upon the diplomatic edition of the White Book of Rhydderch, although readings from the Red Book of Hergest have been adopted when they represent, in my view, the more accurate meaning, or when they supplement significantly the readings from the White Book or supply omissions. I have tried to remain faithful to the text, but it was not always possible to do so and make sense in English. When that happened, I took liberties while remaining true, I hope, to the spirit of the original. For example, I have used the second person plural pronoun throughout; the singular *thou* and its other forms are archaic in English and tend to convey a quaintness that does not exist in the original, where the two forms are used only to distinguish number, not politness and familiarity.

The Taliesin and Gwion Bach tales are translated from the late seventeenth-century manuscript National Library of Wales MS. 6209E, copied by David Parry (an amanuensis of Edward Lhuyd) from the sixteenth-century text of Elis Gruffydd. Gruffydd's copy, NLW MS. 5276D, unfortunately lacks a leaf. Lady Guest did not have access to this manuscript; her translation of the tale, which differs substantially from the one offered here, was based on eighteenth-century Welsh manuscript sources.

The notes in Sir Ifor Williams's *Pedeir Keinc y Mabinogi* were of great assistance in working out some of the more resistant passages in the four branches, as was his edition (and the later one by Dr. Brynley Roberts) of the tale of "Lludd and Lleuelys." And of course scholarship published since the appearance of the Joneses' translation has shed considerable light on many of the problems presented by the material translated here.

The head-notes to each tale are designed to help the reader who is approaching these tales for the first time. The style and content of the stories does not conform to that of the usual short story that modern readers are familiar with, or even to the "fairy-tales" of traditional cultures. Themes are often confused, narrative threads dropped, and events sometimes are so bizarre that comprehension is difficult, to say the least. The head-notes will discuss briefly and generally the thematic and stylistic elements of each tale.

But however helpful these head-notes may be as brief guides to the individual tales, they cannot serve as an introduction to the tradition that underlies them. To do that properly, we must try to understand why tales were grouped together in a particular way as *mabinogi* and what the ingredients of individual tales were. We should like to know what the relationship among various tales was and what purpose they served. Because we are dealing with traditional material, we cannot isolate the Welsh stories, but must examine them in the light of tales that survived in the medieval repertory of a sister Celtic country, Ireland. When the meaning of the story is still obscure, we must draw on evidence from other Indo-European cultures. This enterprise will involve us in some rather technical matters, but it is hoped that the non-specialist will find enlightment in the pages of the Introduction, once he has become familiar with the tales.

It is difficult to know where to begin to acknowledge the abundant assistance this work has received. First of all, I must express my appreciation to the Committee on International Exchange of Persons (Fulbright Program), which made it possible for me to work in Wales on a senior research fellowship during 1973–74. The hospitality of the University College of Wales at Aberystwyth and its Principal, Sir Goronwy Daniel, provided a very pleasant interlude from my teaching duties at the University of California. More specifically, the Department of Welsh made me feel very much at home and did its utmost to facilitate my work at every stage. Nor could I have accomplished even a small part of the labors I undertook without the splendid and expert advice and assistance I received from the staff members of the National Library of Wales. To them and to the Librarian, Mr. David Jenkins, I extend my sincere thanks. To Dr. R. Geraint Gruffydd, Professor of Welsh at Aberystwyth, and Dr. Brynley Roberts I owe a very special debt. Both read the translations (and in the case of the Taliesin material, my transcription of the manuscript as well) and offered numerous valuable suggestions. Most of these were gratefully accepted, but others I resisted, determined for one reason or another that my reading was defensible; the responsibility for any failure, therefore, is entirely my own. It was my great good fortune that during the same period Aberystwyth was the residence of the distinguished American linguist and Celticist, Professor Eric Hamp of the University of Chicago. It is a pleasure to acknowledge his tutelage and friendship. More recently, my colleague, Professor

Daniel Melia of the University of California at Berkeley, and my former professor at Harvard University, Charles W. Dunn, read the complete typescript and offered many valuable suggestions; I am very grateful to both of them. Finally, there is a kind of support and encouragement that is difficult to specify, so manifold are its dimensions. I have left that acknowledgment to the dedication page.

P. K. F.

Los Angeles
August 1976

Introduction

The word *mabinogi* applies properly to only the first four tales collected and translated here.[1] They are otherwise known as the "four branches," a designation whose precise meaning is as yet not clear. For that matter, neither is the term *mabinogi* understood clearly, although we shall try to shed some light on it. "Lludd and Lleuelys" and "Culhwch and Olwen" are purely native tales; the former reaches back into Celtic antiquity and has analogues in Irish mythological tradition, and the latter, despite its resemblance to international types of this tale and its well-known folktale motifs, is firmly rooted in native tradition. "The Tale of Gwion Bach" and its sequel "The Tale of Taliesin" come from late manuscripts, but together they are a mine of information about the archetypal poet of Welsh tradition. A fair amount of attention has been given to purely external aspects of some of these tales, that is, to problems of dating, social customs, language, and so on, but they have been slighted more than most works of medieval literature in the matter of criticism.[2] There are good reasons why they have been ignored, and it is one of the purposes of the present introduction to offer some critical perspectives on the tales as literature.

[1] The form *mabinogion* (ms *mabynnogyon*) occurs only at the end of "Pwyll." *Mabinogi* and its variant spellings occurs at the end of the other three branches, and it is clear that *mabinogion* is a scribal error. The suffix *-(i)on* is a very common plural ending in Welsh, and Lady Charlotte Guest assumed that *mabinogion* was the correct form and referred to all of the tales found in the White Book and Red Book. Because the tales became widely known under this designation, scholars have not seen fit to correct the error, and even the Joneses refer to "the eleven stories of the Mabinogion."

[2] Sir Edward Anwyl analyzed the structure and composition with characteristic insight and erudition in "The Four Branches of the Mabinogi" (see Select Bibliography). A brief biography and bibliography of the work of this important Welsh scholar by Dr. Brynley F. Roberts can be found in *Transactions of the Honourable Society of Cymmrodorion* (1968), pp. 211–264. More recently, P. L. Henry has made an important contribution with his structural analysis of "Culhwch and Olwen."

All of these tales with the exception of the Gwion Bach and Taliesin narratives occur in more or less complete versions in the White Book of Rhydderch (*Llyfr Gwyn Rhydderch*, A.D. 1300–1325) and the Red Book of Hergest (*Llyfr Coch Hergest*, 1375–1425). Fragments occur in manuscripts earlier by a hundred years or so, but they need not concern us here. It is clear that the tales are older than the manuscripts, but how much older we do not know. Sir Ifor Williams believed that the four branches belonged to about the middle of the eleventh century; "Culhwch and Olwen" may be a century earlier. The linguistic data that served to support those dates has been seriously challenged recently by Dr. T. M. Charles-Edwards and Professor Eric Hamp, and it appears that cultural criteria are a surer guide to the antiquity of the tales.[3] The Taliesin material, though not extant in any manuscript prior to the sixteenth century, is set in the time of King Arthur and Maelgwn, a sixth-century king of Gwynedd.

These stories occupy the central position in medieval Welsh literature, and they have been the focus of numerous studies. W. J. Gruffydd was the first to study the mythological aspects systematically and in detail, and his work has been continued with particular success by Professor Proinsias MacCana. Mrs. Rachel Bromwich has shed much light on the composition of the tales in her *Trioedd Ynys Prydein* and in other studies, and Professor Kenneth Jackson has analyzed the tales with respect to international popular tradition. Yet in spite of the labors of these and other scholars over the years, there is much in the *mabinogi* and other medieval Welsh narratives that remains obscure.

As to the former, it has long been recognized that the word contains the regular Welsh word for 'son, boy,' *mab*. It was thought, therefore, that the tales had something to do with youth, either tales for boys, perhaps for their edification, or apprentice tales for those learning the story-telling art. Alternatively, it was noticed that *mabinogi* translates Latin *infantia* in a fourteenth-century apocryphal gospel of the boyhood of Jesus. On the basis of the French form of the word, *enfance*, it was thought that the tales were histories of the birth, boyhood deeds, later feats of arms, of certain heroes. The difficulty in all of these guesses is that they

[3] For full references to the work of these and other scholars mentioned in this section, see the Select Bibliography.

fit none of the four branches of the *mabinogi*, nor do they fit the four branches as a whole.

This is not the place to examine the theories expounded by W. J. Gruffydd on the *mabinogi*, but it is appropriate to acknowledge that he was essentially correct, though he went too far. He believed that the four branches originally told of the birth, youth, marriage, and death of a single hero, Pryderi, and that Pryderi was virtually identical with the British god Maponos. Professor Hamp has recently offered a brilliant explanation of the word *mabinogi*, in which he demonstrates (conclusively, in my view) that the word originally meant "the (collective) material pertaining to the god Maponos."[4] He rearranges the genealogical chart produced by W. J. Gruffydd to suggest that part of what we have in the four branches concerns the father of Maponos, Gwri (= Pryderi).

It is important to emphasize that we are dealing with a collection of material, and that only part of it deals, or dealt originally, with Maponos. A glance at the end of "Branwen" shows us that smaller episodes were known independently, episodes such as "The Assembly of Bran," "The Avenging of the Blow to Branwen," "The Feasting in Harlech," "The Singing of the Birds of Rhiannon," and so on.[5] These quasi-independent episodes or bits of lore were part of the storehouse of tradition on which story-tellers and poets alike could draw to inform their art. Sometimes the storyteller refers to lore outside the context of his narrative, lore that he knows but has chosen not to incorporate or elaborate; at the end of the fourth branch, for example, he says, "and according to the lore (i.e., inherited tradition) he was lord of Gwynedd after that."

These references within the texts to adventures, tales, bits of lore, and the like, suggest to me that *mabinogi* was an extensive collection of more or less related adventures, related sufficiently for them to be metaphorically conceived as branches, rather than as independent tales and that each branch consisted of episodes of

[4] "Mabinogi."

[5] Cf. Loth's remark, "on peut, à la vérité, distinguer dans le *Mabinogi* et ses *branches*, des cycles qui se sont mêlés et confondus" (*Les Mabinogion*, p. 43); similarly, Anwyl: "it is clear from the Four Branches themselves that they presuppose previous stories, not unprobably in a written form . . . the stories here enumerated [in "Branwen"] were probably originally distinct and condensed by the writer of Branwen and the earlier part of Manawyddan [sic] into one narrative" (*Zeitschrift für Celtische Philologie*, II, 127).

related lore (in Welsh, *cyfarwyddyd*) and adventures (*cyfrangau*). In Irish tradition, we find *dindshenchas* 'lore of famous places,' *cóir anmann* 'fitness of names,' and other homogeneous collections that served as the raw materials, as it were, for the tales, which were classified by the native storytellers according to types (e.g., adventures, wooings, elopements, raids).

If we accept this eclectic theory of the composition of the *mabinogi*, that is, that each branch represents a collection of more or less related lore, our understanding of the material and its treatment by the redactor is improved. It means that we can look at isolated episodes, examine their structures, compare them with related episodes elsewhere in Celtic and Indo-European, and thus grasp their meaning more fully. It offers an explanation of why the quality of the redactor's work is so high within individual sections and episodes, and why continuity between these sections is often lacking or poor.

Let us test the method and examine one of the episodes in detail. In "Pwyll," after Teyrnon has returned the boy Gwri to the court of Pwyll and the meal has finished, Teyrnon explains how he happened to find Gwri: 'and he told them the entire adventure concerning the mare and the boy' (*menegi y holl gyfranc am y gasec ac am y mab*). If we were to list the episodes that constitute this branch, in the way that the contents of the second branch are given at the end of "Branwen," we would see clearly that one of them is *Cyfranc Caseg a'r Mab* 'The Adventure of the Mare and the Boy.' I would suggest that it had a separate existence and perhaps was known independently by that name. There was more to it than we find in the first branch, and some of it found its way into the third branch. External evidence shows that, from a mythological point of view, it must have been one of the most significant narratives in the tradition, reaching back to some event that was central enough to Celtic society to generate a variety of literary reflexes.

Cyfranc Caseg a'r Mab had its origins in a myth concerning a horse-goddess and fertility deity, attested among the continental Celts in the name of Epona.[6] This divinity was widely known, and her worship is documented over a large area of the continent.

[6] See Jan de Vries, *Keltische Religion* (Stuttgart, 1961), esp. pp. 123–127 and references there.

There are remains of monuments and inscriptions to her in what is now Germany, France, Switzerland, and Austria, and she was worshipped in Rome itself. She was a favorite even with Roman cavalry units, and Apuleius says that one could see statues set up in her honor in stables. Juvenal and Minucius Felix extend her association to mules and asses. The connection with cavalry and beasts of burden is underscored by her very name, for the element *ep-*, cognate with Latin *equ-us* and Greek *hipp-os,* means 'horse.' She is sometimes depicted mounted on a horse, which always is at an amble, is sometimes accompanied by birds, and is sometimes holding a bag. Other monuments show her seated, surrounded by horses or foals. She has various nicknames, one of which is *regina* 'queen.' The Romans celebrated her feast on December 18, between the Consualia (December 15) and the Opalia (December 19), and we should remember that Consus himself was identified with Poseidon Hippios. The important point here is that Epona was associated in the calendar of feasts with the hippomorphic sea god and fertility deity.

The name of the heroine of the first branch, Rhiannon, comes from an earlier form **Rīgantonā* that means "great queen goddess," and brings to mind the Roman given epithet of Epona, *regina.* The narrative or *cyfranc* that concerns Rhiannon, *Cyfranc Caseg a'r Mab*, begins with a feast in Arberth at which great hosts are present. After the nobles have eaten, Pwyll, the chief, and his men depart for the mound of Arberth. As they are sitting upon the mound, they see a maiden mounted on a pale-white horse travelling along the road. Her horse moves at an easy amble, never increasing its pace, and yet no one of the assembled company is able to overtake her. Eventually, she stops and Pwyll succeeds in winning her hand in marriage. It is important to note in this section that there is a competitor for her favors and her hand, and that the successive marriage dates are one year apart, and therefore on the same day as that on which Pwyll had assembled his feast.

Eventually, a son is born to Rhiannon and Pwyll, but, under mysterious circumstances, he disappears. Rhiannon is accused of having destroyed her child, and as a punishment is required to sit by the horse block and carry visitors to the court on her back. The story switches at this point to introduce Teyrnon Twrf Liant, a neighboring lord. Teyrnon has a mare that foals every May eve, but the offspring disappear. This year he decides to be vigilant; he overcomes a monster that tries to steal the new-born colt, and when he returns to the mare he finds not only the rescued colt but a baby boy (Rhiannon's son) as well.

Teyrnon and his wife pretend they are the boy's parents and rear him. He enjoys a precocious development, like that of Lleu Llaw Gyffes in the fourth branch (and most heroes), but besides that we hear of his fondness of horses, and that he would ask the grooms to let him take them to water. Teyrnon's wife suggests that the colt be broken in and given to the boy, since "it was the night you found the boy that the colt which you rescued was born." Teyrnon replies that he will not oppose her suggestion, but that he will let her give the horse to the boy. From then on, she takes charge and gives the orders to the grooms. In the end, the boy and his colt are restored to Rhiannon and Pwyll.

That, briefly, is the substance of *Cyfranc Caseg a'r Mab* as we find it in the first branch of the *Mabinogi*. As Gruffydd saw, there is some reconstruction to be done here, and he supplied numerous hypothetical lost links in order to reconstruct the *mabinogi* as a whole and the first and third branches in particular. But Gruffydd was looking in vain when he sought in the *mabinogi* an original story that told of the birth, boyhood deeds, wooing, marriage, and tragic death of Pryderi. Such a cycle may have existed, but the four branches are not its direct descendant.

The matter of Rhiannon's punishment is central to the underlying myth. Gruffydd suggested that in the original she had been accused of giving birth to a foal, and that is why she was given the punishment of acting like a horse. But in her hippomorphic aspect she would be expected to give birth to a foal (and that is exactly what happens in the complementary tale of Teyrnon), and there could be no punishment for that, certainly. Analyzing the tale structurally, we might say that she has been deprived of her equine divinity, demoted to beast of burden for failing her function as progenitor. But on a purely literary level, I think that two things influenced Rhiannon's punishment: (1) it was a punishment well-known in the medieval period, as Dr. Brynley Roberts has pointed out,[7] and (2) Rhiannon's hippomorphic character had not been

[7] "Penyd Rhiannon," *Bulletin of the Board of Celtic Studies*, XXIII (1970), 325–327.

forgotten; it had survived with sufficient force to influence this part of the tale.

Irish versions of "The Adventure of the Mare and the Boy" are found in two stories. One is *Noínden Ulad*, 'The Debility of the Ulstermen,'[8] and it may be summarized as follows: a woman appears one day to the widower Crunnchu and begins keeping house for him. She eventually discloses her identity, saying that she is Macha daughter of Sainreth mac Imbaith, or 'Nature of the Sea.' She insists that he must not mention her existence to anyone, and while she stays with him his prosperity increases. At the king's assembly, however, Crunnchu boasts that his wife can outrun the king's horses. He is compelled by the king to bring her to the assembly, where before everyone she is forced to race against the royal horses. Alas, she is pregnant. Still, she wins the race and as she crosses the finish line she gives birth to twins—a boy and a girl. Thereupon, she utters a curse, saying that in their time of greatest need, the Ulstermen will all be stricken with pangs of childbirth. There is no further mention of the twins, except that it is from them (*emain* 'twins') that the capitol of Ulster takes its name, Emain Macha. The pertinent facts are that, at a king's assembly, a woman races against his horses and, while thus behaving like a horse, gives birth. The equine associations of Macha do not end there, and we turn now to *Compert Con Culainn* 'The Birth of CúChulainn.'[9]

There are two versions of this tale, and they differ rather significantly, but I shall take account of that in the summary that follows. King Conchobor and his men set out to hunt a flock of birds that have been ravaging Emain Macha. Night overtakes the party, and they find themselves guests of a man and his pregnant wife. In one of the versions, Conchobor insists that the woman sleep with him; it is his right to sleep with the wife of every man in his realm, and thus he is nominally the husband of every woman in his kingdom and potentially the father of every child. This is

[8] Trans. in *Ancient Irish Tales*, ed. by Tom Peete Cross and Clark Harris Slover with revised bibliography by Charles W. Dunn (New York, 1969), pp. 208–210.

[9] Trans. by Thomas Kinsella, *The Tain* (London, 1969), pp. 21–25; trans. from a different manuscript in *Ancient Irish Tales*, pp. 134–136. For the Irish text, see the edition by A. G. Van Hamel, *Compert Con Culainn and Other Stories* (Dublin, 1933).

appropriate to the sovereign in his role of guarantor of fertility. In this instance, because the woman is pregnant, she is not forced to have intercourse with the king but lies next to him. In the morning, the boy who is later to be known as CúChulainn is found in the folds of Conchobor's cloak. In one of the versions, a mare standing outside the door gives birth to twin colts at the moment the woman delivers. In the morning, the house, man, wife, and birds have all disappeared; only the boy, the colts, and the king and his party remain. The boy is given to the king's sister to raise, and she declares that he will be treated exactly like her own son Conall Cernach, *conid cumma lem 7 bid e Conall Cernach* 'and he will be the same in my mind as though he were Conall Cernach.' The congenital horses turn out to be exceptional, but one is greater than the other, and is called Liath Macha, 'The Grey of Macha.' When CúChulainn is finally killed, the Grey of Macha returns to the water, whence, presumably, it came. There is an obvious twinning element here, for the text implies that Conall and CúChulainn are twins, although as we can see from other stories in the cycle, Conall is victorious only over mortal opponents, whereas CúChulainn establishes his superiority over the supernatural as well.[10] Similarly, while the one horse exceeds ordinary horses in beauty, speed, and the like, the Grey of Macha is supernatural.

In these two Irish tales, we glimpse once again the remnants of a myth operating at both the hippomorphic and anthropomorphic levels. Macha, daughter of the Sea, appears as one who insures prosperity. Compelled to behave like a horse, she runs against the king's horses and delivers twins while in that equine role. Elsewhere, twin horses are born of Macha (the supernatural one is *liath* 'grey' like the *canwelw* 'pale-white, whitish' horse upon which Rhiannon rides) under circumstances that also yield the birth of the hero. At least one of these horses is of the sea, but both become associates of the hero.

We might well ask at this point what kings have to do with horses, and what mares have to do with kings. I do not think it is possible to supply an answer that goes beyond the reasonable assumption that horses were important to a society in which the

[10] The supremacy of CúChulainn against supernatural opponents is the major theme of the tale "Bricriu's Feast," trans. in *Ancient Irish Tales*, pp. 254–280.

warrior aristocracy figures so prominently. But, structurally, the myths that underly medieval Irish and Welsh tales reaffirm repeatedly the female and equine nature of sovereignty. When an Irish king espoused his kingdom, he became responsible for fertility in the land, among other things. One aspect of this responsibility was enacted ritually, and has been recorded for us by Giraldus Cambrensis. In Book III, Chapter 25 of *Topographia Hibernica*,[11] he recounts what he calls a "monstrous" ritual he heard reported in Tirconnell in the North of Ireland. When a king was to be inaugurated, says Giraldus, all of the people of that land were assembled in one place, and a white mare was led into their midst. He who was to be inaugurated king, in front of all assembled there, publicly comported himself like a horse and acknowledged himself to be one. The meaning of Giraldus' outraged Latin, is, as Julius Pokorny recognized, that the king had sexual intercourse with the mare.[12] Afterwards, according to Giraldus, the mare was cut up and cooked in a broth. The king sat in a bath prepared from this, and, without use of a cup or even his hands, drank of the broth about him, while he and all the people consumed the meat of the mare.

Schröder discussed this reference long ago, and compared it with a rite described in the Sanskrit *Aśvamedha*, where the roles are reversed—there, it is the queen and a stallion who symbolically mate.[13] The purpose, said Schröder, was to make the generative power of the hippomorphic fertility god effective in the earth. The explanation offered by Schröder sheds some light, I believe, on the stories we have been considering. Sovereignty, female, was elusive. There was competition for the kingship, several suitors trying to espouse the kingdom, of which only one could be successful. To put it another way, there was one on whom the lady Sovereignty bestowed her favors or was forced to do so. The king mated with her, and the result was prosperity in the land. In myth, the mating has two reflexes, human and equine, depending on whether it functions on the anthropomorphic (king and queen) or zoomorphic (mare and stallion) level. When the two levels overlap in nar-

[11] Trans. by John J. O'Meara (Dundalk, 1951), p. 93.

[12] *Zeitschrift für Celtische Philologie*, XVI (1926), 123.

[13] "Ein Altirischer Krönungsritus und das Indo-germanische Rossopfer," *Zeitschrift*, XVI (1926), 310–312.

ratives, the boy and the horse become inseparably bound to each other's fate.

We can be quite sure that the king was cast in the role of stallion at the ritual recounted by Giraldus, for it is borne out by onomastic evidence.[14] The people of Tirconnell were Uí Néill, descendants of Niall Noígiallach, whose father was Eochu Mugmedón.[15] The root of the name Eochu, and Eochaid with which it is frequently confused, is *ech-* 'horse,' the Irish equivalent of *ep-* that we find in Gaulish Epona. Indeed, Irish tradition abounds with the name. The chief over the Túatha Dé Danann, the Dagda, was otherwise called Eochaid Ollathair 'Eochaid Great-father.' Bres, half Fomorian, half Túatha Dé Danann, who guarantees fertility in exchange for his freedom in "The Second Battle of Magh Tuiredh," is otherwise known as Eochaid Bres. Several of the husbands of Medb (English Maeve), the personification of sovereignty in the Ulster cycle of tales, are called Eochaid, and her father is yet another Eochaid.

We have one more thread to pick up in this fractious Celtic narrative of "The Adventure of the Mare and the Boy," and that is the connection with the sea. We have seen that the Grey of Macha appears to have come from the sea, and that Macha is once called daughter of the Nature of the Sea, and we may now explore further marine associations. In the fourth branch of the *mabinogi*, Math induces birth in Aranrhod. She delivers twins, one of whom is christened Dylan; he immediately makes for the sea and assumes its nature. One is tempted to believe that whoever sired this child also came from the sea, although the principles of genetics do not always dictate the shape of mythic narrative. The other of this pair is Lleu Llaw Gyffes, whose name is cognate with that of the Irish Lugh, foster-son of Manannán mac Lir, the Irish sea god. (According to the story of his birth, CúChulainn was the reincarnation of Lugh.)

[14] The evidence of proper names and their signification must be used cautiously, as D. Ellis Evans points out; see his "A Comparison of the Formation of Some Continental and Early Insular Celtic Personal Names," *Études Celtiques*, XIII (1972–1973), 171–193.

[15] T. F. O'Rahilly showed that Irish tradition confused Niall's father with Eochu Domlén (? = Eochu mac Echach Domlén), but it was not the epithet that was significant in the name; see *Early Irish History and Mythology* (Dublin, 1946), pp. 221–222.

Perhaps one of the most striking examples of the horse-king and his marine affiliation is in the *Compert Brese* 'The Birth of (Eochaid) Bres,' interpolated into the "Second Battle of Magh Tuiredh."[16] It tells how Eri daughter of Delbaeth was watching the sea one day when she saw a vessel of silver on an unusually becalmed surface. Its extent seemed great to her although she could not determine its shape. The tide brought it to land, and she saw that it held a man of very fair form, yellow-haired, dressed in gold cloth and ornaments, with two silver spears. The man addressed her as though his visit had been planned or fore-ordained. He lay with her, identified himself as Elotha son of Delbaeth, king of the Fomorians, and prophesied to her that she would bear a son of their union, and that he would be called Eochaid Bres. Following the prophecy, he went back as he had come. Eri's child enjoyed a prodigious development, growing at twice the rate of ordinary lads, so that he reached a growth of fourteen years at the end of his seventh. Later Eochaid Bres became king in place of the unfit Nuadha, and reigned until the Túatha Dé Danann expelled him. When he asked his mother for information concerning his own race, she took him to the hill whence she had seen the vessel of silver, then to the strand where she gave him the ring left by Elotha. Then they set out together for the land of the Fomorians.

Now there is in all of this the operation of paronymy, wherein the name Fomorian suggested 'the people from the sea' (*fo* + *mor*). The etymology is generally considered spurious, though it is by no means inconceivable that Fomorian could be an alternative name for the Túatha Dé Danann. Anyone who has read around in that masterpiece of muddled medieval miscellany, the *Lebor Gabála*, knows that the genealogies of the Túatha Dé Danann and the Fomorians overlap in many places and are almost hopelessly confused. Both Elotha and Eri have the same patronym, and are perhaps brother and sister. It may be, of course, that the name Fomorian is simply the marine appellation of the descendants of Danu/Anu, the Túatha Dé Danann. But I leave that interesting and tantalizing question for the moment, and conclude simply that a king of the Túatha Dé Danann who bore the appropriate soubriquet (*Eoch* 'horse'), was sired by a gold and silver youth who

[16] Ed. and trans. by Whitley Stokes, *Révue Celtique*, XII (1891), 52–130, 306–308; *Ancient Irish Tales*, pp. 28–48.

came in on the tide and departed the same way. These motifs seem to have an affinity for each other elsewhere in Celtic tradition; in "Culhwch and Olwen," the shepherd Custennin falsely claims that Culhwch was found in the sea with a gold ring around his finger, and in the Irish "The Death of Connla," CúChulainn's only son comes in from the sea wearing his gold band of identification.

In his analysis of the *mabinogi*, W. J. Gruffydd showed that Manawydan son of Llŷr 'son of the Sea' must have been the father of Pryderi. His arguments were based in part on the Irish *Compert Mongán* 'The Birth of Mongán,' and he was no doubt correct in adducing that parallel. My own view is that the third branch preserves the detritus of a myth wherein the sea-god mated with the horse-goddess; this view is supported by evidence from the first branch and the parallels we have considered from elsewhere in both Irish and Welsh. In the first branch, Teyrnon is the ersatz father of Pryderi (he and his wife pretend that the foundling is their own son and, in fact, they raise him) and lord of the mare that foals on the night Pryderi is found. Teyrnon is called Twrf Liant, an epithet which very possibly means "tempestuous flood," so that he may be Lord of the Raging Sea–a fitting title for the sea deity. In the third branch the relationship between the marine and equine divinities finds a variant expression: Manawydan son of the Sea becomes the father of Pryderi by marring Rhiannon. The Romans understood this close association between the horse goddess and the hippomorphic sea god when they fitted Epona into their calendar.

I have devoted a good deal of space to "The Adventure of the Mare and the Boy" and its mythological ramifications, because I wanted to show that it is possible to isolate episodes in the four branches, and to suggest that they existed independently. I do not suggest that these narratives survived as myths in the strict sense of that word, but their mythic significance may well have been understood in a general way by an eleventh-century audience. In their introduction to *The Mabinogion*, Thomas Jones and Gwyn Jones stated that the matter of the *mabinogi* is "mythology in decline." That may be true, yet we must not assume that the meaning of the tales was lost to a contemporary audience. We are not yet sufficiently familiar with the structure of medieval prose–and certainly not medieval Welsh prose—to know how these tales were received by an audience in the eleventh, tenth, or earlier centuries. Structural analysis suggests that the myths reflected in these tales were very much alive and that the story-teller was very much aware of them. For example, the first branch appears to confront the problem of the failure of the horse-goddess to guarantee fertility and generate a hero (at the anthropomorphic level) and a foal (at the hippomorphic level). For that failure, she is punished by being deprived of her divinity and reduced to the function of beast of burden (to wit, Rhiannon carried men on her back). The story is successfully resolved, that is, it has a happy ending, in that the hero and foal are restored and so is Rhiannon to her proper role as consort of the king and guarantor of fertility. In the second branch, it is the destruction of horses that causes Branwen to be removed from her place as consort of the king of Ireland and to be reduced to performing menial tasks. But in this branch there is no restoration; Branwen dies and the two kingdoms are virtually destroyed. These sub-structures are veiled by a literary fabric woven in the interests of the tales' audiences, but it is difficult to believe that the story-teller who put together the versions we have was not aware of the general drift of the myth, even though his primary concern was the telling of a good tale.

The same concern with regeneration is evident in the fourth branch. The punishment of Gilfaethwy and Gwydion, wherein their uncle turns them into pairs of animals and they beget offspring on each other, enforces the notion that the punishment for unlawful intercourse (rape) is for the offenders to experience the pangs of childbirth. The episode is reminiscent of that in Irish tradition where Macha gets revenge upon the Ulstermen for tampering with her procreative powers by making them all experience the pangs of childbirth. The punishment of Math's nephews, then, may be structurally significant, and but a repetition of the underlying theme of the whole tale. As Lévi-Strauss says, "repetition has as its function to make the structure of the myth apparent."[17]

The views advanced here are unquestionably speculative, and they are intended only to show that structural studies of the *mabinogi* might well reveal something of the compositional tech-

[17] "The Structural Study of Myth," in *Myth: A Symposium*, ed. Thomas A. Sebeok (Bloomington, 1958), p. 105.

niques of medieval Welsh literature.[18] Within the various episodes there is a skillful use of language, of characterization, of dramatic irony, and other rhetorical and narrative devices that we associate with the literary art. But the episodes are never completely harmonized in a given tale, and there are inconsistences. It is this episodic character and the inconsistencies that suggest to me, more than anything else, that the materials of the tales were of great antiquity; however much the redactor elaborated the super-structure, the sub-structure remained intact.

Another striking example of the survival of the kernel of myth occurs in the tale of "Culhwch and Olwen." At the level of folk-tale, it belongs to a widely known type, "the giant's daughter." A number of motifs known to students of the international folktale are clustered here: the jealous stepmother, love for an unknown and unseen maiden, the oldest animals, the helper animals, and the impossible tasks are perhaps the most obvious. But the combination of these motifs and the universality of the tale types are features of the super-structure of the tale, and they belong to the later development of an ancient myth, the key to which lies in the opening paragraph of the tale.

It is a commonplace concerning Celtic heroes (indeed, heroes in most cultures), that there is some confusion over parentage. This is usually because the hero has both divine and human parents. In the instance of CúChulainn there is multiple conception, accounting for the fact that he is both the son and reincarnation of Lugh and the son of Sualtam, a mortal. The opening of "Culhwch and Olwen" is not so explicit in the matter of conception, but I believe that it can be shown that the strange events recounted there preserve a very nearly obscured account of the origins of Culhwch. According to the tale, Cilydd's wife becomes pregnant, goes mad, and wanders in the wastes. She returns to her senses just as she is about to give birth, an event that takes place among swine and in the presence of a swineherd. It is the swineherd who brings the boy to court, and the boy is named Culhwch 'pig-run,' because that is where he was found.

[18] Professor Daniel Melia has done an excellent study of the Irish *Táin Bó Cúalnge* 'The Cattle Raid of Cooley' in his 1972 Harvard University doctoral dissertation (unpublished), but the field is otherwise largely ignored. See also Melia's "Parallel Versions of 'The Boyhood Deeds of CúChulainn,'" *Forum for Modern Language Studies*, X (1974), 211–226.

In order to get at the underlying significance of this bizarre account, let us reconsider the events of the birth of Pryderi in the first branch of the *mabinogi*. He was found with a mare and a colt, and eventually brought to court by Teyrnon and restored to Pwyll and Rhiannon. I have tried to show that the narrative is merely taking account of different levels of the myth of the horse-goddess: at one of the levels her offspring was a hero, at another a foal. Her mate was the sea god, explained in the story as a neighboring lord, Teyrnon, who merely found the boy and later brought him to court. I would like to suggest now that the first paragraph of "Culhwch and Olwen" reflects a tradition about the birth of another kind of hero, associated with the god known in Gaul as Moccus (Welsh *moch*, Irish *mucc* 'pig'). In that tradition, the myth recounted the circumstances of the birth of a hero sired by the swine-god. All that remains in our tale is the location of the birth, a pig-run, and the role of the swine-herd in delivering the boy to the court. In the story of Pryderi, too, we are left with the location of the epiphany, the horse-stable, and the role of the mare's lord in bringing the boy to court.

There is no denying that the swine was an important animal among the Celts, and the references to it are commonplace.[19] In addition to its domestic and economic importance, it may well have been the animal held most sacred by the Celts. At the divine level, besides the Gaulish Moccus, the boar turns up as alter ego of Diarmuid in the Irish tale of Diarmuid and Grainne.[20] Diarmuid's foster-brother is said to have been killed by Diarmuid's father. He was changed into a boar, and it was decreed that he would have a life as long as Diarmuid's; he became Diarmuid's nemesis and the two die in combat with one another (another fairly clear instance of the myth operating simultaneously at both the anthropomorphic and zoomorphic levels). The major episode of "Culhwch and Olwen," of course, is the boar hunt, where Arthur the hunter pursues Twrch Trwyth (and his double, Ysgithrwyn). The episode is strongly reminiscent of the boar fight in the Irish tale known as "The Chase of Síd na mBan Finn,"[21] where the object of the chase

[19] See, e.g., Anne Ross, *Everyday Life of the Pagan Celts* (London and New York, 1970), pp. 169–170.

[20] Translated in *Ancient Irish Tales*, pp. 370–421.

[21] Ed. and trans. by Kuno Meyer in *Fianaigecht* (*Todd Lecture Series*, XVI, Dublin, 1910), pp. 64ff.

is also of supernatural if not divine proportions.

"Culhwch and Olwen" is much more episodic than any of the four branches, yet its unusual opening and its central episode assure us that it carries on traditions associated with a Celtic swine divinity. One of his manifestations was the ferocious though noble and rational opponent of such divine hunters as the Welsh Arthur and the Irish Finn; on the continent he was assimilated to the Roman god Mercury; his human form is to be associated with such characters as Culhwch and, perhaps, Hychdwn Hir, the "tall swine" turned champion, born to Gwydion and Gilfaethwy while they were in the shape of boar and sow in the tale of "Math." As these traditions become obscured, only those elements that had dramatic or some other entertainment value survived with any vigor, although the mythological connections were not entirely lost. The result is a story about a boy whose paternity is confused by the presence of a swineherd, and whose name, bearing the word for a pig, is explained in typical onomastic fashion. Even though the basic type of the story is that of the lad performing various difficult tasks to win the giant's daughter, the major episode is Arthur's hunt of the great boar. No doubt the doublet episode of the hunt of Ysgithrwyn Pen Baidd developed out of one of Twrch's epithets, *ysgithr wyn* 'shining tusks." By the same token, a differentiation occurred so that the epithet *gwrych ereint* 'silver bristles' became yet another boar and a kind of lieutenant to Twrch Trwyth. It is interesting to note that the corresponding Irish words, *torc* and *tríath*, mean both "boar" and "chieftain, hero," suggesting that the tradition of the swine god as ferocious fighter survived in Ireland as well. In Cormac's Glossary (early tenth century), we read *Orc* [a young pig] *trēith .i. ainm do mac rīgh: trīath enim rex uocatur* '*orc* of a *tríath*, that is, a name for the son of a king: for a king was called a *tríath*';[22] it is tempting to think that herein lies a potential literary source for the remark, made by Arthur, that the boar "had been a king, but God changed him into a swine for his sins."

"The Tale of Gwion Bach" and "The Tale of Taliesin," which together form a continuous saga about the birth and boyhood deeds

[22] *Sanas Cormaic* (*Anecdota from Irish Manuscripts*, iv, 1912), p. 86.1018.

of the poet/prophet Taliesin, are straightforward narratives with virtually no textual confusion or complexity. There are no awkward transitions here, no seams behind which we can glimpse a sub-structure that might give a clue to the underlying mythical significance of the material. And yet when we look outside the saga at the wider traditions about Taliesin, we see a good deal of confusion and complexity.

Taliesin is known from the earliest extant Welsh sources, and he is mentioned by Nennius in the *Historia Brittonum* as one of five poets distinguished for their poetry in the late sixth century, the others being Aneirin, Blwchbardd, Cian (called Gwenith Gwawd "Wheat of Song"), and Talhaearn Tad Awen. To Aneirin is ascribed the sixth-century Welsh poem *Y Gododdin*, which celebrates elegiacally the valor of a band of warriors who fought against the expanding Anglo-Saxon kingdom of Northumbria. Nothing remains of the work of the other three. Of the work of Taliesin, a good deal remains, most of it preserved in a thirteenth-century manuscript called "The Book of Taliesin." But there is an inconsistency in the types of poems attributed to this most famous of Welsh poets; there are panegyrics in praise of known historical figures, religious poems, and most peculiar of all, those litanies of metamorphoses sometimes called transformational poems.[23] The primary source of all this material is the thirteenth-century Book of Taliesin, but there are a number of other poems not found there that occur with great regularity in manuscripts from the sixteenth to the eighteenth century. In this latter category of manuscripts we usually find at least a fragment of the *Hanes* or "Tale" of Taliesin; rarely do we find in them any of the poems from the Book of Taliesin, and we are tempted to conclude that there were two independent traditions about Taliesin, one concerning a genuine poet, one a legendary shape-shifter. This was Sir Ifor Williams' conviction and he maintained that the transformational poems in the Book of Taliesin were to be understood in terms of the "folk-tale" of Taliesin, that is, in terms of the shape-shifting that goes

[23] The poems of the "historical" Taliesin have been edited by Sir Ifor Williams and discussed often. But aside from Sir Ifor's discussion in *Chwedl Taliesin* (Cardiff, 1957), the tale has been neglected, owing largely to the unavailability of a satisfactory text. I have identified over two dozen manuscripts that contain at least part of the tale, and I hope to publish an edition soon.

on in the first part, "The Tale of Gwion Bach."[24] The eulogies and elegies to such known historical persons as Urien and his son Owain, and those alone, he asserted, are the poems of Taliesin, "the bard who is mentioned in the *Historia Brittonum* . . . This Taliesin is a genuine historical figure—not a legendary character who combines the powers of a magician, a sorcerer, and a prophet."

In order to understand the relationship between these two apparently distinct poets and the widely divergent contexts of the poems attributed to them, it is essential to turn back to an earlier Celtic society. The practice of poetry among the Celts had explicitly magical overtones, and the poet was undestood to have supernatural and divinatory powers. This is most clearly manifested in the early Irish tales and other documents such as Cormac's Glossary, where the ritual of divination known as *imbas forosna*, one of the three things that characterized poets and poetry, is described. These powers are alluded to by the ethnographers of classical antiquity in their commentaries on the Celts, and there is a celebrated reference to divinatory practices in Wales in the works of Giraldus Cambrensis, who lived in the twelfth century. Keating knew about similar practices in Scotland as late as the seventeenth century. Taken together, this evidence points to the belief that in Celtic tradition the poet had the power to loose his spirit to seek out knowledge, in whatever quarter that was to be had. I have discussed elsewhere the possible connections of this notion with shamanistic practices,[25] and it seems that these powers are related to the ability to shift shape and are connected as well with the idea of the transmigration of souls in which there is ample evidence to suggest the Celts believed.

Against this background was projected the image of the archetypal poet, seer, diviner, prophet. In Irish, one of his names is Amergin, who in the quasi-historical *Lebor Gabála* recites a poem as the Sons of Míl land in Ireland, in which he claims to be many things, including a wave, a salmon, a sword, a plant, and a spear. As O'Rahilly rightly saw, Amergin has been "borrowed from Irish

24 See the Introduction in the English version of Sir Ifor Williams' *Canu Taliesin: The Poems of Taliesin,* prepared by Professor J. E. Caerwyn Williams (Dublin, 1968), esp. pp. xv–xix.

25 See the discussion and references in Patrick K. Ford, *The Poetry of Llywarch Hen* (Berkeley, Los Angeles, and London, 1974), pp. 58ff.

mythology," the seer of the pantheon, wisdom itself.[26] In Welsh, one of his names is Taliesin; he claims that he was not created from a mother and father but from the elements, and he has been in existence since the dawn of creation.[27] He has been all things, knows what is, what has been, what will be; he will endure till doomsday. He is, therefore, the repository of supernatural and otherworldly knowledge, the ultimate divine projection of the Celtic poet whose intensive wisdom (the literal meaning of *druí*, *derwydd* 'druid,' *imbas*, *cyfarwydd*, and other words associated with the scope of poetic activities among the Celts) was his hallmark. The tale that Elis Gruffydd recorded for us in the sixteenth century was still sensitive to the tradition that Taliesin had existed among the Welsh for hundreds of years under different names, and the shapeshifting powers of Gwion Bach are but one manifestation of the polymorphic powers of the archtypal poet.[28]

The waters of this native tradition have been muddied somewhat by the influx of classical and Judeo-Christian traditions. Here, as elsewhere in Irish and Welsh, the confluence of these traditions produced some interesting results. Materials from the non-native cultures were often joined clumsily onto the other, so that instead of assimilation we have agglutination; in the place of "Christian coloring" of native sagas or the like, we find references to New Testament events inserted into the tales. For example, in the Irish Ulster Cycle, King Conchobor dies a victim of his own rage upon hearing the news of Christ's crucifixion, although the events that lead to Conchobor's death have nothing whatsoever to do with the events of the Passion. This technique of grafting from one tradition onto another is not very satisfying artistically, but it does ease the task of distinguishing the native from the non-native. In the poem that Taliesin recites in response to the queries of Maelgwn Gwynedd (below, p. 117), Old Testament, Classical, and Welsh traditions come together with a resounding thud: we meet Absalon and Alexander, Lucifer and Gwydion. There is Noah's ark, Nimrod's tower, Aranrhod's prison, and the survivors of Troy. Though

26 *Early Irish History and Mythology*, p. 199.

27 See Appendix: *Cad Goddeu*, esp. 11. 74ff.

28 Merlin was believed to have been identical with Taliesin, but existing in another time and place. See Patrick K. Ford, "The Death of Merlin in the Chronicle of Elis Gruffydd," *Viator*, VII (1975), pp. 379–390.

the speaker of these lines dwelt in the land of the Trinity, he issued forth from the womb of the witch Ceridwen. There is not better evidence that the Taliesin material passed through many hands, each embellishing its shape with learning from classical and Biblical sources.[29]

Emerging from these poems, then, and the transformational poems in the Book of Taliesin is the figure of the eternal, divine poet and prophet, essentially amorphous yet paradoxically having many shapes. The prose tale itself tells how this archetypal poet first acquired wisdom, and is analogous to tales in Irish that explain how Finn acquired wisdom, and to those in Scandinavian that tell how Odin gained poetry and wisdom. In all three traditions there is a cauldron of poetry or inspired wisdom, and there is a contest over the custody of it.

One of the Irish versions tells how Finn, who was still called Demne at this time, goes to his namesake Finn Éces to learn poetry.[30] Finn Éces had been waiting on the banks of the Boyne for seven years to catch the salmon of Wisdom, and when the fish is finally caught, young Demne is given the task of cooking it in a cauldron of water. As he is doing so, some of the steam escapes and burns his thumb. When he puts the thumb into his mouth to ease the pain, he immediately knows all things, and is renamed Finn by his tutor. There is no overt hostility here, but the wisdom that resided in the salmon was intended for Finn Éces, and instead was acquired by the boy.

In the Old Norse *Skáldskaparmál*, Odin drinks up all the mead

[29] There is a superficial resemblance between this poem and portions of the apocryphal "Wisdom of Sirach," where personified Wisdom claims to have existed from all time:

> I issued from the mouth of the Most High,
> And covered the earth like a mist.
> I lived on the heights,
> And my throne was on the pillar of cloud.
> I alone compassed the circuit of heaven,
> And I walked in the depth of the abyss.
> I owned the waves of the sea and the whole earth
> And every people and nation.

The Apochrypha, trans. by Edgar J. Goodspeed (Chicago, 1938; rptd. New York, 1959), p. 268. Cf. Proverbs 8:22–31 and the notes to those verses in R.B.Y. Scott, *Proverbs, Ecclesiastes* (The Anchor Bible: Garden City, New York, 1965).

[30] "The Boyhood Deeds of Finn," *Ancient Irish Tales*, pp. 360–369.

of poetry from the kettle and two crocks that are in the possession of the giant Suttung.[31] Suttung pursues Odin, both of them assuming the shape of an eagle. Odin returns safely to the Aesir and gives the mead to "those men who can compose poetry."

In our story, the cauldon of inspiration is being brewed for Afagddu, the hideous son of the witch Ceridwen. The lad Gwion Bach positions himself so that the magical drops that spring from the cauldron alight on himself instead of upon Afagddu, and Gwion acquires the wisdom. Thereupon he is pursued by Ceridwen, both changing their shapes several times in the course of the chase. In the end, Gwion is swallowed up by Ceridwen; nine months later, he is reborn as Taliesin, the gifted poet and prophet. Like Finn, his name is changed after he has acquired wisdom.

Clearly, the tales of Gwion Bach and Taliesin cannot be lightly dismissed as "folktale" or late developments. Perceptible in them and in their attendant poems, despite the layering of successive generations and external influences, lies the myth of the primeval poet, in whom resided all wisdom.

The structures of the tales discussed here reveal their mythological orientation, and the tales survived because the myths they reflected, however much in decline, were still an important part of the traditions of medieval Wales. But it is evident that the primary interest in the tales on the part of the redactor and his audience was in their entertainment value. The storyteller's art is everywhere in evidence, and though he could not alter his inherited materials at will, for that would have done violence to the myth, he could and did suit them to his own purposes and to the tastes of his audience. The divine characters who play out these events are not always "invested with a physical and moral grandeur" as the translators of *The Mabinogion* asserted. These characters, like those in medieval Irish sagas, received no consistent treatment from the redactor of their tales, and if there is mythology in decline here, it is mainly a decline in reverence. Math has great dignity, it is true. But think of Manawydan building his tiny gal-

[31] Snorri Sturluson, *The Prose Edda,* trans. by Jean I. Young (Berkeley and Los Angeles, 1964), pp. 102–103. Older versions of the myth are found in the *Hávamál*, and are discussed by Turville-Petre, *Myth and Religion of the North* (New York, 1964), pp. 36–37.

lows to hang a pregnant mouse; think of Pwyll bungling his way toward marriage with the tough-minded Rhiannon. The author of the *mabinogi*, like the author of many an Irish saga, had a highly developed sense of humor and of the absurd, and he knew how to use this sense to relieve the tension or offer his own comments on the events he chronicled—however serious they may have been in origin.[32]

Let us examine in some detail here the contributions of the redactor or storyteller to this body of ancient and traditional material. The first episode in "Pwyll" deals with the exchange of shapes between Pwyll and Arawn, king of Annwfn, and with Pwyll's adventures in the Otherworld. It is difficult to see what this episode has to do with the rest of the tale. W. J. Gruffydd suggested that it represented a confused version of a motif that occurs in Irish tradition. In the original story, he proposed, a king of the Otherworld changes places with a mortal king in order to beget a hero in the mortal's wife. The theme occurs in the tale of Mongán, and there may be a vestige of it in the tale of King Arthur's conception. But of course no such event takes place in the version before us, and one might suggest as well that the episode comes from an annual battle, such as that waged between Gwyn and Gwythr for the hand of Creiddylad, daughter of Lludd Llawereint, in the tale of "Culhwch and Olwen" (below, p. 151). There, the battle is said to be fought every year on May first, and whoever is victorious on Doomsday shall have the maiden. The battle between Hafgan and Arawn is also an annual battle, but the quarrel is said to be over land and not over a woman, although the woman is very nearly the focal point of the story.

The action begins with a hunt, a very common device in medieval literature to move the characters and the action to the edge of the Otherworld. Pwyll is separated from his men, just as in the third branch Pryderi is isolated in the course of a hunt. His exchange with Arawn is a very wooden one, based in part on protocol between nobility of differing ranks. As T. M. Charles-Edwards has shown, these customs belong to ancient Celtic society and do not imply a knowledge of Norman feudal practices.[33] The

[32] For an evaluation of audience and story-teller in medieval Ireland, see Kathleen Hughes, *Early Christian Ireland* (Ithaca, New York, 1972), pp. 182ff.

[33] "The Date of the Four Branches"; see Select Bibliography.

result of their conversation is that Pwyll agrees to atone for his insult to Arawn by going to Annwfn in Arawn's shape and fighting an enemy king of the Otherworld, Hafgan. In the meantime, Arawn takes Pwyll's shape and governs Dyfed. Whether or not the purpose of this visit to the Otherworld and its mythological significance had been forgotten by the eleventh century, we shall never know. But we do know that the redactor's chief interest and, perhaps, that of his audience, lay in the exchange itself. The dramatic situation is excellent: an Otherworldly figure with the power to shape-shift spends a year ruling mortals disguised as their king. In the meantime, the transformed mortal is in the land of the perfected. He is astonished by the beauty of the place, "the most beautifully ornamented buildings anyone had seen . . . the most splendid and best equipped troop that anyone had ever seen." But best of all, Pwyll is given "the fairest woman you have ever seen to sleep with you every night." The situation is full of possibilities, and one can only regret that other versions of this narrative have not survived. Our redactor shows great skill in his balanced handling of the drama: Pwyll finds her everything that Arawn had promised and more; she is not only beautiful and beautifully dressed, she is the noblest and gentlest woman he has ever conversed with. But when they get into bed together, he turns his face to the wall! And from that time on, no matter how tender they were toward one another during the day, he spent every night of that year with his face toward the wall.

After Pwyll has defeated Hafgan and united Annwfn, he returns to the place where he and Arawn originally met, and Arawn restores them to their proper shapes. Arawn's return to Annwfn is treated next, and the redactor builds the tension for the scene that is to come by reminding us that Arawn's host experienced no special elation on seeing him, for they had not been aware of his absence. He, however, felt great pleasure when he saw them. When the day is done, he and his wife go to bed; the language here is very similar to that used when Pwyll first goes to bed with the woman. What Arawn's wife expected, no doubt, was that which she had been accustomed to for the past year, for the man was, in her view, the same. But her mate does not turn his face to the wall on this night: "first he talked to her, then engaged in affectionate play and made love to her."

The humor inherent in this little scene fired the imagination of our redactor, and once again his genius and his restraint are evident. There is an admirable economy in the passage that follows, and yet the tension is built and sustained as surely as any narrator could do it with all the supralinguistic tools at his disposal.

> "Dear God!" she thought, "what a different mind he has tonight from what he has had for the past year!"
>
> And she thought for a long time. And after her musing, he awoke and said something to her, and again, and a third time. But he got no answer from her.
>
> "Why don't you speak to me?" he asked.
>
> "I tell you," she replied, "that I haven't spoken this much for a year under these circumstances."
>
> "Why," he said, "we have talked continually."
>
> "Shame on me," she said, "if from the time we went between the sheets there was either pleasure or talk between us or even your facing me—much less anything more than that—for the past year!"

And Arawn reflects for a moment, a reflection that amounts to a "double-take," as it dawns on him that Pwyll has not had sexual relations with his wife but has remained chaste the whole year. Then he tells her the truth.

In this scene and the corresponding scene in which Pwyll discovers that his rule has been improved upon by the supernatural king in his absence we have evidence for a highly developed literary tradition sprung from a vigorous oral one. The tale abounds with motifs common to international popular tradition, as Professor Kenneth Jackson has shown; in this instance, the motif of the chaste friend is apparent. But it is not the matter of chastity that interests the author, it is the ironic consequences of it. Arawn imagined that Pwyll would act out his role fully: "You will have my shape and manner, so that neither chamberlain, nor officer, nor any other who has ever followed me shall know that you are not me." When Pwyll abstained from part of the routine, Arawn had some explaining to do. The characters come to life in consequence of the author's attention to the irony of the situation and his humorous treatment of it. No explanation is offered for Pwyll's continence, and here—as elsewhere in the first branch—he seems a retiring, almost spineless character whose every move must be made for him. He is no less passive in the presence of Arawn's wife than in the presence of Arawn himself and, in the next episode, in the presence of Rhiannon. Arawn is depicted as a powerful and vigorous hunter and a capable lover; his wife is a willing mate, more than willing, perhaps, if there is irony or sarcasm even in her words, "I confess to God . . . as far as fighting temptations of the flesh and keeping true to you goes, you had a solid hold on a fellow."

This is not an isolated instance of the author's interest in the "battle of the sexes." Indeed, he seems to be at his narrative best when reporting conversations between men and woman and probing the psychological realities of the relationships between them. This is especially true in the third and fourth branches, but there are traces of the same deftness in "Branwen" too.

I suggested earlier that the redactor moved rather woodenly between the episodes that form his tale, and that the myths survived with sufficient strength that he could not alter them significantly. Had he had a freer hand in constructing his tales I think we would find a sustained brilliance in each of the branches. But such is not the case; when his interest and imagination are sparked his work shines, and when they are not, the work lacks life. He was clearly interested in the exchange between Pwyll and Arawn, but he shows little interest in the unusual meeting between Pwyll and Rhiannon. Clothed in resplendent garments, she rides by the magical mound of Arberth, site of most of the unusual occurrences in the first and third branches, on her supernatural horse. Pwyll says, "Men . . . does any of you know the horse-woman?" His words are as flat as any he utters throughout the scene, and it is not until Rhiannon herself speaks that the encounter comes to life. After exhausting every means at his disposal to overtake her, Pwyll cries out to her to stop. Her swift and decisive reply with its waspish rebuke comes to typify this forth-putting heroine: "I will wait gladly," she said, "and it had been better for the horse if you had asked it long ago."

This relationship is maintained with great consistency, and throughout the story, Pwyll is portrayed as a bungling incompetent, saved from the consequences of his own incompetence by the resourceful Rhiannon. The characterization is exploited adeptly by the author in the wedding feast scene. Pwyll welcomes the suppliant (as he was obliged to do, of course), and grants him his boon without reservation. The suitor has come, as we know, to take Rhiannon away, and Pwyll's unbounded generosity very nearly allows him to succeed. Note that in "Culhwch and Olwen," Arthur is more circumspect: "You shall have what your head and tongue may claim," he tells Culhwch, even though he does not know his identity yet, "except my ship and my mantle, Caledfwlch my sword, Rhongomiant my spear, Wynebgwrthucher my shield, Carnwennan my knife, and Gwenhwyfar my wife." A worldly-wise lord is the maker of that offer, but Pwyll is not such a one. Rhiannon's reaction is right in character, and Pwyll falls silent as she castigates his dim wits. Again, we glimpse the genius of our author in handling dramatic tension: the successful and crafty Gwawl stands before the crestfallen Pwyll, while Rhiannon unfolds the plan whereby Gwawl will be outwitted and she and Pwyll reunited. Rhiannon's plan is a complicated one and takes some time to reveal; when she has finished, Gwawl says, impatiently, "it's high time I had an answer to what I asked."

All of this is the contribution of our eleventh-century redactor or author. The mythological underpinnings are barely evident: the goddess with equine associations, choosing to bestow her favors on one lord, though there is competition for them. The boast of Medb, personification of sovereignty in Irish tradition, comes to mind: "I never had one man without another waiting in his shadow." The bag that Rhiannon gives to Pwyll, a bag of endless bounty, symbol of fertility and prosperity, is surely to be identified with the bag the goddess Epona is so often depicted holding. The time is night, when nearly all of the action of the first branch takes place, and clearly the most important if not most auspicious time for the Celts, for Caesar says that the Celts "measure all divisions of time not by the number of days, but by that of nights."[34] Just as the year began with the dark half (Irish *samhain*, November 1), so the twenty-four hour day began with the dark half (Welsh *wythnos* 'week,' literally, 'eight nights'). The action is spaced not according to ordinary temporal calculations, but at one year intervals; it is reckoned not by profane time, but by sacred time.

[34] *Gallic War*, Book VI, chapter 18.

The vigor of Rhiannon vis à vis the passivity of Pwyll is perhaps a purely Celtic phenomenon. It is in part a literary reflex of the mythological tradition we have discussed in detail, wherein elusive Sovereignty bestows her favors, albeit capriciously, on those that seek kingship. The same vigorous, forth-putting female figure is to be found in Irish tradition in Queen Medb, with her passive partner, the frequently cuckolded Ailill. She turns up again in the *mabinogi* in Aranrhod. But even though the type seems invariable, the several characterizations are fully dependent upon the skills and purposes of the authors. Aranrhod, for example, is nearly identical with the widely-known jealous step-mother type. In "Culhwch and Olwen" and the Irish *Fingal Rónáin*[35] this domineering and dangerous Celtic female is in fact the step-mother.

But against such assertive femininity, the *mabinogi* poses another type. Branwen, Blodeuedd, and Cigfa are shy, cautious, almost retiring. Branwen has nothing to say in the matter of her betrothal, nothing to say in the matter of her punishment, and dies the death of one frustrated over the inability to control destiny: she dies of a broken heart. Rhiannon, on the other hand, *decides* to accept her punishment only after conferring with her counsellors, and her mate is a man of her own choice.

Cigfa provides an interesting comparison with Pwyll: whereas he remained chaste in a relationship so admirably probed by the author, she is certain that her own is about to be compromised. Again, the motif of the chaste friend is brilliantly manipulated. Pryderi and Rhiannon have vanished, and their two mates are left alone. There is no exchange of identity here, no offer of a tempting partner to sleep with, only father-in-law and daughter-in-law. But the situation is potentially compromising, and the author plays skilfully on the psychological tension. Cigfa at first says nothing, but her meaning is clear. Manawydan, however, says too much, and it is in this imbalance of dialogue that the author has conveyed the real humor of the scene.

> When Cigfa daughter of Gwyn Gloyw, wife of Pryderi, saw that there was no one in the court but she and Manawydan, she wept

[35] The early part of *Fingal Rónáin* is somewhat similar to "Culhwch and Olwen"; for a translation of this excellently constructed tale, see *Ancient Irish Tales*, pp. 538–545.

> until she didn't care whether she was still alive or dead. What Manawydan did then was to look at her.
>
> "God knows," he said, "you're mistaken about it if you weep for fear of me. As God is my guarantor, you have never seen a truer friend than you will have in me, as long as God may wish you to be thus. I swear to God, if I were beginning my youth I would keep true to Pryderi, and for you yourself will I keep it; fear not," he said. "I swear to God," he continued, "you will get the companionship you wish from me, according to my ability, while God wills us to be in this stress and strain."

It has often been noted that the fourth branch is the most complex of the *mabinogi* tales; it is, in the sense that there is less apparent continuity between its numerous episodes than is found in the other three branches. I have tried to suggest above some of the mythological detritus that informs that tale, and therein lies the key to the tale's sub-structure. But here it is the super-structure, the cortex, that interests us, especially the characterization of Blodeuedd. Her name indicates her origin, for she was fashioned from flowers, though the bloom never left her and she was the most beautiful maiden anyone ever saw. The author wastes no time on the conjugal affairs of Lleu and his bride, but removes the husband from the scene almost immediately and launches into the episode of Blodeuedd's infidelity. This episode and its consequences occupy a full quarter of the tale, and much of it is dialogue. Lleu has little to do with it; Blodeuedd is depicted as one who easily loses her heart and is capable of using her husband's desire for her as a lever to pry from him knowledge of how his death may be achieved. The fact that a hero's death can only be encompassed by a combination of unlikely circumstances is typical of many literatures, but the circumstances are rarely as preposterous as these or accomplished by such charade.

The love that Blodeuedd and the adulterer Gronw feel for each other is unlike any sort of love depicted in the other branches, but is reminiscent of the love that Gilfaethwy feels for Math's footholder, Goewin, and the debilitating sort of love that later came to characterize the courtly lover. Gilfaethwy's love is unilateral, however: "Gilfaethwy son of Dôn set his mind on the maid, and fell in love with her to the extent that he did not know what to do about it. Even his color, his appearance and his general condition worsened for love of her, so that it was not easy to recognize him." In the case of Blodeuedd and Gronw, the love is mutual, but not less debilitating: "What Blodeuedd did was to look at him, and as she gazed, her entire being was filled with love of him. And he noticed her, too, and the same feeling was awakened in him as awakened in her." While Gilfaethwy has to resort to a complicated ruse and then rape to satisfy his urge, Blodeuedd and Gronw enjoy a hasty requital: "Nor did they put off past that night embracing each other; they slept together the same night." Neither of these loves bears any close relationship to the love Culhwch feels for Olwen. His is a cursed loving; he neither wills it nor resists it. She feels nothing for him, and responds to him only as the tale type requires. The author of the four branches, on the other hand, shows a remarkable sophistication in dealing with the ideals and realities of human love. He can with equal success probe the subtle and not so subtle feeling of lover, beloved, and cuckolded.

In this introduction, I have used the words "redactor" and "author" for lack of a better word. We do not know who "authored" these tales, though it is quite certain that a single person was responsible for the final shape of the four branches of the *mabinogi*, and that he was not the same person who gave us the final shape of the other tales translated here. The tales and the episodes that constitute them were part of the repertory of a learned class of men who transmitted their lore orally; there were differences of detail in the performances of different reciters. We do not know whether the version copied down by our nameless scribe was that taken down from a prominent contemporary storyteller or was the scribe's own version. But in either case, he or his patron or his audience must have felt that it was an "authoritative" version. He might have added with justifiable pride and in the spirit of the scribe who wrote down "The Cattle Raid of Cooley" in the twelfth-century Book of Leinster: "A blessing on every one who shall faithfully memorize the Táin as it is written here and shall not add any other form to it."[36]

The colophon testifies not only to the Irish scribe's adherence to the "version" he has recorded, but his approval of its style and

[36] *Táin Bó Cúalnge* from the Book of Leinster, ed. and trans. by Cecile O'Rahilly (Dublin, 1967), p. 272.

language. He knew that some of his story was "the deception of demons," that is, remnants of the old beliefs, the pre-Christian traditions, and that some of it was "poetic figments," the conscious stylistic contributions of a skilful narrator. If our Welsh redactors, authors, scribes, were conscious that the tales they transmitted contained the "deceptions of demons," they did not say so. Fortunately for us, they were content to pass on the branches of their tradition that had survived, quickened with an artistic vitality that varied according to the gifts of the individual performers. Their work is our most important index of tradition and the literary art in medieval Wales.

SELECT BIBLIOGRAPHY

Bibliography

RACHEL BROMWICH, *Medieval Celtic Literature* (Toronto, 1974).

Editions

J. GWENOGVRYN EVANS and SIR JOHN RHŶS, *The Text of the Mabinogion and Other Welsh Tales from the Red Book of Hergest* (Oxford, 1887), diplomatic edition.

J. GWENOGVRYN EVANS, *The White Book Mabinogion* (Pwllheli, 1907), diplomatic edition.

BRYNLEY F. ROBERTS, *Cyfranc Lludd a Llefelys* (Dublin, 1975).

DERICK S. THOMSON, *Branwen Uerch Lyr* (Dublin, 1961).

R. L. THOMSON, *Pwyll Pendeuic Dyuet* (Dublin, 1957).

SIR IFOR WILLIAMS, *Cyfranc Lludd a Llevelys*, 2nd ed. (Bangor, 1932).

——, *Pedeir Keinc y Mabinogi* (Cardiff, 1930; new ed. 1951).

Translations

LADY CHARLOTTE GUEST, *The Mabinogion* (London, 1838–1849); text and translation, including "Taliesin."

THOMAS JONES and GWYN JONES, *The Mabinogion*, rev. ed. (London and New York, 1974); Everyman's Library, no. 97; first published by Golden Cockerel Press, 1948.

T. P. ELLIS and JOHN LLOYD, *The Mabinogion, A New Translation* (Oxford, 1929).

LOTH, J., *Les Mabinogion*, 2nd ed. (Paris, 1913).

William Owen Pughe, "Pwyll,"*Cambrian Register,* 1795.
———, "Pwyll," (revised), *Cambro-Briton,* February, 1821.
———, "Math son of Mathonwy," *Cambrian Quarterly,* 1829.

Discussion

Edward Anwyl, "The Four Branches of the Mabinogi," *Zeitschrift für Celtische Philologie,* I (1896), 277–293; II (1898), 124–133; III (1900), 123–134.

R. A. Breatnach, "The Lady and the King: A Theme of Irish Literature," *Studies,* XLII (1953), 321–336.

Rachel Bromwich, "The Chracter of Early Welsh Tradition" in H. M. Chadwick et al., *Studies in Early British History* (Cambridge, 1959), pp. 83–136.

———, *Trioedd Ynys Prydein* (Cardiff, 1961).

T. M. Charles-Edwards, "The Date of the Four Branches of the Mabinogi," *Transactions of the Honourable Society of Cymmrodorion,* 1970, pp. 263–298.

T. P. Ellis, "Legal References, Terms and Conceptions in *The Mabinogion," Y Cymmrodor,* XXXIX (1928), 86–148.

Patrick K. Ford, "A Fragment of the Hanes Taliesin by Llywelyn Siôn," *Études Celtiques,* XIV (1975), 449–458.

———, "The Poet as *Cyfarwydd* in Early Welsh Tradition," *Studia Celtica,* X–XI (1975–1976), 152–162.

W. J. Gruffydd, "Mabon fab Modron," *Y Cymmrodor,* XLII (1930), 129–147.

———, *Math vab Mathonwy* (Cardiff, 1928).

———,*Rhiannon* (Cardiff, 1953).

Eric P. Hamp, "Mabinogi," *Transactions of the Honourable Society of Cymmrodorion,* 1974–1975, pp. 243–249.

———, "On Dating and Archaism in the Pedeir Keinc," *Transactions of the Honourable Society of Cymmrodorion,* 1972–1973, pp. 95–103.

P. L. Henry, "Culhwch and Olwen–Some Aspects of Style and Structure," *Studia Celtica,* III (1968), 30–38.

Kenneth H. Jackson, *The International Popular Tale and Early Welsh Tradition* (Cardiff, 1961).

———, "Some Popular Motifs in Early Welsh Tradition," *Études Celtiques,* XI (1964–1965), 83–99.

A. O. H. Jarman and Gwilym Rees Hughes, *A Guide to Welsh Literature Vol. I* (Swansea, 1976), esp. chaps. vii, ix.

Thomas Jones, "The Early Evolution of the Legend of Arthur," *Nottingham Medieval Studies,* VIII (1964), 3–21; translated from the Welsh by Gerald Morgan.

E. J. LLOYD, "*The Mabinogion* as Literature," *The Celtic Review*, VII (1911), 164–174; 220–248.

R. S. LOOMIS, ed., *Arthurian Literature in the Middle Ages* (Oxford, 1959).

PROINSIAS MACCANA, *Branwen Daughter of Llŷr* (Cardiff, 1958).

———, *Celtic Mythology* (London, 1970).

———, "The Theme of King and Goddess in Irish Literature," *Études Celtiques*, VII (1955), 76–114; 356–413; VIII (1958), 59–65.

JOHN MORRIS-JONES, "Taliesin," *Y Cymmrodor*, XXVIII (1918), 1–290.

THOMAS PARRY, *A History of Welsh Literature*, translated by H. I. Bell (Oxford, 1955).

ALWYN REES and BRINLEY REES, *Celtic Heritage* (London, 1961).

Other

T. P. CROSS and CLARK SLOVER, *Ancient Irish Tales*, with revised bibliography by Charles W. Dunn, New York, 1969.

THE TALES

Annwyn

Other world

Arawn

(1)

1. change world
2. change colors red + white
3. change shapes (Arawn)

(4) 1. change shapes Math

G. = Gwydion

Pwyll, Prince of Dyfed

The first branch of the *mabinogi* is set in Dyfed in southwest Wales. It concerns Pwyll, prince or lord of that region, his adventures in the Otherworld, his marriage to Rhiannon, and the birth of their son, Pryderi. Adventures in the Otherworld are common enough in romance, but in medieval Celtic literature they play a large role. It is often difficult to distinguish between the Otherworld and the world of ordinary mortals, and movement between the two is effected with little or no difficulty. There are certain standard devices used to mark the passage from one into the other; the most common of these is the chase or the hunt. Typically, an Otherworldly animal lures his pursuers until he gets them within the territory of the Otherworld, but in our tale, Pwyll is simply hunting, when he becomes separated from his companions. No other territorial markers signal the entry into the Otherworld, nor is the return from the Otherworld indicated by any precise demarcation. The only indication for the audience that the Otherworld is at hand is the color of the other hunter's hounds, for red and white are the colors of animals of the Otherworld in Celtic tradition.

Just as movement between the two worlds is affected without difficulty, so is movement between shapes, and Pwyll and Arawn accomplish their transformations easily. In this branch, the power to shift shapes rests with the Otherworldly king, Arawn; in the fourth branch there is no opposition of worlds, and there it is Math and his nephew Gwydion who possess the power of shape-shifting. Math uses a rod of magic to change the shapes of Gwydion and Gilfaethwy against their wills; Gwydion changes his and his companions shapes without any instrument.

The exchange between Pwyll and Arawn is the only instance of shape-shifting in the first branch, but there are many other instances of magic. The horse on which Rhiannon rides is magical, for although its pace is slow and steady, the fastest horses in Pwyll's stables are unable to catch it. The mound from which Rhiannon is first seen is a magical place, and we should remember that hills and mounds played a special part in the religious observances of the Celts. The mound at Arberth has special significance in the third branch also; it is the place from which Manawydan and his companions witness the disappearance of every living thing from the land, and the place on which Manawydan secures the restoration of life and propserity for Dyfed. In the second branch, the rock of Harlech is the place from which the action of the tale begins and the site of the Otherworld feast. Other instances of magic in the tale of "Pwyll" include Rhiannon's bag, which can never be filled except by the recitation of a special formula, the annual disappearance of the foals from Teyrnon's mare, and the unusual circumstances of the discovery of Rhiannon's baby.

It is difficult to account for the lack of continuity in the story; for example, once Pwyll has received his new title, *Pen Annwfn* 'Lord of the Otherworld,' the story-teller shows no further interest in Arawn or in Annwfn, and the story seems to begin to anew. Some scholars have seen this as evidence for the corrupt state of the text, and have sought to reconstruct the opening episode in such a way that it results in the birth of Pryderi. But such reconstruction does too much violence to the text we have before us, and it is probably unnecessary anyway. What the opening episode does quite clearly is establish Pwyll's Otherworldly connections and account for the fact that he was, mortal Prince of Dyfed or not, a head or lord of the Otherworld. From that point on, the story proceeds in a linear way through the events of the courtship of Rhiannon, the marriage, the birth, loss and restoration of Pryderi.

The punishment of Rhiannon is bizarre, but it provides an important clue to the mythological identity of this character. Because she was accused of having destroyed her own child, Rhiannon was driven from her place beside Pwyll, and sentenced to spend seven years at the horse block outside the court, to tell her story (presumably the story of how she killed her own offspring) to those she thought might not know it, and to offer to carry strangers up to the court on her back. In other words, she was to fill the role of horse. Scholars have long seen in this a connection between Rhiannon and the goddess known as Epona worshipped by the Celts on the Continent. The name Epona means "Divine Horse," and although she is depicted as human, there is no doubt that she was originally one of the numerous deities in animal form worshipped by the Celtic peoples. There are numerous and widespread depictions of Epona, showing her seated upon a horse proceeding at an amble, surrounded by birds, foals, or holding a bag or cornucopia. It appears that the first branch preserves the memory of this Celtic goddess and the detritus of a myth that told about her mating and giving birth.

The characterization of Rhiannon is strong and sure; she is assertive and dominant, often domineering. It is clear from her first entrance that she will accomplish her ends despite the ineptness of her intended mate. She has no equal in characterization anywhere in these tales.

Pwyll, Prince of Dyfed, was lord over the seven cantrefs of Dyfed. One time he was in Arberth, his principal court, and it came into his head and mind to go hunting. The part of his realm he wished to hunt was called Glyn Cuch. He set out that night from Arberth, and came as far as Pen Llwyn Diarwya; there he stayed that night. The following day at dawn he rose, and came to Glyn Cuch to let his hounds loose in the woods. He sounded his horn, began to muster the hunt, and set off behind his dogs—but he got separated from his companions. As he was listening to the cry of his hunting-pack, he heard the cry of another, and they were not the same; the other was coming toward his own. He could see a clearing in the woods, a kind of level field, and as his own pack reached the edge of the clearing, he could see a stag in front of the other. Toward the middle of the clearing, the pack chasing the stag overtook it and bore it to the ground.

He looked at the color of the hounds, not bothering to look at the stag, and of all the hunting dogs he had seen in the world, he had never seen dogs the color of them. Glittering bright white was their color, and their ears red: the redness of the ears glittered as brightly as the whiteness of their bodies. Thereupon, he came to the dogs and drove off the pack that had killed the stag, feeding his own pack on it.

As he was feeding the dogs, he saw a horseman coming up behind the pack on a large dapple-gray horse, a hunting horn about his neck, wearing a pale grey garment for hunting gear. Thereupon, the horseman came to him, saying as follows:

"Chieftain," he said, "I know who you are, but I will not greet you."

"Well," said the other, "perhaps your rank does not require it."

"God knows!" he exclaimed, "it is not the obligation of my rank that prevents me."

"What else, Chieftain?" asked the other.

"I swear to God," he said, "your own ignorance and your discourtesy."

"What discourtesy have you seen in me, Chieftain?"

"No greater discourtesy have I seen in a man," he replied, "than driving off the pack that killed the stag, and feeding your own pack on it; that," he continued, "was discourtesy. And though I shall not take revenge upon you, I swear to God," he said, "I will have you satirized to the value of a hundred stags."

"Chieftain," he said, "if I have committed a wrong, I will sue for peace with you."

"On what terms?" asked the other.

"Such as your rank may require, but I don't know who you are."

"I am a crowned king in the land from which I hail."

"Lord," he said, "good-day to you! What land do you come from?"

"Annwfn," he replied, "I am Arawn, King of Annwfn."

"Lord," he said, "how shall I gain peace with you?"

"Here is how you shall gain it," he began. "A man whose realm borders on mine makes war on me continually. He is Hafgan, a king of Annwfn. For delivering me from his oppression—and you can do that easily—you will have peace from me."

"I will do that gladly," he replied, "tell me how I can accomplish it."

"All right," he said, "here is how you shall do it. I will form a strong bond with you in this way: I will put you in my place in Annwfn, and give you the fairest woman you have ever seen to sleep with you every night. You will have my shape and manner, so that neither chamberlain, nor officer, nor any other who has ever followed me shall know that you are not I. And that until the end of a year from tomorrow, when we meet in this place."

"Well," he said, "though I be there until the end of the year, what information will I have to find the man of whom you speak?"

"He and I are due to meet a year from tonight at the ford," he explained, "and you be there in my place. Give him but a single blow; he will not survive that. And though he may beg you to strike again, don't—however he may plead with you. No matter how many more I would give him, he would attack me the next day as well as before."

"Well," said Pwyll, "what shall I do with my kingdom?"

"I will arrange that no man or woman in your realm shall know that I am not you," said Arawn, "I will go in your place."

"Gladly," said Pwyll; "I will set forth."

"Your path will be smooth and nothing will obstruct you until you come to my realm; I will be your guide."

He escorted him until he saw the court and dwellings.

"There," he said, "is the court and the realm in your power. Approach the court; there is none in it that shall not know you. And as you observe the practices there, you will come to know the court's customs."

He approached the court, and inside he could see sleeping quarters, halls, and chambers, and the most beautifully ornamented buildings anyone had seen. He went into the hall to change his dress. Lads and young attendants came to assist him in removing his gear, and each greeted him as he came. Two horsemen came to remove his hunting garments and dress him in gold brocade.

The hall was set in order, and then he could see entering a warband and hosts—the most splendid and best equipped troop that anyone had ever seen; the queen was with them, the fairest woman anyone had ever seen, dressed in a glittering gold brocaded garment. Thereupon, they washed, went to the table, and sat in this way: the queen on his one side and the earl (he supposed) on the other. He began to converse with the queen, and as for talking with her, she was the noblest and gentlest in her nature and her discourse of any he had ever seen. And they passed the time in food and drink, with songs and entertainment. Of all the courts he had seen on earth, this was the court best supplied with food and drink, gold vessels, and royal treasures.

The time came for them to go to sleep, and to sleep they went, he and the queen. As soon as they got into bed, he turned his face toward the edge of the bed, with his back toward her. From that moment until the next morning, he spoke not a single word to her. On the following day there was tenderness and loving discourse between them, but whatever affection would be between them during the day, there was not a single night for the rest of the year different from the first night.

He spent the year in hunting, in songs and festivity, in affection and conversation with friends, until the night of the encounter came: a night remembered as well by the most remote inhabitant of the entire land as it was by him. He came to the appointed place, accompanied by nobles of his realm. The moment he came to the ford, a horseman arose and spoke as follows:

"Men," he said, "listen well: this encounter is between the two kings, and between their two bodies alone. Each of them is a claimant against the other, and that concerning land and territory. And each of you can stand aside and leave it between them two."

Thereupon, the two kings made for the middle of the ford to clash. At the first blow, the man who was in Arawn's place struck Hafgan in the middle of the boss of his shield so that it split in half and all the armor shattered, and Hafgan went the length of his arm and spear over his horse's rump to the ground, a mortal thrust in him.

"Chieftain," said Hafgan, "what right did you have to my death? I claimed nothing from you nor do I know any cause for you to kill me, but for God's sake," he said, "since you have begun to kill me, finish!"

"Chieftain," said the other, "I could regret doing what I did to you. Find someone who will kill you, I will not."

"My loyal nobles," Hafgan said, "take me hence; my death is assured. I have no means to support you any longer."

"Men of mine," said the man who was in Arawn's place, "take accounts and find out who owes allegiance to me."

"Lord," said the nobles, "all owe it, for there is no king over all of Annwfn except you."

"Well," he said, "those who come in peace, it is proper to receive, but those who do not come peacefully, let them be compelled by sword."

And then he received homage of the men and began to take possession of the land. By noon of the next day the two realms were in his power.

And then he set out for his rendezvous, and came to Glyn Cuch. When he arrived, Arawn king of Annwfn was waiting for him. They greeted each other.

"Well," said Arawn, "may God repay you your friendship—I have heard about it."

"Yes," said the other, "when you reach your land you will see what I have done for you."

"For what you have done on my behalf, may God repay you."

Then Arawn restored Pwyll, Prince of Dyfed, to his own shape and form, took for himself his own form and shape, and set out for his own court in Annwfn. It gave him pleasure to see his host and his retinue, since he had not seen them for a year. But on their part, they had not felt his loss, so there was nothing extraordinary about his coming. He passed that day in pleasure and joy, sitting and conversing with his wife and his nobles. And when the period of entertainment was past and it was time to sleep, to sleep they went. He got into bed, and his wife went to him. First he talked to her, then engaged in affectionate play and made love to her. She had not been accustomed to that for a year, and she thought about that.

"Dear God!" she thought, "what a different mind he has tonight from what he has had for the past year!"

And she thought for a long time. And after her musing, he awoke and said something to her, and again, and a third time. But he got no answer from her.

"Why don't you speak to me?" he asked.

"I tell you," she replied, 'that I haven't spoken this much for a year under these circumstances."

"Why," he said, "we have talked continually."

"Shame on me," she said, "if from the time we went between the sheets there was either pleasure or talk between us or even your facing me—much less anything more than that—for the past year!"

And he thought, "Dear Lord God, it was a unique man, with strong and unwavering friendship that I got for a companion." And then he said to his wife, "Lady," he said, "don't blame me. I swear to God," he said, "I haven't slept with you since a year from last night nor have I lain with you."

And he told her the entire adventure.

"I confess to God," she said, "as far as fighting temptations of the flesh and keeping true to you goes, you had a solid hold on a fellow."

"Lady," he said, "that's just what I was thinking while I was silent with you."

"That was only natural," she answered.

Meanwhile, Pwyll, Prince of Dyfed, came to his realm and country. And he began to query the nobles of the country about what their governance had been during that year compared with what it had been prior to that.

"Lord," they said, "your discernment has never been so good: never have you been so amiable a fellow; never have you been so ready to spend your gain; your rule has never been better than this past year."

"I swear to God," he said, "it is right for you to thank the man who has been with you: here is the story, just as it was"—and Pwyll told it all.

"Well, Lord," they said, "thank God you acquired that friendship. And the governance we got, you'll not withdraw from us, surely!"

"I will not, I swear to God," said Pwyll.

From that time on, they began to strengthen their friendship, and sent each other horses, hunting dogs, hawks, and treasures of the sort that each supposed would give pleasure to the other. Because of his living for that year in Annwfn and ruling it so successfully, and bringing the two realms together by virtue of his bravery and valor, his name, Pwyll, Prince of Dyfed, fell out of use, and he came to be called Pwyll, Head of Annwfn, thenceforth.

One time he was in Arberth, his chief court, and a feast had been prepared for him and the great numbers of men with him. After the first sitting Pwyll rose to take a walk, and proceeded to the top of a mound that was just above the court, called the Mound of Arberth.

"Lord," said a member of the court," it is a characteristic of the mound that any noble who sits upon it shall not leave it without the one of two things: either he will be wounded or suffer an injury, or he will see a marvel."

"I am not afraid of being wounded or injured in the midst of such a host as this, but I would be pleased if I could see a wonder. I will go to the mound and sit," he declared.

He sat on the mound. As they were sitting, they saw a woman mounted on a great, majestic pale-white horse, dressed in brilliant gold silk brocade, coming along the main road that ran past the mound. To anyone who saw it, the horse appeared to have a slow, steady gait as it came even with the mound.

"Men," said Pwyll, "does any of you know the horse-woman?"

"No, Lord," they replied.

"One of you go meet her," he said, "to find out who she is."

One of them rose, but when he got to the road to meet her, she had gone by him. He pursued her as quickly as he could on foot. The more he hastened, the farther she got from him. When he saw that it did not avail him to pursue her, he returned to Pwyll and said to him, "Lord," he said, "no one in the world will succeed in following on foot."

"Well," said Pwyll, "go to the court, take the fastest horse you know, and go out after her."

He took the horse and away he went. When he reached the plain, he put spurs to the horse, but the more he spurred the horse, the farther she would be from him. She held the horse to the same pace she had begun. His horse balked; when he realized that his horse had refused the pace, he returned to where Pwyll was.

"Lord," he said, "it doesn't avail anyone to follow yonder lady. I knew of no horse in the realm swifter than that one, yet I didn't succeed in pursuing her."

"Well," said Pwyll, "there is some mysterious meaning in that; let us go to the court."

They went to the court and spent that day.

The next day they arose, and they passed the day until it was time to eat. After the first sitting, Pwyll said, "Well, let us go—the same group as yesterday—to the top of the mound. And you," he said to one of his lads, "bring the fastest horse in the field you know, right away."

The lad did that, and they went to the mound, the horse with them. As they were sitting, they saw the woman mounted on the horse, the same garment about her, coming the same way.

"There," said Pwyll, "is the horse-woman we saw yesterday. Be ready, my fellow," he said, "to find out who she is."

"Lord," he said, "I will, gladly."

Thereupon, the horse-woman came level with them. The lad mounted the horse, but before he had settled himself in his saddle, she had gone past him and put distance between them. She maintained no pace other than she had the day before. He set the horse at an amble, supposing that because of how slowly his horse travelled he would overtake her. But that did not work. Then he gave the horse his reins, but he was no nearer to her than if he were at a walk; the more he spurred his horse, the farther she would be from him, though her pace was no greater than before. Since he saw it did not avail him to pursue her, he turned back and came to where Pwyll was.

"Lord," he said, "the horse has no power other than what you saw."

"I saw;" he replied, "no one will succeed in pursuing her. But I swear to God," he said, "she had business with someone here, if obstinacy would allow her to tell it. But let us go to the court."

They went to the court and spent that night in songs and entertainment, as they were content to do. The next day they whiled away the hours until it was time to eat. When they finished the food, Pwyll said, "Where is the company we were yesterday and the day before at the top of the mound?"

"Here, Lord," they said.

"Let us go to the mound to sit," he said, "And you," he said to his groom, "saddle my horse well and bring him to the road, and bring my spurs with you."

The fellow did that, and they came to the mound to sit. They had scarcely been there a moment when they saw the horse-woman coming the same way, looking as she did before, travelling at the same pace.

"Lad," said Pwyll, "I see the horse-woman. Bring my horse."

Pwyll mounted the horse, and no sooner had he done so, than she was past him. He turned after her, and let the lively prancing horse set its own pace. He supposed that at the second or third bound he would overtake her. But he was no nearer to her than before. He urged the horse on to its swiftest pace. And he saw that it did no good to pursue her. Then Pwyll called out; "Maiden," he said, "for the sake of the man you love most, wait for me!"

"I will wait gladly," she said, "and it had been better for the horse if you had asked it long ago."

The maiden stopped and waited, removed the part of her head piece that was supposed to be about her face, and fixing a look upon him, began to converse with him.

"Lady," he said, "whence do you come, and what is the nature of your travel?"

"I travel on my business," she said, "and I am pleased to see you."

"I welcome you," he said.

And he thought that the faces of all the maidens he had ever seen were unpleasant compared with her face.

"Lady," he said, "will you tell me any of your business?"

"Yes; I swear to God," she said, "my principle business was trying to see you."

"That is the best business you could come for in my estimation," said Pwyll, "But will you tell me who you are?"

"I will, Lord," she said, "I am Rhiannon daughter of Hyfaidd Hen, and I am being given to a man against my will. I have never desired any man, and that because of loving you. And I still don't desire one, unless you reject me; it is to know your answer to that that I have come."

"I swear to God," said Pwyll, "my answer to you is this: if I could choose from all the women and maidens in the world, 'tis you I would choose."

"Well," said she, "if that is what you want, set a date with me before I am given to another man."

"The sooner the better for me," said Pwyll, "and let it be wherever you like."

"All right, Lord," she said. "A year from tonight, in the court of Hyfaidd Hen, I will arrange for a feast to be ready by the time you arrive."

"Gladly," said he, "and I will be there."

"Lord," she said, "stay well! and remember to keep your promise. And now I shall depart."

They separated, and he went toward his retinue and his host. Whatever questions they would have concerning the maiden, he would turn to other matters.

They passed the year from then on until the appointed time, when Pwyll arrayed himself with a hundred horsemen, and set out for the court of Hyfaidd Hen. He came to the court, and they welcomed him; there was a multitude to greet him with great gladness and many preparations. All the resources of the court were placed at his disposal. The hall was arranged and they went to the tables. This is how they sat: Hyfaidd Hen on one side of Pwyll and Rhiannon on the other; after that each according to his rank. They ate and celebrated and conversed.

At the beginning of the after-dinner entertainment, they saw a large, noble, brown-haired fellow enter, wearing silk brocade. When he came to the fore-court of the hall, he saluted Pwyll and his companions.

"God's welcome to you, friend, go sit down," said Pwyll.

"No," he replied, "I am a suppliant and I will do my business."

"Do it gladly," said Pwyll.

"Lord," he began, "my business is with you, and I have come to make a request of you."

"Whatever you ask of me, as far as I am able to get it, you shall have it."

"Och!" exclaimed Rhiannon, "why do you respond so!"

"He did so, Lady, and in the presence of nobles," said the other.

"Friend," said Pwyll, "what is your request?"

"You are sleeping tonight with the woman I love most, and it is to ask for her and the feast and the preparations that are here that I have come."

Pwyll fell silent, for there was no response he could give.

"Be silent as long as you like," said Rhiannon. "Never has a man been more feeble-witted than you have been."

"Lady," he said, "I didn't know who he was."

"That's the man to whom they wanted to give me against my will," she said, "Gwawl son of Clud, a man of hosts and riches. But since you said what you did, give me to him lest dishonor befall you."

"Lady," he replied, "I don't know what sort of answer that is; I could never bring myself to do what you say."

"Give me to him," she said, "and I will see to it that he shall never have me."

"How will that be?" asked Pwyll.

"I will put in your hand a small bag," she said, "and keep it safely with you. He will ask for the feast and the provisions and the preparations, but that is not yours. I will give the feast to the retinue and the hosts," she continued, "and that will be your answer as to that. As for me," she said, "I will set a date with him, for a year from tonight, to sleep with me. At the end of the year, you be up in the orchard as one of a hundred horsemen, and have this bag with you. When he is in the midst of his pleasure and revelry you come in wearing threadbare clothing, and have the bag in your hand," she explained, "and ask nothing but the bag full of food. I will bring it about," she said, "that even if all the food and drink of these seven cantrefs were put into it, the bag would be no fuller than before. And after a great deal has been thrown into it, he will ask you, 'will your bag ever be full?' You will reply that it will not, unless some very powerful nobleman gets up and tramples the food in the bag with his feet, saying 'enough has been put in here.' And I will see to it that he goes to trample the food in the bag. When he does, twist the bag so that he goes head over heels into it. Then knot the strings of the bag. Have a hunting horn around your neck, and when he is bound up in the bag, sound your horn and that will be a sign between you and your horsemen. When they hear your horn, let them descend upon the court."

"Lord," said Gwawl, "it's high time I had an answer to what I asked."

"As much as you asked," said Pwyll, "of that which is my power you shall have."

"Friend," said Rhiannon, "as for the feast and the provisions here, I have given them to the men of Dyfed, to the retinue and the hosts that are here. I will not allow it to be given to anyone else. A year from tonight, however, a feast shall be made ready in this court for you, friend, to sleep with me."

Gwawl departed for his realm. Pwyll came to Dyfed. Each of them passed that year, until the appointed time for the feast that was in the court of Hyfaidd Hen. Gwawl son of Clud came to the feast that was arranged for him; he approached the court and they welcomed him. Pwyll Pen Annwfn came to the orchard—one of a hundred horsemen—just as Rhiannon had commanded him, and the bag with him. Pwyll wore wretched rags and had oafish boots on his feet. When he knew they had begun the after-dinner entertainment, he went forth to the court. After he came to the forecourt he saluted Gwawl son of Clud and his company of men and women.

"May God provide for you, and God's welcome to you," said Gwawl.

"Lord," said the other, "may God repay you. I have business with you."

"Your errand is welcome," he said, "and if your resquest is

reasonable, gladly will you have it."

"It is reasonable, Lord," said the other, "I ask it only from want. This is what I request: this small bag that you see full of food."

"That is a modest request," he said, "and you shall have it, gladly. Bring food for him," he ordered.

A great number of servers arose and began to fill the bag. But despite what they put in it was no fuller than before.

"Friend," said Gwawl, "will your bag ever be full?"

"No, I swear to God," he replied, "no matter what is put in it, until a noble endowed with land, territory, and wealth rises up and tramples the food in the bag, saying 'enough has been put in here'."

"Great Lord," said Rhiannon to Gwawl, "get up quickly."

"I will, gladly," he said.

And he rose up and put his feet in the bag; Pwyll twisted it so that Gwawl went head over heels into the bag, then he closed it quickly, tied the strings, and sounded his horn. Instantly, the war band was upon the court, and the entire host that had come with Gwawl was seized and put in their own fetters. Pwyll cast off the rags, oafish boots, and shabby clothing that he had worn.

Each of his own men as they came in, would strike the bag a blow, and would ask, "what do we have here?" "A badger," the others would reply. This is the sort of game they played, each would strike the bag a blow, either with his foot or with a stick. Thus they played with the bag; each as he came in would ask, "what is this game you are playing?" "The game of Badger-in-the-Bag" they would answer. That was the first time that "Badger-in-the-Bag" was ever played.

"Lord," said the man in the bag, "if you would listen to me, killing me inside a bag is no death for me."

"Lord," said Hyfaidd Hen, "he speaks truly, and it is right for you to hear him. That is no death for him."

"Well," said Pwyll, "I will deal with him according to your counsel."

"Here is your advice," said Rhiannon then. "You are in the position where it falls to you to satisfy suppliants and minstrels. Let him dispense on your behalf, and take a pledge from him that there shall never be redress nor vengeance for it; that's enough punishment for him."

"He shall get that gladly," said the man in the bag.

"And I shall accept it, gladly," said Pwyll, "on the advice of Hyfaidd and Rhiannon."

"That is our advice," they said.

"I accept it," said Pwyll. "Find sureties to go on your behalf."

"We will act as sureties for him," said Hyfaidd, "until his own men are free to go on his behalf."

And thereupon he was released from the bag, and his chief followers were freed.

"Ask Gwawl for sureties now," said Hyfaidd. "We know who should be taken from him." Hyfaidd enumerated the sureties.

"State your terms yourself," said Gwawl.

"I am satisfied with the way Rhiannon stated them," said Pwyll.

The sureties went on those terms.

"Well, Lord," said Gwawl, "I am wounded, I have received a grievous injury, and I need to bathe. With your permission I will depart. And I will leave nobles here on my behalf to answer all those who may make requests of you."

"Gladly," said Pwyll, "do that."

Gwawl went off toward his own land.

The hall was then prepared for Pwyll and his host, and the host of the court as well. They went to the tables and sat down—they seated themselves that night just as they had the year before. They ate and revelled, and it came time to go to sleep. Pwyll and Rhiannon went to the chamber and spent the night in pleasure and contentment.

Early on the next day, Rhiannon said, "Lord, arise, and begin satisfying the minstrels, and refuse none who may seek goods."

"Gladly will I do that," said Pwyll, "today and every day while the feast lasts."

Pwyll rose and caused a proclamation to be made, requiring all suppliants and minstrels to appear, and telling them that each would be satisfied according to his pleasure and his whim; that was done.

The feast was consumed, and while it lasted, none was refused. When it ended, Pwyll said to Hyfaidd, "Lord, I will set out for Dyfed in the morning with your permission."

"Well," said Hyfaidd, "may God make smooth your path. Set a time and date when Rhiannon shall follow you."

"I swear to God," said Pwyll, "we will leave here together!"

"Is that the way you want it, Lord?" asked Hyfaidd.

"It is, I swear to God," answered Pwyll.

The next day they set out for Dyfed and made for the court at Arberth. A feast had been prepared for them, and the best men and women in the land and in the realm were assembled before them. Neither man nor woman of them went away from Rhiannon without being given some special gift, either a brooch or a ring or some precious stone.

They ruled the land successfully that year and the next. But in the third year, the men of the land began to feel sad within themselves at seeing the man they loved so much as their lord and foster-brother without an heir. And they summoned him to them. It was in Presseleu in Dyfed that they met.

"Lord," they said, "we know that you are not the same age as some of the men in this land, and we are afraid that you might not have an heir from the woman who is with you. So for that reason, take another wife that you may have an heir from her. You will not last forever, and though you would like to remain as you are, we will not tolerate it from you."

"Well," said Pwyll, "we have not been together long, and much may happen yet. Be patient with me until the end of the year: we will arrange to meet a year from now, and I will act according to your advice."

The appointment was made, but before the time was up, a son was born to him, and in Arberth he was born. On the night of his birth, women were brought in to watch over the boy and his mother. What the women did, however, was sleep, and Rhiannon, the boy's mother, too. Six was the number of women brought in. They kept vigil for a part of the night, but then, however, before midnight, each fell asleep; toward dawn they awakened. When they awoke, they looked where they had put the boy, but there was no sign of him there.

"Och!" exclaimed one of the women, "the boy is surely lost!"

"Indeed," said another, "it would be a small punishment to burn us or slay us on account of the boy."

"Is there any counsel in the world for that?" one of them asked.

"There is," said another, "I have good counsel."

"What is it?" they asked.

"There is a staghound bitch here," she said, "and she had puppies. Let us kill some of the pups, smear Rhiannon's face and hands with the blood, cast the bones before her, and swear that she herself has destroyed her son. And our affirmation will not yield to her own."

They decided on that. Toward day Rhiannon awoke and said, "Ladies, where is my boy?"

"Lady," they said, "don't ask us for your son. We have nothing but bruises and blows from struggling with you, and we have certainly never seen ferocity in any woman as much as in you. But it did us no good to fight with you; you have destroyed your son yourself, so do not seek him from us."

"You poor things!" exclaimed Rhiannon, "for the sake of the Lord God who knows all things, don't lie to me! God, who knows everything, knows that's a lie. If it is because you are afraid, I confess to God, I will protect you."

"God knows," they said, "we would not suffer harm to befall us for anyone in the world."

"Poor things," she said, "you'll suffer no harm for telling the truth."

But despite what she would say either in reason or with emotion, she would get only the same answer from the women.

Thereupon Pwyll Pen Annwfn rose, along with the retinue and the hosts; it was impossible to conceal what had happened. The news went through the land, and every nobleman heard it. The nobles met and sent emissaries to Pwyll, to ask him to divorce his wife for having committed an outrage as reprehensible as she had done.

"They have no cause to request that I divorce my wife, save that she bear no children," Pwyll told them. "I know she has children, and I will not divorce her. If she has done wrong, let her be punished for it."

Rhiannon, for her part, summoned to her teachers and men of wisdom. And when it seemed more appropriate to her to accept her penance than to haggle with the women, she accepted her punishment. This was the punishment handed down to her: to be in that court in Arberth for seven years, to sit beside the mounting block that was outside the gate each day, to tell her story to all who came whom she thought might not know it, and to offer to those guests and distant travellers who would allow it to carry them on her back to the court; only rarely would one allow himself to be carried. And thus she spent a part of the year.

At that time, Teyrnon Twrf Liant was lord over Gwent Is Coed, and he was the best man in the world. In his house was a mare, and there was neither stallion nor mare fairer than she in his kingdom. On the eve of every May day she would foal, but no one knew what became of her foal. One night, Teyrnon conversed with his wife.

"Wife," he said, "we are remiss in allowing our mare to bear issue each year without us getting any of them."

"What can be done about it?" she asked.

"God's vengeance on me," said he, "if I do not find out what destruction is carrying off the colts: tonight is May eve."

He had the mare brought into the house, armed himself, and began the night's vigil. As night fell, the mare gave birth to a large, handsome colt; it stood immediately. Teyrnon rose to inspect the stoutness of the colt, and as he was so engaged, he heard a great commotion, and after the commotion, a great claw came through the window, and grasped the colt by the mane. Teyrnon drew his sword and cut off the arm from the elbow, so that that part of the arm and the colt remained inside with him. At the same time, he heard a roar and wail together. He opened the door and rushed headlong in the direction of the noise, but he could see nothing because of the night's darkness. He pursued the sound, following it. Then he remembered having left the door open, and went back. At the door there was a small boy all wrapped up in a mantle of silk brocade! He took the boy to him and, indeed, the boy was strong for his age! He fastened the door and went to the room where his wife was.

"Wife," he said, "are you asleep?"

"No, Lord," she replied, "I was, but when you came in I awoke."

"Here is a son for you if you like," he said, "something you never had."

"Lord," she said, "what kind of an adventure was that?"

"Here is the whole story," said Teyrnon, and he told it all.

"Well, Lord," she asked, "what kind of clothing is on the boy?"

"A silk brocaded coverlet," he replied.

"He is the son of gentlefolk," said she, "And, Lord," she continued, "it would be a pleasure and comfort to me–if you wished it; I would bring women into league with me, and I would say that I was pregnant."

"I will go along with you on that gladly," he said.

And so it was done. They had the baby baptized, in the way it was done then. The name they gave him was Gwri Golden-Hair, for all the hair on his head was as yellow as gold.

The boy was fostered in the court until he was a year old. Before his first birthday he was walking firmly and was stronger than a three-year-old big for his age. The boy was nurtured a second year, and as strong as a six-year-old he was. Before the end of the fourth year, he was bargaining with the stable-boys to let him lead the horses to water.

"Lord," said his wife to Teyrnon, "where is the colt you rescued the night you found the boy?"

"I have entrusted it to the stable-boys," he replied, "and ordered them to look after it."

"Wouldn't it be good for you, Lord," she said, "to have it broken in and given to the boy? For it was the night you found the boy that the colt that you rescued was born."

"I will not oppose that," said Teyrnon. "I will let you give it to him."

The horse was given to the boy, and she came to the grooms and to the stable-boys to order them to look after the horse, and have it broken in by the time the boy took up horsemanship and had need of it.*

In the meantime, they had heard rumors about Rhiannon and her punishment. Because of the treasure he had found, Teyrnon

* Ms. *chwedyl y wrthaw* is a crux. I translate on the basis of the Irish cognate *scél* which can mean 'affair, business' and take this to mean that as horseman, the boy will have business with the horse (*y wrthaw*).

listened to the report and inquired earnestly about it, until he heard from many of those multitudes that came to the court increasing complaints of the wretchedness of Rhiannon's state, and her punishment. What Teyrnon did then was to think about it, and look closely at the boy. In the matter of appearance, he began to realize that he had never seen a son so like his father as the boy was to Pwyll Pen Annwfn. Pwyll's features were known to him, for he had been his "man" before that. And after that, he became concerned about how wrong it was for him to keep the boy with him, knowing that he was another man's son. The first chance he had to speak privately with his wife, he told her that it was not right for them to keep possession of the boy and let so great a punishment fall on a woman as good as Rhiannon because of it—and the boy a son of Pwyll Pen Annwfn.

Teyrnon's wife agreed to send the boy to Pwyll.

"And three things we shall get from that, Lord," she said, "thanks and gratitude for releasing Rhiannon from the punishment she suffers, the thanks of Pwyll for fostering his son and returning him to him, and the third thing—if he be a gracious man—the boy will be our fosterling, and will always do his best for us."

And they settled on that counsel. No later than the next day, Teyrnon readied himself as one of three horsemen, the boy with them as the fourth, mounted on the horse Teyrnon had given him. They set out for Arberth, and it was not long before they arrived there. As they approached the court, they saw Rhiannon sitting beside the mounting block. When they came opposite her, she said, "Lord, go no farther. I will carry each of you to the court; that is my punishment for killing my own son and destroying him."

"Noble Lady," said Teyrnon, "I don't suppose that any of these will get up on your back."

"Let go who will," said the boy. "I will not."

"God knows," said Teyrnon, "we won't either."

They went to the court, and were welcomed joyously. They were beginning to celebrate a feast in the court; Pwyll himself had just come from a circuit of Dyfed. They went to wash and to the hall. Pwyll received Teyrnon joyfully, and they sat down. Teyrnon sat between Pwyll and Rhiannon, and Teyrnon's two companions above Pwyll with the boy between them. When the eating was finished, at the beginning of the festivities, they conversed.

What Teyrnon did was relate the whole adventure of the mare and the boy, how he and his wife had claimed the child as their own, and how they had reared him.

"And you see here," said Teyrnon, "your son. And whoever accused falsely did wrong. When I heard the torment you suffered, I was sorry and I grieved. I suppose there is no one in this entire company who does not know the boy is Pwyll's son," said Teyrnon.

"No one doubts it," everyone answered.

"I swear to God," said Rhiannon, "if it is true, I have been delivered of my anxiety (*pryder*)."

"Lady," said Pendaran Dyfed, "you have named your son well: Pryderi. And that fits him best: Pryderi son of Pwyll Pen Annwfn."

"See whether his own name doesn't fit him better," said Rhiannon.

"What name has he?" asked Pendaran Dyfed.

"We named him Gwri Golden-hair."

"Pryderi," said Pendaran Dyfed, "shall be his name."

"It is most fitting," said Pwyll, "to take the boy's name from the word his mother uttered when she received good news about him."

And they decided on that.

"Teyrnon," said Pwyll, "may God repay your fostering of this boy up until now. And it is right for him, if he be a gracious man, to compensate you."

"Lord," said Teyrnon, "there is no one in the world that grieves for him more than the woman who raised him. It is proper for him to remember me and this woman for what we have done for him."

"I swear to God," said Pwyll, "while I live, I will uphold you and your realm–as long as I am able to uphold my own. If he survives, it will be even more fitting for him to uphold you than for me. And if it be your counsel, and that of these nobles, since you have raised him until now, we will give him to Pendaran Dyfed to foster from now on; you will be his companions and his foster-fathers."

"That," they said, "is good counsel."

And then he handed over the boy to Pendaran Dyfed, and the

nobles of the land took charge of him. Then Teyrnon Twrf Liant set out with his companions for his land and realm, full of fellowship and joy. But he didn't go before he had been offered the fairest gems, the finest horses, and the most admired dogs. But he wanted nothing.

Then they dwelt in their realm, and Pryderi son of Pwyll Pen Annwfn was fostered with loving care—as was proper—until he was the most splendid lad, the fairest, and the most accomplished in every feat, of all those in the kingdom. In this way, years and years passed, until Pwyll Pen Annwfn's life ended, and he died. And then Pryderi ruled the seven cantrefs of Dyfed successfully, beloved by the realm and the people around him. Later, he gained the three cantrefs of Ystrad Tywi and the four cantrefs of Ceredigion; these are called the seven cantrefs of Seisyllwch. Pryderi son of Pwyll Pen Annwfn was engaged in that conquest until it occurred to him to marry. The one he wanted was Cigfa daughter of Gwyn Gohoyw son of Gloyw Gwallt Lydan son of Casnar Wledig of the nobility of this island.

And so ends this branch of the Mabinogi.

Branwen Daughter of Llŷr

The tale of Branwen concerns the family of Llŷr and is set in Mid-Wales. The family includes Bendigeidfran, whose name consists of the adjective *bendigeid* 'blessed' and *Bran,* his brother Manawydan, and their sister Branwen. There has been some debate over this last name, some holding that it is a corruption of *bronwen* 'fair or white breast,' others holding that it is simply a feminine form of Bran plus the feminine adjective *gwen* 'white, holy.' The patronym, Llŷr, is clearly the Welsh form of the ordinary word for "sea," which turns up in Irish as *ler* (gen. *lir*). Manawydan has his Irish counterpart in Manannán mac Lir, and Bran the Blessed may have a counterpart in the Irish Bran, the central figure in "The Voyage of Bran." Certainly all of these characters have something to do with the sea, but the relationships between the Irish and Welsh characters and the ways in which they function in their respective narratives have by no means been clearly established. In addition to Branwen, Manawydan, and Bendigeidfran, two half brothers appear in the story, Nisien and Efnisien. Efnisien is malevolent, and it is his deed that precipitates war between the Irish and the Welsh; it is also his sacrifice that permits the Welsh to win a kind of victory at the end. Nisien plays virtually no role at all, although from the description of him at the beginning of the story, he is the one we would expect to bring the final victory and counteract his brother's wickedness.

The story itself deals with a wedding of convenience between Branwen and Matholwch, a king of Ireland. It is interesting to see how different the character of Branwen is from the character of Rhiannon. The latter is solely responsible for her choice of mate and brings about the match despite numerous obstacles. Branwen has no voice whatsoever in the negotiation, and is simply a pawn to secure an alliance between the Irish and the "Isle of the Mighty." Her half brother Efnisien, however, expects to have a voice in her betrothal, and when he is not consulted, he takes revenge by multilating horses that belong to Matholwch. This is a gross insult to a man who has every right to expect the protection due a visiting king, and it is only by payment of his honor price and bestowing additional gifts that Bendigeidfran can persuade him to remain at court. His departure under such circumstances would bring dishonor to Bendigeidfran, of course, and loss of honor was tantamount to loss of life in Celtic society. After the wedding feast, Matholwch returns to Ireland with Branwen, and a child is born to them eventually. Matholwch, like Pwyll, is weak, and in due time his nobles and advisers convince him that he has not had sufficient reparation for the wrong done him in the destruction of his horses. At their suggestion, Branwen is driven from his side, and compelled to work as a common scullery maid. In this condition, she trains a starling to recognize her brother, and when he learns of his sister's condition he invades Ireland to liberate her. The matter is nearly settled peacefully when Matholwch offers to install their son as monarch, but Efnisien interferes, casting the boy headlong into the fire, thereby beginning the war that results in the destruction of Ireland and very nearly all of the men of the "Isle of the Mighty." Only seven men escaped from that battle. When they return to Wales, Branwen, reflecting on the carnage that has been wrought because of her, dies of a broken heart.

The seven survivors, accompanied by the head of Bendigeidfran, spend seven years at Harlech, the site of the opening of the tale, then eighty years at Gwales. These two feasting halls provide the best description in medieval Welsh narrative of the Celtic Otherworld; it is a place of endless food and drink, heavenly music, complete absence of pain and sorrow, and timelessness. The feasting was presided over by the head of Bendigeidfran, and seems to have had a special place in early Welsh tradition, for it has a name of its own, "The Assembly of the Noble Head." This section constitutes important evidence for our knowledge of early Celtic belief, for we know that the early Celts were headhunters, and that heads of friends and foes alike had special cult significance. Eventually, the head of Bran is buried in London, where its magical power was strong enough to ward off any plague, so long as it remained buried there.

"Branwen" is the only branch of the *mabinogi* in which a significant portion of the setting shifts outside of Wales. The geographical association with Ireland is bolstered by thematic associations, and scholars (especially MacCana, *Branwen: A Study of the Irish Affinities*) have noticed a strong Irish influence in this branch of the *mabinogi.* For example, the cauldron of rejuvenation (or rebirth, or plenty, but always having something to do with fertility and prosperity) is an important motif in early Irish tradition. It has also been suggested that the tale may be a euhemerized version of a raid on the Otherworld, such as is recounted in a poem from the Book of Taliesin, "The Spoils of Annwfn." There, Arthur and his men undertake an expedition to Annwfn (the

Otherworld), whose treasures include a magical cauldron. From that expedition, only seven returned, just as in our tale. Yet another version may be imbedded in Arthur's expedition to Ireland to acquire the cauldron of Diwrnach, recounted in "Culhwch and Olwen." In place of the Otherworld, we have Ireland, an attempt to substitute a geographical reality for the mythical land of the living. But "euhemerized" is scarcely the word to describe our story; Bendigeidfran is literally larger than life and accomplishes the journey to Ireland by wading. Once there, he lies down across the river Shannon to make a bridge for his men. His seat in Wales is Harlech, identified later in the tale as site of the Otherworld feast. It should be noted that the discrepancy in size between Bendigeidfran and his fellows causes no difficulty to the story-teller, and we are reminded once again that in these tales there is complete freedom of movement in size, shape, and time.

Bendigeidfran son of Llŷr was crowned king of this island, and was invested with the crown of London. One day he was in Harlech in Ardudwy, a court of his. He and his brother Manawydan son of Llŷr were sitting on the rock of Harlech above the sea, along with his mother's two sons, Nisien and Efnisien, and other nobles besides, as befitted the company of a king.

His two half-brothers were sons of Euroswydd by his own mother, Penarddun daughter of Beli son of Mynogan. One of these lads was a good fellow; he could bring peace to opposing hosts when they were most wrathful—that was Nisien. The other could incite his two brothers to fight when they were most affectionate.

As they were sitting thus, they could see thirteen ships coming from the south of Ireland, approaching them at a smooth and swift pace. The wind was behind them and they drew near rapidly.

"I see ships yonder," said the king, "and they're coming boldly to land. Ask men of the court to arm and go find out their intentions."

The men armed and went down to meet them. After seeing the ships up close, they were certain that they had never seen better equipped ships than those. Fair, shapely, splendid pennants of brocaded silk were aloft.

And then one of the ships pushed ahead of the others, and they could see a shield being raised above the ship's rail, the tip of the shield up, in a sign of peace. And the men drew near to them until they could hear each other's conversation. They put down boats and, as they approached the shore, greeted the king. The king could hear them from where he was on the rock above them.

"May God prosper you," he said, "and welcome. Whose ships are these, and who is chief over them?"

"Lord," they replied, "Matholwch, king of Ireland, is here; the ships are his."

"What does he want?" asked the king. "Does he wish to come to land?"

"He has business with you, Lord," they said, "and he does not want to come to land unless he can accomplish his business."

"What sort of business does he have?" asked the king.

"He seeks an alliance with you, Lord," they said. "He has come to ask the hand of Branwen daughter of Llŷr, and if it please you, he wishes to unite the Isle of the Mighty with Ireland that they might be stronger."

"Well," said he, "let him land, and we will take counsel about that."

"I will go gladly," he said.

He landed and was welcomed. And there was a great assembly in the court that night between his retinue and that of the court. First thing in the morning they took counsel. What they decided was to give Branwen to Matholwch. She was one of the three chief ancestresses in this island, and the fairest maid in the world. A date was set to sleep with her in Aberffraw, and then they left there, Matholwch and his hosts setting out in their ships, Bendigeidfran and his own retinue over land, until they reached Aberffraw. In Aberffraw they sat down and began the feast. This is how they sat: Manawydan son of Llŷr on one side of the king of the Isle of the Mighty, Matholwch on the other side, and Branwen daughter of Llŷr together with them. They were not in a house, but in tents, for Bendigeidfran had never been contained in a house.

They began the festivities, and they continued to celebrate and converse. When they saw that the time for festivities had passed and it was time to sleep, to sleep they went. And that night Matholwch slept with Branwen. The next day they arose, and the officers began to discuss the division of the horses and the lads, and they divided them in every region as far as the sea. Then one day, Efnisien, the troublesome one of whom we spoke above, happened upon the preserve of Matholwch's horses, and asked whose they were.

"These belong to Matholwch, king of Ireland," they said.

"What are they doing here?" he said.

"The king of Ireland is here, he has slept with Branwen, your sister, and these are his horses."

"Is that the way they act concerning a maiden as fine as that—my own sister—giving her away without my permission? They could have done no greater insult to me," he said. And thereupon he lunged at the horses, cutting their lips to the teeth, their ears down to the head, and their tails to the rumps, and where he could get a grip on them, he cut their eyelids to the bone. And thus he disfigured the horses so that no use could be made of them.

The news came to Matholwch: they told him about the maiming and ruining of the horses so that there was no use that could be made of them.

"Well, Lord," said one, "you have been disgraced, and they did that to you on purpose."

"God knows, I am amazed that, if they wanted to disgrace me, they would bestow on me a maiden so good, so noble, and so beloved by the people."

"Lord," said another, "it is manifest; there is nothing left for you but to return to your ships."

And thereupon, they made for their ships.

The news came to Bendigeidfran that Matholwch was departing the court without petition, without leave. Messengers were sent to him to inquire the reason; they were Iddig son of Anarawg and Hyfaidd Hir. Those men overtook him and asked him what he was planning to do and why he was going away.

"God knows," he told them, "If I had known it, I would not have come here. I have been completely disgraced. No one has ever embarked on a worse mission than this. And a remarkable thing has happened to me."

"What is it?" they queried.

"That Branwen daughter of Llŷr, one of the three chief ancestresses of this island and daughter to the king of the Isle of the Mighty, was given to me to sleep with, and then I was disgraced. It is a wonder to me that the insult was not perpetrated before so good a maiden was given to me."

"God knows, Lord, it was not through the will of the one to whom the court belongs," they said, "nor any in his counsel that that insult was done to you. And though that act of contempt and trick is an insult to you, it is an even greater one to Bendigeidfran than to you."

"Yes," he said, "I suppose. Yet he cannot undo that insult."

Those men returned with that answer to the place where Bendigeidfran was, and they told him what Matholwch had said.

"Well," he said, "there is nothing to be gained by his going in hostility, and we will not allow it."

"Well, Lord," they said, "then send messengers after him."

"I will," he replied. "Arise Manawydan son of Llŷr and Hyfaidd Hir and Unig Glew Ysgwyd, and go after him; tell him he shall have sound horses for every one that was ruined. In addition, he shall have as his honor-price a measure of silver as thick as his finger and as long as himself, and a gold plate as broad as his face. Tell him what sort of man did that, and that it was done against my will; that the man who did it is my half brother—we have the same mother—and that it is not easy for me to kill or destroy him. Let him call on me," he said, "and I will arrange whatever peace he may wish."

The messengers went after Matholwch and told him all that in a friendly way, and he listened.

"Men," he said, "let us take counsel."

They deliberated among themselves, and they decided that if they rejected that offer, it was likelier that their disgrace would be increased than that their compensation would increase. And they decided to accept it; they returned to the court in peace. The tents and pavillions were arranged for them according to the proper arrangement of a hall, and they went to eat. And as they had begun to sit at the start of the feast, so they sat then.

Matholwch and Bendigeidfran began to converse, and indeed, it seemed to Bendigeidfran that Matholwch's discourse was listless and forlorn, whereas previously he had been continually merry. He thought that the chieftain was dispirited because of how little recompense he had received for the wrong done him.

"Good sir," said Bendigeidfran, "you are not as good a talker tonight as you usually are. If that is because you consider your compensation slight, it shall be increased according to your will; and tomorrow your horses will be paid to you."

"Lord," he said, "may God repay you."

"I will make your compensation complete," said Bendigeidfran. "I will give you a cauldron with a special property: should a man of yours be killed today, cast him into the cauldron, and by tomorrow he will be as good as ever—but he will be without speech."

And the other thanked him for that, and became exceedingly happy over it. The next day his horses were paid to him, as long as tame horses lasted. From there they took him to another commote, and he was paid in colts until the payment was complete. And for that reason, that commote was called Tal-ebolion (payment of colts) thenceforth. And for the second night they sat down together.

"Lord," said Matholwch, "how did you come by the cauldron you gave me?"

"It came to me from a man who had been in your country. And for all I know, he got it there."

"Who was that?" he asked.

"Llassar Llaes Gyfnewid," replied the other. "He came here from Ireland with Cymidei Cymeinfoll, his wife; they had escaped from the iron house in Ireland when it was made white-hot around them. I am amazed that you do not know anything about that."

"I do know something of it, Lord," he said, "and I will tell you as much as I know. I was hunting one day in Ireland, atop the mound above a lake in Ireland called Lake of the Cauldron. And I saw a great yellowish-red haired man coming from the lake, and a cauldron on his back. He was a large, enormous man, too, with an uncompromising look about him. His wife came behind him, and if he was big, more than twice his size was she. They came up to me and greeted me."

"Well," said I, "what is the nature of your travel?"

"Just this, Lord," said the man, "at the end of a fortnight and a month this woman will conceive, and the boy born of that pregnancy at the end of a fortnight and a month will be a fully armed warrior."

"I took them in and maintained them, and they were with me

for a year. In that year I kept them ungrudgingly; from then on it was begruduged me. Before the end of the fourth month they were making themselves loathed and unwanted in the land, insulting, molesting, and pestering noble men and women. From then on my people rose up about me, petitioning me to renounce them, and giving me a choice: either my kingdom or them. I put myself in my people's counsel as to what should be done with them. They would not go of their own accord, nor could they be compelled by force of arms. Then, in their dilemma, they had a chamber made entirely of iron; when it was ready, they summoned all there were of blacksmiths in Ireland there, and all the owners of tongs and hammers, and had coal piled as high as the roof of the chamber. Then they had an endless supply of food and drink served the woman, her husband, and her children. When they saw that they were drunk, they kindled the fire around the chamber and blew the bellows that had been placed around the house—one man to each two bellows—and began to blow the bellows until the house was white-hot around them. And then they took counsel in the midst of the chamber; he waited until the iron wall was white, and from the intense heat, he charged the wall with his shoulder and broke out through it, his wife behind him. Only he and his wife escaped from there. And then, I suppose, Lord," said Matholwch to Bendigeidfran, "he came over to you."

"Then, surely," said the other, "he came here and gave the cauldron to me."

"How did you receive them, Lord?"

"I divided them throughout the land, and they are numerous and thriving everywhere, and strengthening the places in which they happen to be with the best men and arms anyone has ever seen."

They continued their discourse that night, and their song and celebration, as long as it pleased them. And when they saw that it was more profitable for them to go to sleep than to sit longer, they went to sleep. Thus they spent the period of the feast in pleasure. When it was finished, Matholwch and Branwen set out for Ireland. Their thirteen ships set out from Abermenai, and came to Ireland.

In Ireland there was an exceedingly great welcome for them. No great lord or lady in Ireland would come to see Branwen to whom she didn't give either a brooch or a ring or a precious gem that would be remarkable to see given away. In all that, she spent that year in high regard, and she had full complement of praise and companions. And then she conceived, and after the appropriate time passed a son was born to her. The name they gave the boy was Gwern son of Matholwch; he was given in fosterage to the best place for men in Ireland.

And then in the second year, there was a murmuring in Ireland over the insult that Matholwch had received in Wales, and the humiliation he had had over the horses. And his foster brothers and the men closest to him began to reproach him for it, not concealing it. Then an uprising in Ireland, so that he could have no peace until he got revenge for it. The revenge they took was to drive Branwen from his chamber, and force her to cook for the court; they had the butcher–after he would finish butchering each day–come to her and strike her a blow on the ears. Thus was her punishment carried out.

"Now, Lord," the men said to Matholwch," place a prohibition on ships, barges, and coracles, now, so that none may go to Wales; whatever Welshmen come here, imprison them and do not let them return lest they find this out."

And they agreed to that.

They maintained this position for not less than three years. During that time Branwen raised a starling at her kneading trough, taught it speech, and explained to it what kind of man her brother was. She wrote a letter describing the punishment and dishonor that had befallen her, bound it beneath the bird's wing, and sent it toward Wales. The bird came to this Island, and found Bendigeidfran at one of his assemblies one day in Caer Seint in Arfon. It alighted on his shoulder and ruffled its feathers until the letter was discovered, and it was perceived that the bird had been raised among men. He took the letter and looked at it; when he had read it, he grieved to learn of the punishment on Branwen. Beginning there, he had messengers sent to muster the entire island, and issued a complete summons to the one hundred and fifty-four districts of the land, all the while bewailing his sister's punishment. Then they took counsel, and decided to go to Ireland and leave seven men as leaders here, along with their seven horsemen, with Caradawg son of Bran as the chief over them. Those men were left in Edeirnon, and because of that the name Seith Marchawg (seven horsemen) was given to the township. The seven were Caradawg son of Bran, Hyfaidd Hir, Unig Glew Ysgwyd, Iddig son of Anarawg Curly-haired, Ffodor son of Erfyll, Wlch Lip-bone, Llashar son of Llassar Llaes Gyfnewid, and Pendaran Dyfed as a young lad with them. These seven remained as the seven caretakers to look after his island, and Caradawg son of Bran was the head caretaker over them.

Bendigeidfran and the host we have mentioned sailed toward Ireland. The sea was not deep then: he went through the shallows; they were but two rivers called Lli and Archan. Later, the sea expanded when it inundated the lands. But at that time he walked, taking all there was of string music on his back, and made for Ireland.

Matholwch's swineherds were on the sea-shore on a certain day, busy watching their swine. And because of the sight they saw on the sea, they came to Matholwch.

"Lord," they said, "may you prosper."

"God prosper you," he said. "Do you have news?"

"Lord," they replied, "we have remarkable tidings; we have seen a forest on the sea where we have never seen a single tree."

"That is an amazing thing," he said. "Did you see anything else?"

"We did, Lord," they answered. "We saw a large mountain beside the forest and it was moving; and there was a high ridge on the mountain, with a lake on either side of it. The forest, the mountain, and all the rest of it was moving."

"Well," he said, "there is no one here who knows anything about that unless it be Branwen. Ask her."

Messengers went off to Branwen.

"Lady," they asked, "what do you suppose that is?"

"Though I am no Lady," she said, "I know what it is: it is the men of the Isle of the Mighty coming over after hearing of my punishment and dishonor."

"What is the forest that was seen on the sea?" they asked.

"Masts of ships and yard arms," she replied.

"Och!" they exclaimed. "What was the mountain that was seen alongside the ships?"

"That was Bendigeidfran, my brother," she replied, "coming

through the shallows; there was never a ship that could contain him."

"What was the high ridge with the lakes on either side?"

"He," she said, "looking at this island—and he is angry: the two lakes on either side of the ridge are his eyes alongside his nose."

Then all the fighting men of Ireland and the coastal districts were summoned quickly, and they took counsel.

"Lord," said his men to Matholwch, "the only advice is to withdraw across the Shannon (a river that was in Ireland), putting the Shannon between you and him, and destroy the bridge that's over it. There are magnetic stones at the bottom of the river, so that neither ships nor vessels can cross it."

They retreated across the river and destroyed the bridge.

Bendigeidfran and his ships came to land, and approached the river bank.

"Lord," said his men, "you know the peculiarity of the river, that none can go across it—nor is there a bridge over it. What do you advise for a bridge?"

"Nothing, except that he who is chief shall be a bridge," he replied. "I will be a bridge."

Then was first uttered that saying, and it has become proverbial.

And then after he had lain down across the river, planks were placed across him, and his hosts went over—across him. Then as soon as he rose, messengers of Matholwch came toward him, saluted him, and gave him greetings from Matholwch his kinsman, saying that he had nothing but good intentions toward Bendigeidfran.

"And Matholwch gives the kingship of Ireland to Gwern son of Matholwch, your own nephew, your sister's son, and he is bestowing it in your presence, for the wrong and insult that was done to Branwen. And provide for Matholwch wherever you like—either here, or in the Isle of the Mighty."

"Well," said Bendigeidfran, "can I not take the kingship myself? But, perhaps I will take counsel over your offer. But until something else comes from you, you will get no answer from me."

"Well," they said, "we will come to you with the best response we can get; wait for our message."

"I will wait," he said, "if you come quickly."

The messengers went forth, and came to Matholwch.

"Lord," they said, "prepare a better response for Bendigeidfran. He would have none of the offer we took to him."

"Men," said Matholwch, "what is your counsel?"

"Lord," they replied, "there is but one counsel. He has never found room in a house. Construct a house in his honor, in which he and the men of the Isle of the Mighty may be quartered in one part, and you and your host in the other. Put your kingship into his power, and do homage to him. And from the honor accorded him in making the house—something he has never had—he will conclude peace with you."

And the messengers took that offer to Bendigeidfran, and he went into counsel. What they decided on was to accept that. All that was done through the advice of Branwen, and she did that lest the country be destroyed.

The peace was arranged, and the house built, large and fine. But the Irish conceived a ruse: they fixed a peg on every side of each of the one hundred columns that were in the house, and hung a hide bag on each peg, with an armed warrior inside each. What Efnisien did was to come inside ahead of the host of the Isle of the Mighty, and cast a hard and merciless glance around the house. He noticed the hide bags along the posts.

'What's in this bag?" he asked one of the Irishmen.

"Flour, friend," said he.

What the other did then was to feel around him until he found his head, and squeezed his head until he could feel his fingers meet in the brain, through the bone. Then he left him and put his hand on another, saying, "What do we have here?"

"Flour," answered the Irishman.

And then he played the same trick on each of them, until only one of the entire two hundred remained. He went up to that one asking, "What do we have here?"

"Flour, friend," said the Irishman.

And then he felt around him until he found his head, and as he had squashed the heads of the others, he squashed that head. He could feel battle gear on that one, and he did not leave him until he killed him. Then he sang an *englyn*:

> There is in this bag a form of flour,
> Champions, battlers, fighters in the fray,
> From warriors, battle-ready.

After that the hosts entered the house: the men of the Isle of Ireland on one side, and the men of the Isle of the Mighty on the other. And as soon as they sat down there was accord between them, and the kingship was bestowed on the boy.

Then, after peace was declared, Bendigeidfran called the boy to him. From Bendigeidfran the boy went to Manawydan, and all who saw him loved him. Nisien son of Euroswydd called the boy to him from Manawydan; the boy went graciously.

"Why doesn't my nephew–my sister's son–come to me?" said Efnisien. "Even if he weren't king of Ireland I would gladly act kindly toward him."

"Let him go, gladly," said Bendigeidfran.

The boy went to him cheerfully.

"I confess to God," Efnisien said to himself, "doing what I shall now do will seem a perverse outrage to the family."

And he rose up, took the boy by the feet, and without delay, before any man in the house could lay a hand on him, he thrust the boy headlong into the fire. When Branwen saw her son seared in the fire, she tried to bound into the fire from where she was sitting between her two brothers. Bendigeidfran grasped her in his one hand, his shield in the other; at that, everyone in the house leapt up, and the greatest uproar ever seen by the company of a single house took place, everyone seizing his weapons. Then said Morddwyd Tyllion, "Warriors of Gwern, beware Morddwyd Tyllion."

And as each gathered up his arms, Bendigeidfran held Branwen between his shield and his shoulder. The Irish began to kindle a fire beneath the cauldron of rebirth. Corpses were thrown into the cauldron until it was full, and the next morning they rose up fighting as well as before, except they could not speak. But when Efnisien saw the corpses, and no room at all for the men of the Isle of the Mighty, he thought, "Dear God, alas! that I have caused this desolation of men of the Isle of the Mighty! And shame on me unless I find a way to deliver them from this."

He hid himself, then, among the Irish corpses, and two bare-bottomed Irish came and threw him into the cauldron as an Irishman. He stretched himself out in the cauldron, then, until the cauldron broke in four pieces, and his heart as well. From that came such victory as the men of the Isle of the Mighty got, and their only victory was the escape of seven men. But Bendigeidfran was wounded in the heel by a poison spear.

The seven who escaped were Pryderi, Manawydan, Glifieu Eil Taran, Taliesin, Ynawg, Gruddyeu son of Muriel, and Heilyn son of Gwyn Hen. And Bendigeidfran ordered his head to be cut off.

"And take the head and carry it to Gwynfryn (white mount) in London," said Bendigeidfran, "and bury it with its face toward France. You will be on the road for a long time: you will be feasting in Harlech for seven years with the birds of Rhiannon singing to you, and the head will be as good company for you as it ever was when it was on me. Then you will be in Gwales in Pembroke eighty years, and until you open the door toward Aber Henfelen—in the direction of Cornwall—you can remain there, and the head, untainted, will be with you. But from the time you open the door you cannot remain there; go to London and bury the head. Now set out for the other side."

Then his head was struck off, and the seven men and Branwen as the eighth began the crossing; they landed in Aber Alaw in Talebolion, and they sat down and rested. She looked at Ireland and at the Isle of the Mighty—what she could see of them.

"Dear Son of God," she said, "alas, that I was born! Two good islands have been destroyed because of me."

And she sighed deeply, and thereupon her heart broke. They made a four-sided grave for her, and buried her there on the shore of the Alaw. After that the seven travelled towards Harlech, and the head with them. As they were going, they encountered a company of men and women.

"Do you have any news?" asked Manawydan.

"No," they replied, "unless it be the conquest of the Isle of the Mighty by Caswallawn son of Beli, and his being crowned king in London."

"What happened to Caradawg son of Bran," they asked, "and the seven that were left with him in this island?"

"Caswallawn overcame them, killing six, and Caradawg died

of grief from watching the sword kill his men and not knowing who killed them. Caswallawn had put a magic mantle about him, so that no one could see him killing the men—only the sword. Caswallawn did not wish to kill him, for he was a nephew—son of his first cousin (he was one of the three men whose hearts broke from grief). Pendaran Dyfed, who was a young lad in their company, escaped to the woods," they said.

They went to Harlech then, and settled in; a boundless supply of food and drink commenced. As they began to eat and drink, three birds came and began singing some songs to them, and all the songs they had ever heard were coarse compared to that one. They were a distant vision seen above the waves, yet they were as clear to them as if they were together with them. And they were at that feast for seven years.

At the end of the seventh year, they set out for Gwales in Pembroke. There was a fine royal palace for them there, high above the sea, with a great hall; they went to the hall. They could see two doors open, and a third one closed; that one faced Cornwall.

"You see there," said Manawydan, "the door we are not to open."

That night they lacked for nothing, and took pleasure there. And of all the grief they had witnessed and experienced, they had no memory of it or of any sorrow in the world. And there they spent eighty years; they were not aware of spending a more pleasurable nor lovelier time than that ever. None could tell by the others that any time had passed since they came, nor was the presence of the head any less comfort to them than when Bendigeidfran had been living with them. And because of those fourscore years, that was called The Assembly of the Noble Head. (What went to Ireland was The Assembly of Branwen and Matholwch.)

One day Heilyn son of Gwyn did something.

"Shame upon my beard," he said, "unless I open the door to see if what they say about it is true."

He opened the door, and looked out on Cornwall and Aber Henfelen. And when he did, the degree of loss they had suffered, the number of kinsmen and friends they had lost, and the amount of ill that had befallen them was as vivid as if they had encountered it on the spot; and most of all concerning their lord. From that moment they could not rest, but set out for London with the head. However long they were on the road, they arrived in London and buried the head in Gwynfryn.

That was one of three fortunate interments when it was interred—and one of three unfortunate disinterments when it was disinterred, for no oppression would ever reach this island from across the sea while the head was secreted there. And thus does this account tell their tale; it is called The Men Who Set Out From Ireland.

In Ireland none were left alive, except five pregnant women in a cave in the wastes of Ireland. And these five women simultaneously bore five sons. They raised these five boys until they were big lads, who turned their thoughts on women, and desired to have them. And then each slept side by side with each other's mother, and they inhabited the land and dwelt in it, dividing it between the five of them. They still call the five districts of Ireland from that division. And they examined the land where battles had been fought, and collected gold and silver until they were wealthy.

And that is how this branch of the Mabinogi ends: the incidents of Branwen's Slap—which was one of the three unfortunate slaps in this island, the occasion of The Assembly of Bran—when the hosts of one hundred and fifty-four districts went to Ireland to revenge Branwen's slap, The Feasting in Harlech—which lasted seven years, The Singing of the Birds of Rhiannon, and The Assembly of the Head—which lasted eighty years.

Manawydan Son of Llŷr

There is an expressed continuity between this branch and the preceding one, the story of Branwen, for it begins with a reference to the seven who escaped from Ireland and the burial of Bendigeidfran's head in London. But we soon leave the children of Llŷr, and return to Dyfed and Rhiannon and Pryderi, so that this story has an organic connection with both the first and second branches. Pryderi and Manawydan, two of the seven who escaped from Ireland, set out for Dyfed, and Manawydan is persuaded to wed Rhiannon. At the celebration of the feast of Arberth, a magical mist descends upon the mound where the company has gathered, and when it lifts no living thing is left in the land, only Manawydan and Rhiannon, and Pryderi and his wife, Cigfa. The four live alone in the land, apparantly content with their lot, for two years. Then Manawydan becomes discontent and suggests that they go into England and make their living by practising various crafts. They begin by making saddles, but their work is so fine that they nearly ruin the business of the other saddlers in the town, who conspire to slay them. Pryderi would like to oppose them, but at Manawydan's urging they remove to another town. There, they make shields, and again, the other craftsmen threaten to slay them. In a third town they take up shoemaking, and when they are opposed by the other shoemakers, they decide to return to Dyfed.

One day as they are out hunting, they are lured by a gleaming white boar to a beautiful fort where Pryderi becomes entrapped. Rhiannon chastises Manawydan for abandoning his companion, and in seeking him, she too becomes trapped in the magical fort. Cigfa and Manawydan are now alone in Dyfed, and Manawydan decides once again to go into England and work at a craft. The results are the same as before, for this is but a repetition of the earlier episode, and the two return to Dyfed. This time, Manawydan engages in agricultural activities, but he has difficulty harvesting his crop. Through vigilance, he discovers a horde of mice ravaging the crop, and he manages to catch one of the band. He discovers that the horde is the transformed warband of Llwyd, a friend of Gwawl, Rhiannon's unsuccessful suitor from the first branch. Gwawl was treated rather unceremoniously in the game of "Badger-in-the-Bag," and it was to avenge that wrong that the war band had come to destroy Manawydan's crops. It was for that reason, too, that the land of Dyfed was enchanted and Rhiannon and Pryderi trapped in the fort. Manawydan offers to exchange the mouse he has caught—actually, Llwyd's pregnant wife—for the safe return of Rhiannon and Pryderi, removal of the enchantment from the land, and a vow that vengeance never be taken on them again.

The connection with the first branch is reinforced in several ways. Rhiannon is a strong, assertive character, consistent with her portrayal in "Pwyll." For most of the story, Manawydan is a retiring, conciliatory figure, closely resembling Rhiannon's husband in the first branch. He has no desire for land (though it is entirely possible that this alienation from land reflects his essential marine nature), he forsakes Pryderi without trying to free him from the fort, and retreats from his persecutors in England, much to the dismay of first Pryderi and then Cigfa. Like Pwyll, who remains chaste for an entire year in the company of the most beautiful woman in the world, Manawydan is a completely trustworthy and chaste friend to Pryderi. He takes great pains in reassuring Cigfa, after the disappearance of Rhiannon and Pryderi, that although they are entirely alone in the land he will remain a true friend, and would do so even if he were a young man again.

There is a good deal of magic in this branch. The enchantment that covers the land is a good example of the power of a hostile force to rob the land of its fertility, a motif that has a second expression in the destruction of Manawydan's crops. We are reminded of the plagues recounted in the tale of "Lludd and Lleuelys," and the efforts to secure protection from such forces by talismanic means, such as the burial of Bendigeidfran's head on a sacred mound in London in the second branch. The imprisonment of Pryderi is achieved by a typical device; a magical animal of the Otherworld lures the hunters to an Otherworld terminal, in this instance a huge fort, sitting upon ground where there has hitherto been no building at all. Inside is a fountain, a golden bowl secured to silver chains, and all that resting upon a marble slab. When Pryderi (and later, Rhiannon) takes hold of the bowl, the magic binds him fast. Eventually, in the wake of a thunder peal and descending mist, the fort with its prisoners disappears. The motif is found with very slight changes in the romance of Owain, "The Lady of the Fountain" (the Middle English "Ywain and Gawain," Chrétien's *Yvain*).

Shape-shifting is a feature of this tale, too, although it is clear that the story-teller meant to turn shape-shifting to literary advantage here. The shape-shifting in the first branch is simply to accommodate Arawn's ends, to allow the mortal Pwyll to fight his battle without the enemy Hafgan being the wiser. In the fourth branch, it is used variously; Gwydion changes his shape to dupe Pryderi, Math uses it to punish his nephews, and it occurs rather unaccountably in a scene that should result in the death of Lleu. But nowhere is it used self-consciously by the story-teller to achieve dramatic effect. The scene in which Manawydan pursues the pregnant mouse is a delightfully humorous one. Later, the absurdity of the situation begins to emerge as Cigfa finds herself in the role of advocate for the poor creature. The final scene, in which Manawydan proceeds to the sacred mound at Arberth, erects a gallows at its highest point, fixes the crossbeam, and finally fits the string about the pregnant mouse's neck is one of the most bizarre and one of the most delightful episodes in Medieval Welsh literature. The drama is perfectly sustained in this section, as Llwyd in three separate disguises attempts to swerve Manawydan from his awful task and rescue his wife. He eventually succeeds, but only after releasing Dyfed, Rhiannon and Pryderi. Manawydan acts in a deliberate and cunning way here, unlike the faltering, indecisive character he is in the earlier part of the tale.

At the very end, we find that Rhiannon's punishment during her incarceration has consisted in wearing the collars of asses about her neck, reaffirming thereby her connection with Epona, the Celtic goddess who was associated with horses and asses. Pryderi's imprisonment has been compared with that of other famous prisoners, namely Mabon son of Modron in the tale of "Culhwch and Olwen" and Gweir, the prisoner of Caer Siddi in "The Spoils of Annwfn." It may even be, as some have suggested, that these are but different names for the same divine hero who had been, at one point, a celebrated prisoner.

After the seven men we have spoken of above buried Bendigeidfran's head in Gwynfryn in London with his face toward France, Manawydan looked at the town of London and at his companions, gave up a sigh, and was seized with great grief and longing.

"Dear Almighty God!" he said. "Alas for me; I am the only one with no place to go tonight!"

"Lord," said Pryderi, "don't be so depressed as that. Your cousin is king of the Isle of the Mighty, and though he wrongs you, you have never claimed land and territory, for you are one of the three humble chieftains."

"Well," said the other, "even though that man is my cousin,

I am grieved at seeing anyone in my brother Bendigeidfran's place, and I cannot be happy in the same house with him."

"Will you take any other advice?" asked Pryderi.

"I should," he replied. "What is it?"

"The seven cantrefs of Dyfed were left to me," said Pryderi, "and my mother Rhiannon is there. I will bestow her upon you, as well as possession of the seven cantrefs. And though you have no wealth but those seven cantrefs, there aren't seven better cantrefs. Cigfa daughter of Gwyn Gloyw [*sic*] is my wife," he said, "and though the realm will be mine in name, the enjoyment of it will be yours and Rhiannon's. And if you wish wealth at all, perhaps you would accept that."

"I don't, chieftain," he said, "but may God repay your fellowship."

"The best fellowship I am capable of shall be yours if you want it."

"I do, friend," he replied, "may God reward you. I will go with you to see Rhiannon and to look at the realm."

"You do well," said the other; "I suppose that you have never listened to a woman whose discourse was better than hers. Since she has been in her prime, there has been none finer than she, nor is her appearance unpleasant now."

They set out, and however long they were on the road, they came to Dyfed. By the time they reached Arberth, a feast had been prepared for them, made ready by Rhiannon and Cigfa. And then Manawydan and Rhiannon sat and conversed, and as a result of that conversation, his heart and mind grew tender toward her, and he relished the thought that he had never seen a woman whose beauty and fineness was more replete than hers.

"Pryderi," he said, "I accede to what you proposed."

"What proposal was that?" asked Rhiannon.

"Lady," said Pryderi, "I have given you as wife to Manawydan son of Llŷr."

"I agree to that, gladly," said Rhiannon.

"I am glad," said Manawydan, "and may God reward the man who has given me his friendship so unstintingly."

Before that feast came to an end, she was slept with.

"Enjoy what remains of the feast," said Pryderi, "and I will go into England to tender homage to Caswallawn son of Beli."

"Lord," said Rhiannon, "Caswallawn is in Kent, and you can enjoy this feast and wait until he is nearer."

"We shall await him," he said.

And they enjoyed that feast, and began to go on circuit of Dyfed, hunting it and taking their pleasure. As they travelled the land, they realized that they had never seen a land more habitable, nor better hunting grounds, nor one more plentiful in honey and fish. And friendship grew among the four of them, so that none wanted to be without the others either day or night. During that time, Pryderi went to Caswallawn in Oxford to tender homage to him. He was received with great joy, and thanked for his allegiance. When he returned, Pryderi and Manawydan took up their feasts and their leisure again.

They commenced a feast in Arberth, for it was the chief court, and every honorific occasion was commenced there. And after the first feeding that night, while the attendants were eating, they strolled out, the four of them, and went to the mound of Arberth, and the host with them. As they were sitting, there was a tumultuous clatter, and concurrent with the sound, a mist falling, so that not one of them could see the other. After the mist, then, it brightened everywhere. And when they looked in the places where they had seen flocks and cattle and habitations before then, no one could see anything whatsoever—neither house, nor animal, nor smoke, nor fire, nor dwellings, only the court buildings, and those empty, deserted, desolate, without men or animals in them, their own companions lost without their knowing anything of their whereabouts; only they four remained.

"Dear Lord God," said Manawydan, "where is the court's retinue and the rest of our own company? Let's go look for them."

They came to the hall, but there was no one. They searched the chamber and the sleeping quarter, but they saw no one. Neither in the mead cellar nor in the kitchen was there anything but emptiness.

The four of them began to partake of the feast, and they hunted and took their pleasure. Each of them wandered through the land and the realm to see what they could of either houses or habitations, but they could see nothing of any kind except wild animals. And when they had used up the feast and their supplies, they began to support themselves on game, fish and honey. And thus they passed that year and the next in pleasure. At last, they became discontented, and Manawydan said, "God knows, we will not live like this! We will go to England and try a craft by which we may make our living."

They went toward England, and came as far as Henffordd, where they took up making saddles. Manawydan began to fashion pommels and color them in the way he had seen Llassar Laes Gyfnewid color pommels: he made them blue as the other had done. That process is called now "Calch Llassar" from the practice of Llassar Laes Gyfnewid. The result of that work was that, as long as they could be had from Manawydan, neither pommel nor saddle was purchased from saddlers throughout Henffordd. All the saddlers knew they were losing their profits, and that nothing was being purchased from them except when it could not be had from Manawydan. Thereupon, they met together, and decided to kill him and his companion. The two received warning about that, and they discussed leaving the town.

"I swear to God," said Pryderi, "I don't advise leaving the town, rather we should kill those churls."

"No," said Manawydan. "If we should attack them, we would be in ill-repute, and we would be imprisoned. We had better find another town in which to maintain ourselves."

The four of them went to another town.

"What skill shall we practice?" asked Pryderi.

"We will make shields," replied Manawydan.

"Do we know anything about that?" asked Pryderi.

"We will experiment," the other answered.

They began the work of shields, and designed them after the best-crafted shields they had seen, putting the same color on them as they had put on the saddles. The work grew in success until no shield was purchased anywhere in the town, unless it could not be got from them. They worked swiftly and produced countless quantities, and continued in this way, until their fellow townsmen grew angry and conspired to kill them. A warning came to them, and they heard that the men intended to put them to death.

"Pryderi," said Manawydan, "these men want to destroy us."

"We won't take that from these villains. Let's set upon them and kill them."

"No," said the other, "Caswallawn and his men would hear of

it, and we would be ruined. We will go to another town."

They came to another town.

"What craft shall we take up?" asked Manawydan.

"Whatever you like of those we know," replied Pryderi.

"No," said the other, "we will practice shoemaking. The shoemakers will not have heart enough either to fight us or prevent us."

"I don't know anything about that," said Pryderi.

"I do," said Manawydan, "and I will teach you to stitch; we will not bother with preparation of leather, but buy it already prepared, and make our products from it."

And they started buying the finest cordovan leather they could find in the town; none other than that would he buy, except leather for soles. And he began to make friends with the best goldsmith in the town, had buckles made for the shoes, and the buckles gilded; he watched that carefully until he knew how to do it. And because of that, he was called one of the three golden shoemakers.

As long as it could be had from him, neither shoes nor chaps were bought from any shoemaker in the town. The cobblers realized then that their profits were diminishing, for as Manawydan fashioned the work, Pryderi stitched it. They met and took counsel, and what they decided was to kill them.

"Pryderi," said Manawydan, "the men want to kill us."

"Why do we take that from the thieving villains?" said Pryderi. "Why not kill them all?"

"No replied Manawydan, "we will not fight with them, nor will we remain in England any longer. Let us go to Dyfed, and have a look at it."

However long they were on the road, they came to Dyfed and made for Arberth. They kindled a fire, and began to maintain themselves by hunting; in this way they passed a month. Then they assembled their hounds, hunted, and spent a year there in this way.

One morning Pryderi and Manawydan rose to go hunting. They readied the hounds, and went outside the court. What some of the dogs did was to proceed ahead of the rest, and go to a small thicket that was nearby. As soon as they went into the thicket they retreated swiftly in great agitation and terror, and returned to the men.

"Let's approach the thicket," said Pryderi, "and see what's inside."

They drew near to the thicket, and as they did, a gleaming white wild boar charged out from it. The dogs, then, taking heart from the men, charged him. What he did then was to leave the thicket and retreat a bit from the men. Until the men were near he kept the dogs at bay, without retreating before them. When the men would draw near, he would retreat again and break away. And they followed the boar until they could see a great, lofty fort, newly made, in a place where they had never seen stone nor construction. The boar made for the fort quickly, with the dogs after him. When the boar and the dogs had gone into the fort, they marvelled at seeing the fort where they had never seen any before, and from the top of the mound they watched, and listened for the dogs.

However long they remained thus, they heard nothing from any of the dogs.

"Lord," said Pryderi, "I will go to the fort to seek news of the dogs."

"God knows," said the other, "your decision to go to the fort is not good, for we have never seen this fort, and if you take my advice, you will not go there. The one who put a spell on the land has caused the fort to be here."

"God knows," said Pryderi, "I will not forsake my hounds."

Despite the advice he got from Manawydan, he went to the fort. When he reached it, he could see neither man nor creature, neither the boar nor the hounds, neither house nor dwelling inside. He could see, rather toward the middle of the grounds, a fountain with marble construction around it. At the edge of the fountain up over the marble slab was a gold basin secured to four chains, the chains reaching up into the sky; he could not see where they ended. He was enraptured by the fineness of the gold and by how well-wrought the basin was. He came to where the basin was and took hold of it. As soon as he did so, his hands stuck to it and his feet to the slab he was standing on; his power of speech went from him, so that he was not able to utter a single word. Thus he stood.

Manawydan waited for him until toward the end of the day, and late in the afternoon, when he was certain that he would get no news of Pryderi or the hounds, he returned to the court. When he came in, Rhiannon looked at him.

"Where is your companion and your hounds?" she asked.

"This is what happened," he said, and he told her the whole adventure.

"God knows," said Rhiannon, "you have been a poor friend, and what you lost was a good one."

And saying that, she went out, travelling in the direction he said the man and the fort lay.

She saw the gate of the fort open; it was not concealed from her. She went in, and as soon as she did, she noticed Pryderi sticking to the basin, and went to him.

"Och! Lord!" she exclaimed, "what are you doing here?"

She seized the basin with him, and as soon as she did, her hands stuck to it and her feet to the slab, so that she was unable to utter a single word. Then, as soon as it was night, there came a tumultuous clattering sound, and a mist descended upon them; simultaneously the fort disappeared, and away they went.

When Cigfa daughter of Gwyn Gloyw, wife of Pryderi, saw that there was no one in the court but she and Manawydan, she wept until she didn't care whether she was alive or dead. What Manawydan did then was to look at her.

"God knows," he said, "you're mistaken about it if you weep for fear of me. As God is my guarantor, you have never seen a truer friend than you will have in me, as long as God may wish you to be thus. I swear to God, if I were beginning my youth I would keep true to Pryderi, and for you yourself will I keep it; fear not," he said. "I swear to God," he continued, "you will get the companionship you wish from me, according to my ability, while God wills us to be in this stress and strain."

"May God reward you, I thought as much." And then the maiden rejoiced and was emboldened because of that.

"Well, my friend," said Manawydan, "there is no use our staying here; we have lost our dogs and cannot support ourselves. Let us go into England, where it will be easier to support ourselves."

"Gladly, Lord," she said, "let's do that."

Together they travelled toward England.

"Lord," she said, "what craft will you take up? Do something clean."

"I will take up nothing but shoemaking," he replied, "as I did before."

"Lord," she said, "the tidiness of that work is not suitable to a man as fastidious and as noble as you."

"To that will I apply myself," he replied.

He began his craft, and fashioned his work from the finest cordovan he could find in the town. And as he had commenced doing in the other place, he began decorating the shoes with gold buckles, until the work of all the shoemakers in the town was vain and petty compared to his own. As long as they could be had from him, neither shoes nor chaps were bought from anyone else at all. In this way he spent a year there, until the shoemakers became envious and jealous of him, and a warning came to him indicating that they plotted to kill him.

"Lord," said Cigfa, "why is this endured from the villains?"

"No," he said, "we will go back to Dyfed."

They travelled to Dyfed. When they set out, what Manawydan did was to take a load of wheat with him; they made for Arberth, and settled there. Nothing was more pleasurable to him than seeing Arberth and the territory that he had hunted, he and Pryderi, and Rhiannon together with them. He got accustomed to catching fish and hunting deer in their lair. After that, he began to till the soil, and then he sowed a croft, and a second, and a third. Lo, the wheat sprang up the best in the world, and his three crofts equally successful in growth, so that no one had ever seen wheat finer than that. He passed the seasons of the year. Harvest time came, and he went to look at one of his crofts and it was ripe.

"I'll want to harvest that tomorrow," he said.

He went back that night to Arberth. In the grey dawn of the next morning, he came intending to harvest the croft. When he arrived, there was nothing but naked stalks, each one broken where the ear came off the stalk, the ears completely gone, and the stalks left there bare. He wondered greatly at that, and came to inspect another croft. Indeed, that one was ripe.

"God knows," he said, "I'll want to harvest that tomorrow."

The next day he came bent on harvesting it. But when he arrived, there was nothing but bare stalks.

"Dear Lord God!" he exclaimed, "who is ruining me? I know one thing: the one who has begun to ruin me has nearly succeeded and the land has been ruined along with me."

He came to inspect the third croft. When he did, no man had

ever seen finer wheat, and it was ripe.

"Shame on me," he said, "if I do not stand watch tonight, and whatever ravaged the other wheat will come to ravage this and I'll know what it is."

He took up his weapons and prepared to watch the croft. He told Cigfa all about it.

"Well," she said, "what do you have in mind?"

"I shall guard the croft tonight," he replied.

He went to guard the croft. And as midnight came, so did the greatest commotion in the world; what he did was to keep watching. And there came an enormous host of mice, so huge that one could get neither their number nor extent. But he still knew nothing, until the mice were attacking the croft, each of them climbing along a stalk, bending it down, breaking the ear, and carting it off, leaving the stalk there. He didn't know of a single stalk there that didn't have a mouse on each ear. And they set out along their path, carrying the ears with them. In anger and wrath he struck among them, but he couldn't draw a bead on a single one of them—any more than on gnats or birds in flight. But one was pudgy so that he supposed it could barely move. That one he followed, caught it, put it in his glove, tied the top with a string, and took it with him to the court. He came to the room where Cigfa was, kindled a fire, and hung the glove by the string on a peg.

"What's in there, Lord?" asked Cigfa.

"A thief I caught stealing from me," he replied.

"What sort of thief could you put in your glove?" she asked.

"This is what happened," he answered, and told her how his crofts had been ravaged and ruined, and how the mice had come to the last croft as he watched.

"And one of them was pudgy, and I caught it. It's in my glove, and I will hang it tomorrow. I confess to God, if I had caught them all, I would have hanged them all."

"That's natural, Lord," she said. "Yet it is unseemly for a man as dignified and as noble as you are to hang that sort of vermin. If you would do right, you wouldn't bother about the rodent, but let it go."

"If I could get all of them," he said, "shame on me if I wouldn't hang them all, but what I did get I'll hang."

"Well, Lord," she said, "my purpose is not to act on behalf of this rodent, only to keep you from dishonor. But do as you like, Lord."

"If I knew any reason at all why you should act on its behalf, I would take your advice concerning it, but since I do not, Lady, I intend to destroy it."

"Do it, gladly," she said.

Then he set out for the mound of Arberth with the mouse. At the very top of the mound he pushed two forks into the ground. As he was thus engaged he could see a scholar approaching dressed in cheap, worn old clothes. It had been seven years since he had seen either man or beast; those four had been together, alone until the two were lost.

"Lord," said the scholar, "good-day to you."

"God prosper you, and welcome," he replied. "Whence do you come, scholar?"

"I come from England, Lord, from song-making. Why do you ask?" he said.

"I have not seen a single person here for seven years," he replied, "only four isolated people—and now you."

"Well, Lord, I am passing through this country on my way to my own;" he said, "and what sort of work are you engaged in, Lord?"

"Hanging a thief I caught stealing from me," he replied.

"What kind of thief, Lord?" asked the other. "I see some kind of vermin in your hand, rather like a mouse, and it would ill befit a man as dignified as yourself to deal with such vermin as that. Let it go."

"No, I swear to God," he said, "thieving I caught it, and the law of a thief shall be its lot; it'll hang."

"Lord," said the other, "rather than see a man as noble as yourself involved in this business, I will give you the pound I got begging to let the rodent go."

"No, I swear to God, I will neither release it nor ransom it."

"Do as you like, Lord," he said, "if it weren't degrading to see a man as noble as yourself handling this sort of vermin, I wouldn't concern myself."

And the scholar went off.

As he was placing the crossbeam on the forks, a priest approached on a saddled horse.

"Lord, good-day to you," he said.

"God prosper you," said Manawydan, "your blessing."

"The blessing of God upon you; what sort of work are you doing, Lord?"

"Hanging a thief I caught stealing from me," he replied.

"What sort of thief, Lord?" asked the other.

"Vermin," he replied, "a mouse, in fact. It stole from me, and I am punishing it as one punishes a thief."

"Lord, rather than see you troubling about that vermin, I will ransom it. Let it go."

"I confess to God, I will neither accept payment for it nor will I release it."

"It's true, Lord, it is worth nothing, but rather than see you dirty yourself with that vermin, I will give you three pounds, and you let it go."

"I swear to God," said the other, "I desire no payment than what is owed, namely, hanging."

"Gladly, Lord, work your will."

Away went the priest. The other, then, tied the string around the mouse's neck. As he was raising him up, he saw a bishop's entourage with his baggage and retinue, and the bishop himself approaching. What the other did then was to postpone what he was doing.

"Lord Bishop," he said, "your blessing."

"May God bless you," he said. "What sort of work are you engaged in?"

"Hanging a thief I caught stealing from me," he replied.

"Is that not a mouse I see in your hand?" asked the other.

"Yes," he answered, "and it has committed theft against me."

"Well," said the other, "since I have come just as you were about to execute that vermin, I will ransom it from you. I will give you seven pounds for it, and rather than see a man as noble as you executing so worthless a rodent as that; release it, and you will profit from that."

"No, I swear to God," he said.

"Since you will not release it for that, I offer you twenty-four pounds of ready money if you let it go."

"I will not, I confess to God, even for that much again!" he replied.

"Since you will not release it for that," he said, "I will give you all you see of horses here, and the seven loads of baggage, and the seven horses that carry them."

"I don't want it, I swear to God," he said.

"Since you don't want that, name the price."

"The freeing of Rhiannon and Pryderi."

"You shall have it."

"Not enough, I swear to God."

"What do you want?"

"Remove the magic and enchantment from the seven cantrefs of Dyfed."

"You shall have that, too, now release the mouse."

"No, I swear to God," he said. "I want to know who this mouse is."

"She is my wife, and if she hadn't been, I wouldn't have ransomed her."

"Why did she come to me?"

"To steal," he said. "I am Llwyd son of Cil Coed, and it is I who put the enchantment on the seven cantrefs of Dyfed to avenge Gwawl son of Clud; I did it out of friendship for him. And I avenged on Pryderi the game of Badger-in-the-Bag that Pwyll Pen Annwfn played on Gwawl son of Clud; that was done out of meanness in the court of Hyfaidd Hen. And after hearing that you were inhabiting the land, my retinue came to me, asking that they be turned into mice to ravage your wheat; the first night my own war band came. The next night they came again and destroyed the second croft. The third night my wife and ladies of the court came to me asking that they be transformed; I did it. And she was pregnant; if she had not been, you would not have overtaken her. But since she was and you have caught her, I will give you Pryderi and Rhiannon, and remove the magic and enchantment from Dyfed. I have told you who she is, now release her."

"I will not, I swear to God," he said.

"What do you want?" he asked.

"What I want is this: that there never be an enchantment on the seven cantrefs of Dyfed, and none be put."

"You shall have it," said the other. "Now release her."

"No, I swear to God," he said.

"What do you want?" he asked.

"What I want is this: that this never be avenged on Pryderi and Rhiannon, nor on me."

"You shall have all of that—and God knows, it's a good thing you mentioned that, for if you had not," he said, "the whole affliction would have fallen on your shoulders."

"Yes," he said, "that's why I noted it."

"Now free my wife."

"No, I swear to God, until I see Pryderi and Rhiannon free and by my side."

"Look, here they come," he said.

And, indeed, there were Pryderi and Rhiannon. He rose to meet them, welcomed them, and they sat together.

"Good Sir, free my wife now, for you have gotten all you intended."

"I will, gladly," he said.

And he released her, and the other struck her with his magic wand and transformed her into the fairest young woman anyone had ever seen.

"Look around at the land," he said, "and you will see all the dwellings and habitations as good as ever."

He rose and looked. And when he did, he could see the entire land inhabited, replete with all of its herds and habitations.

"In what kind of servitude were Pryderi and Rhiannon?" he asked.

"The gate-hammers of my court were around Pryderi's neck, and the collars of asses after they had been hauling hay, were around Rhiannon's neck. Such was their prison."

Because of that imprisonment, this account is called the Mabinogi of the Collar and the Hammer. Thus ends this branch of the Mabinogi.

Math Son of Mathonwy

In this branch we are concerned with the family of Dôn, a goddess whose name is equivalent to the Irish Danu, mother of the gods known as the Túatha Dé Danann, and the Gaulish divinity whose name is preserved in the river name Danube (Donau). The tale is set in Gwynedd, in the north of Wales, where Dôn's brother Math is king. Dôn's children, Gwydion and his sister Aranrhod, are two principal characters in the story, but the narrative focuses on the birth, boyhood, marriage, and later career of Aranrhod's son, Lleu Llaw Gyffes.

The tale of Math is a complex one, and it resists both a simple plot summary and a concise statement of its meaning. Myth and magic are everywhere apparent in the tale, and the action is even less realistic than in the other three stories. There are several narrative threads in the tale, some of which are broken abruptly, and others that are frayed, leaving gaps in the fabric of the story. The initial episode, which tells of the love of Gilfaethwy for Goewin and the ruse by which he rapes her, bears no apparent relation to the rest of the story. Gilfaethwy disappears from the narrative, as does Goewin, and although Math subsequently marries her, we discover nothing of her later career. Aranrhod enters the story under rather unusual circumstances, but we have no means to account for her great hostility toward her son Lleu. There is no further mention of the aquatic first son, Dylan, after he takes to the sea immediately after being born, although he turns up elsewhere in Welsh tradition. Aranrhod, too, disappears from the story after she has inadvertantly provided a name for her son. The last third of the story tells of the unfaithfulness of Lleu's wife, his destruction by his wife's lover, his revival by Gwydion, and the punishment of the wife and lover.

Gwydion and his uncle, Math, are both powerful magicians, and the tale is filled with their magic. Gwydion demonstrates his powers when he changes himself and his companions into poets, altering their appearance, presumably, and endowing them with magical poetic powers as well; then, he deceives Pryderi by conjuring splendidly equipped horses, hounds, and arms out of toadstools, and trading them for the swine that Pryderi had received from the Otherworld. Later, he and Math conjure a woman for Lleu out of flowers. This creative magic is associated with Math and Gwydion in the Book of Taliesin poem, "Cad Goddeu," where the persona of the poem asserts that he was created not of a father and mother, but from the elements by Math and Gwydion.

We have to do here, then, with the two supreme magician/creators of early Welsh tradition. Unlike his nephew Gwydion, Math is not a shape-shifter, but he does have the power to shift the shapes of others, even against their wills and the strength of their own magic. Gwydion tries to escape his uncle's anger, but with the aid of the magic rod, Math transforms Gwydion and his brother into various beasts, and condemns them to procreate, alternating sexes over a three-year period. The three offspring of these matings are transformed into fine young boys by the same staff of enchantment, although they are in animal form when they arrive with their parents at Math's court. But here is one of those threads abruptly broken off; no further mention is made of these three in the story. It has been suggested that we have in this episode a reference to a lost tradition about three heroes associated somehow with totem animals, but there is no evidence for the suggestion, and we must be content to drop the three as does the story-teller.

The longest sustained episode in the tale and the most interesting for modern readers, perhaps, is that of the deception of Lleu by his wife Blodeuedd. Here the human element is strongest; Blodeuedd and Gronw fall in love at first sight, and their adulterous affair hatches a plot to slay Lleu, so that the two of them can live together openly. When they succeed and news of the event reaches Gwydion, he is genuinely grieved and cannot rest until he has had some word of his nephew. He searches the land tirelessly, and when he has found Lleu, he takes pains to assemble the best physicians to effect the cure of the wasted lad. The tenderness and love felt by Gwydion for Lleu is in marked contrast to the superficial affections that have motivated Gronw and Blodeuedd. But in spite of the genuinely human emotions that motivate this very well constructed episode, it remains firmly rooted in the magic of Celtic tradition. Lleu's life is governed by certain taboos, and while he has no control over them, he has knowledge of them, so that he need only avoid them to remain safe. Such taboos are frequent in Irish tradition, where they are known as *gessa.* A hero or king knows, for example, that he must never harm birds, or that he must never taste the flesh of a dog, or that he must never refuse a boon requested under certain circumstances, or that he must not proceed in a certain direction around a specified place. Life's road is travelled by steering successfully past these obstacles that threaten destruction. Sometimes the taboos are simple enough and clearly articulated; at other times they are strange, almost perverse, as in those that circumscribe the life of Conaire Mór in the Irish tale, "The Destruction of Dá Derga's Hostel." In many instances, the taboos are in conflict and produce dilemmas, so that the hero cannot help but break one to avoid another. It is this tradition of taboos and circumscriptions that underlies the curious events that lead to the disappearance of Lleu, but here there is no dilemma: Lleu willingly places himself in harm's way in order to ease his wife's pretended anxiety. And while the details of the manner in which he can be slain are bizarre, it should be noticed that the place in which his destiny is to be met is neither terrestial nor profane, and the weapon by which it is to be accomplished is constructed only during sacred time.

Math son of Mathonwy was lord of Gwynedd, and Pryderi son of Pwyll was lord over twenty-one cantrefs in the South, namely, the seven cantrefs of Dyfed, seven of Morgannwg, four of Ceredigion, and three of Ystrad Tywi. In those days, Math son of Mathonwy could only live while his feet were in the lap of a maiden—unless the turmoil of war prevented him. The maiden who was with him was Goewin daughter of Pebin of Dol Bebin in Arfon. And she was the fairest of all the maidens that were known in her time. In those days the permanent court was in Caer Dathl in Arfon; none could go on circuit of the land on his behalf except his nephews, sons of his sister, Gilfaethwy son of Dôn and Gwydion son of Dôn, and the retinue with them.

The maiden was with Math continually. Gilfaethwy son of Dôn set his mind on the maid, and fell in love with her to the extent that he did not know what to do about it. Even his color, his appearance and his general condition worsened for love of her, so that it was not easy to recognize him. What his brother Gwydion did one day was to look at him closely.

"Lad," he said, "what has happened to you?"

"Why," answered the other, "how do I look?"

"You have lost your color and your good looks," he replied. "What has happened to you?"

"Lord brother," he answered, "it won't profit me to confide to anyone what has happened to me."

"Why is that, my friend?" he asked.

"You know," he said, "Math son of Mathonwy's nature: whatever whisper—no matter how small—passes between men, if it falls on the wind he will know it."

"Yes," said Gwydion, "you be quiet now, for I know your thoughts: you love Goewin."

What the other did then, when he realized that his brother knew what was on his mind, was heave the heaviest sigh in the world.

"Keep quiet with your sighs, my friend," he said, "that's not going to cure it. I will arrange a marshalling of the forces of Gwynedd and Powys and Deheubarth, because without that it won't be possible to get the maiden. Be cheerful; I will arrange it for you."

Then they went to Math son of Mathonwy.

"Lord," said Gwydion, "I have heard that some kind of animals that have never been in this island have come to the South."

"What are they called?" he asked.

"Swine (*hobeu*), Lord."

"What sort of animals are they?"

"Small animals, whose meat is better than beef. They are small and they change names; they are called pigs (*moch*) now."

"Whose are they?"

"They belong to Pryderi son of Pwyll—sent to him from Annwfn by Arawn, king of Annwfn." (And they still preserve that name in the word for a side of pork: *hanner-hob.*)

"Well," he said, "how can they be got from him?"

"I will go as one of twelve—disguised as poets—to ask for the swine."

"He can surely refuse you," said the other.

"My plan is not bad, Lord," he said. "I will not come away without the swine."

"Gladly," said the other, "go forth."

He and Gilfaethwy went, and ten men with them, as far as Ceredigion, to the place now called Rhuddlan Teifi; Pryderi had a court there. They came in dressed as bards, and were received joyfully, and Gwydion was seated beside Pryderi that night.

"Well," said Pryderi, "we will be pleased to hear lore from some of those young men there."

"Our custom, Lord," said Gwydion, "is that on the first night we come to a great man, the chief poet recites. I will recite lore gladly."

Then Gwydion was the best reciter of lore in the world. That night he entertained the court with pleasing monologues and lore that was admired by everyone of the court, and Pryderi found it delightful to be entertained by him.

When it was over, he said, "Lord, is it better for anyone to state my business with you than myself?"

"It is not," said the other, "yours is a most accomplished tongue."

"This is my business, Lord: to plead with you for the animals sent to you from Annwfn."

"Well," he said, "that would be the easiest thing in the world were it not for the covenant between me and my country about them, namely, that they should not go from me until twice as many as they have been bred in the land."

"Lord," said the other, "I will be able to free you from those words. This is how: don't give me the swine tonight, but don't refuse me them. Tomorrow I will offer an exchange for them."

That night he and his companions went to their lodge to take counsel.

"Men," he said, "we won't get the pigs by asking for them."

"Well," they said, "by what ruse will they be had?"

"I'll arrange to get them," Gwydion replied.

And then he began to practice his skills, and began to conjure, and he conjured twelve steeds, twelve black white-breasted hunting dogs, twelve collars with leashes on them—anyone who saw them would have thought they were gold, twelve saddles on the horses—where they should have been iron, they were solid gold; the bridles were made in the same way.

He came to Pryderi with the horses and the dogs.

"Good-day, Lord," he said.

"God prosper you," he replied, "and welcome."

"Here is your freedom from the words you spoke last night concerning the swine—that you could not give them nor sell them. You can exchange them for something better. I will give you these twelve horses, outfitted as they are, with their saddles and their bridles, the twelve hunting dogs with their collars and leashes, just as you see them, and the twelve golden shields you see over there." (He had made those out of mushrooms.)

"Well," he said, "we will take counsel."

What they decided was to give the pigs to Gwydion and take the horses, dogs, and shields from him.

They took their leave and set out with the pigs.

"My friends," said Gwydion, "we must move quickly. The enchantment lasts but from one day to the next."

That night they travelled as far as the upper part of Ceredigion, to the place which for that reason is now called Mochdref (swine-town). The next day they took the road, and came across Elenid. That night they were between Ceri and Arwystli–in the town which is also called Mochdref because of that. Thence they went forth, they went as far as a commote in Powys, which is called Mochnant (swine-brook), and they stayed there that night. From there they travelled as far as the cantref of Rhos, and they stayed there that night, in a town still called Mochdref.

"Men," said Gwydion, "we will march these animals into the might of Gwynedd, for they are marshalling behind us."

They reached the highest township of Arllechwedd, and made a pen for the pigs there; for that reason it was called Creuwryon. After making the pen for the pigs, they sought Math son of Mathonwy in Caer Dathl.

When they arrived there, the country was being marshalled.

"What news here?" asked Gwydion.

"Pryderi is marshalling twenty-one cantrefs to come after you," they replied. "It is amazing how slowly you have come."

"Where are the animals you went after?" asked Math.

"They have made a pen for them in the other cantref below," said Gwydion.

Then, lo, they could hear the trumpets and the mustering of the land, and they dressed and went forth until they were in Penardd in Arfon. That night, Gwydion son of Dôn and his brother Gilfaethwy returned to Caer Dathl. The handmaidens were forced out rudely, and Gilfaethwy was put in Math son of Mathonwy's bed with Goewin daughter of Pebin to sleep together; the girl was seduced dishonorably, and slept with against her will that night.

With the dawn next morning, they went toward the place

where Math son of Mathonwy and his host were. When they arrived, the others were going into counsel over where they would await Pryderi and the men of the South. They joined the discussion. What they decided was to wait in the fastness of Gwynedd in Arfon. Between Maenawr Bennardd and Maenawr Coed Alun they waited.

Pryderi attacked them there, and that is where the encounter took place. A great massacre was effected on each side, but the men of the South had to retreat. They retreated as far as the place still called Nant Coll, and they were pursued there. An incalculable slaughter took place there, and they retreated as far as the place called Dol Benmaen. There they rallied and sought a truce, and Pryderi gave hostages for the peace. Gwrgi Gwastra was one of the twenty-four nobles' sons he gave in hostage.

After that they went in peace as far as Traeth Mawr. Because the foot soldiers could not be prevented from shooting at each other as soon as they had come to Melen Ryd, Pryderi sent messengers to request that the two hosts be restrained and that it be left between him and Gwydion, since he had caused it. The message came to Math son of Mathonwy.

"Well," said Math, "I swear to God, if it please Gwydion son of Dôn, I will allow it gladly. I will not compel anyone to fight beyond what lies in our power to do."

"God knows," said the messenger, "Pryderi says that it is only fair for the man who so wronged him to put his body against his, Pryderi's, and let the two hosts stay out of it."

"I confess to God, I will not ask the men of Gwynedd to fight for me; I myself will fight with Pryderi. I will put my body against his, gladly."

That was conveyed to Pryderi.

"Well," said Pryderi, "nor will I ask anyone to assert my right but myself alone."

The two of them went aside, began to arm themselves, and then fought. By dint of strength and force, magic and enchantment, Gwydion won and Pryderi was slain. He was buried in Maen Tyfyawg, above Melen Ryd, and his grave is there.

The men of the South set out with woeful lamentations toward their own land, and no wonder: they had lost their lord, many of their best men, their horses, and most of their weapons. The men of Gwynedd returned home happy and full of high spirits.

"Lord," said Gwydion to Math, "wouldn't it be proper for us to release their lord to the men of the South, the one they pledged to us in truce? We should not imprison him."

"Let him be freed, then," said Math.

And that fellow and the hostages that accompanied him were sent back to the men of the South.

Then Math went to Caer Dathl. Gilfaethwy son of Dôn and the host that had been with him went on circuit of Gwynedd as was their custom, and did not go to the court. Math approached his chamber, and had a place arranged for him to recline, the way he loved to put his feet in the maiden's lap.

"Lord," said Goewin, "seek a maid who may sit beneath your feet now; I am a woman."

"What does this mean?"

"An attack was made upon me, Lord, and that openly, nor was I silent–there wasn't anyone in the court who didn't know it. It was your two nephews who came, Lord, sons of your sister: Gwydion son of Dôn and Gilfaethwy son of Dôn. They raped me and shamed you, for I was slept with in your chamber and in your bed."

"Well," he said, "first, I will do right by you–as far as I am able; as for me, I shall act according to my right. I will make you my wife and will put possession of my realm into your hand."

They did not come to the vicinity of the court then, but lived about the country until a prohibition was enacted against food and drink for them. At first they did not come near Math; then they did.

"Lord," they said, "good-day to you."

"Well," he said, "have you come to make reparation to me?"

"Lord, we are at your will."

"Were it my will, I would not have lost what I did of men and arms. You cannot compensate me for my shame, to say nothing of Pryderi's death. But since you have submitted yourselves to my will, I will begin your punishment."

Then he took his staff of enchantment and struck Gilfaethwy so that he became a good-sized hind. He seized the other quickly, and though he wanted to escape, he could not; he struck him with the same staff so that he became a stag.

"Since you two are inseperable, I will make you travel together and mate in the same manner as the wild beasts in whose shape you are; and when they have offspring, so shall you. A year from today return here to me."

At the end of a year from that very day, he could hear a commotion beneath the chamber wall, and the dogs of the court barking at it.

"See what is outside," he said.

"Lord," said one, "I have looked; there is a stag and hind, and a fawn with them."

Thereupon he rose and went out. When he did, he saw the three beasts; the three he saw were a stag and hind, and a sturdy fawn. What he did then was raise his staff.

"The one of you that has been a hind during the past year, let him be a wild boar this year. He who has been a stag, let him be a wild sow."

And at that, he struck them with the staff.

"The little one, however, I will take; I will have him raised and baptized."

The name given him was Hyddwn.

"Go; one of you shall be a wild boar, the other a sow, and such nature as wild pigs may have let that be yours too. A year from today be here alongside the wall and your offspring with you."

At the end of the year, they could hear the dogs barking beside the chamber wall, and the court gathering around them. Thereupon, he rose and went out. When he came outside, he saw three beasts. The kind he saw were a wild boar, wild sow, and a god-sized piglet along with them. He was strong for his age.

"Well," he said, "I will take this one and have him baptized."

And he struck him with the staff, and he turned into a big, fine, handsome boy. The name he gave him was Hychdwn.

"As for you, the one that has been a wild boar for the past year, let him be a wolf bitch this year, and the one that has been a sow, let him be a wolf."

And he struck them with the staff, and they became wolf and bitch.

"Let your nature be the same as that of the animals in whose shape you are. And be here a year from today beside this chamber wall."

At the end of a year from that day, he heard a turmoil and

barking beside the chamber wall. He rose to go outside, and when he came there, he saw a wolf, a bitch, and a sturdy cub with them.

"I'll take this one," he said, "and have him baptized; his name is determined: Bleiddwn. Three sons you have, and these are they:

Three sons of wicked Gilfaethwy,
Three true champions.
Bleiddwn, Hyddwn and Hychdwn Hir.

Saying that, he struck the two of them so that they returned to their own shape.

"Men," he said, "if you have done me wrong, I have punished you enough, and you have had great shame; each of you bearing the other's child. Have these men bathed and their heads washed, and have them properly dressed."

And that was done. After they had been properly arrayed, they went to him.

"Men," he said, "you got peace, and you shall have friendship. Now give me advice on the sort of maiden I should seek."

"Lord," said Gwydion son of Dôn, "it is easy to advise you: your niece Aranrhod daughter of Dôn, your sister's daughter."

She was summoned to him, and came in.

"Maiden," he said, "are you a maiden?"

"I do not know other than that I am."

Then he took his magician's rod and held it down low.

"Step across this," he said, "and if you are a maiden, I will know it."

She stepped over the rod then, and as she did she dropped a big, fine, yellow-haired boy. What the boy did was to utter a loud cry. After the boy's cry, she made for the door, dropping as she went some little thing from her. Before anyone could have a second glance at it, Gwydion took it, wrapped a brocaded silk coverlet around it and hid it. Where he hid it was in a small chest at the foot of his bed.

"Well," said Math son of Mathonwy, "I will have this one baptized," he said, looking at the sturdy yellow-haired boy. "The name I will give him is Dylan."

The boy was baptized, and as soon as he was, he made for the sea. No sooner had he come to the sea then he took the sea's nature, and swam as well as the best fish in the sea; because of that he was called Dylan Eil Ton. No wave ever broke under him; the blow that caused his death was delivered by Gofannon his uncle, and that was one of the three unfortunate blows.

One day, as Gwydion awoke in his bed, he heard a cry from the chest at his feet. Though it was not loud, it was loud enough for him to hear it. What he did was to rise quickly and open the chest. As he opened it, he saw a little boy, flailing his arms free of the folds of the coverlet and tossing it aside. He cradled the boy between his arms and took him to the town, where he knew there was a woman in milk and he had her nurse the boy. And that year he was nursed. When he was a year old, they thought his stoutness was remarkable were he two years old. In the second year he was a large boy, and able to set out for the court on his own. After he came to the court, Gwydion himself took charge of him. The boy came to know him well, and loved him more than anyone. The boy was raised in the court, then, until he was four years old–and it would be remarkable for a boy of eight years to be as sturdy as he.

One day, he set out for a walk behind Gwydion. What he did was to go to Caer Aranrhod, and the boy with him. When he came to the court, Aranrhod rose up to welcome him, and greeted him.

"God prosper you," he said.

"What boy is that behind you?" she asked.

"This boy is your son," he replied.

"Och, Man! What has come over you to disgrace me, and maintain my shame by keeping him as long as this?"

"If you have no shame greater than my fostering a boy as fine as this, then your shame is a small thing indeed."

"What is your boy's name?" she asked.

"God knows," he replied, "he has no name yet."

"Well," she said, "I put a curse on him, that he shall not have a name until he gets it from me."

"I confess to God," he said, "you are a wicked woman; the boy shall have a name, though it displease you. And you, though you may grieve that you are not a maiden, because of what you are you will never be called maiden now."

Thereupon, he went away angrily, made his way to Caer Dathl, and stayed that night. The next morning he arose, and taking the boy with him, journeyed along the sea-shore between there and Abermenai. And where he found dulse and laminaria, he conjured a ship. From the seaweed and the dulse he conjured cordovan leather—a good deal of it, and dappled it until no one had ever seen fairer leather. Then he rigged a sail on the ship, and he and the boy came in the ship to the entrance of the port of Caer Aranrhod. They began to fashion shoes and stitch them, and they were seen from the fort. When he knew they were being observed from the fort, he took away their own appearance and put another upon them so they could not be recognized.

"What kind of men are in the ship?" asked Aranrhod.

"Shoemakers," they replied.

"Go see what kind of leather they have and what kind of work they do."

They went, and when they arrived he was mottling the cordovan with gold. The messengers returned and told her that.

"Well," she said, "take the measurements of my feet, and ask the shoemaker to make a pair of shoes for me."

He fashioned the shoes, and not in her size, but larger. They brought her the shoes, but they didn't fit.

"These are too big," she said. "He will have the price of these, but let him also make some smaller ones."

What he did was to make the others much smaller than her feet, and send them to her.

"Tell him that none of these shoes fit," she said.

That was told to him.

"Well," he said, "I shall make no shoes for her until I see her foot."

That was told to her.

"Well," she said, "I will go to him."

She came to the ship, and when she did he was designing and the boy stitching.

"Well, Lady," he said, "good-day to you."

"God prosper you," she replied. "I am amazed that you are not able to proportion shoes according to measure."

"I couldn't," he said, "but I can now."

At that moment there was a wren perched on the deck of the ship. What the boy did was to make a cast at it and hit it in the leg between the tendon and the bone. She smiled.

"God knows," she said, "it's with a skilful hand (*llaw gyffes*) that the fair-haired one (*lleu*) has hit him!"

"Well," said the other, "God's curse to you, he has got a name, and a good enough name it is: he is Lleu Llaw Gyffes henceforth."

Then the work vanished into dulse and seaweed, and he occupied himself with it no more. On account of that he was called one of the three golden shoemakers.

"God knows," she said, "you won't be any better for being evil toward me."

"I haven't been evil to you, even so!" he said, and with that he transformed his boy into his own shape, and took his own form.

"Well," she said, "I put a curse on this boy that he shall never take arms until I arm him."

"I swear to God," he said, "that comes from your wickedness, but he shall take arms."

They came toward Dinas Dinlleu, then, and Lleu Llaw Gyffes was raised until he was capable of every kind of horsemanship, and until he was perfected in form, growth and size. Then Gwydion realized that he was getting restless over the lack of steeds and arms, and he summoned him.

"My boy," he said, "you and I shall go on an errand tomorrow; be more cheerful than you are."

"I will," said the lad.

Early in the morning the following day, they arose and took the route that led by the sea up toward Bryn Arien. At the very top of Cefn Cludno they mounted horses and came toward Caer Aranrhod. Then they changed their shapes and went to the gate in the guise of two young fellows, except that Gwydion's countenance was more studied than that of the lad.

"Porter," he said, "go inside and say that bards from Morgannwg are here."

The porter went.

"God's welcome to them; let them in," she said.

They were received with very great joy. The hall was readied, and they went to eat. After they ate, she and Gwydion entertained themselves with tales and lore. Gwydion was a good reciter of lore.

When it was time to leave off the entertainment, a chamber was prepared for them and they went to sleep. Long before morning Gwydion rose, and summoned his might and magic. By the time day was dawning the sounds of turmoil, trumpets and cries were filling the land. When the day came, they heard knocking on the door of the room, and then Aranrhod, asking that they open up. The lad rose and opened the door, and in she came, a maid with her.

"Men," she said, "our position is bad."

"Yes," he said, "we have heard trumpets and shouts; what do you suppose it is?"

"God knows," she said, "we can't see the color of the sea for the multitude of ships, and they're coming to land as fast as they can. What shall we do?"

"Lady," said Gwydion, "there is no counsel for us but to shut ourselves inside the fort and defend it as best we can."

"Well," she replied, "may God reward you! Defend it—you will find plenty of weapons here."

Then she went after the weapons. She returned accompanied by two maidens, and they had arms for two men.

"Lady," he said, "you dress this young man, and the maidens will assist me to dress. I hear the roar of men coming."

"I will do that gladly," and she outfitted him completely, and did it cheerfully.

"Have you finished outfitting that young man?" he asked.

"I have," she replied.

"Then I have finished, too," he said. "We will divest ourselves of our arms now, for we have no need of them."

"Och!" she exclaimed, "Why? A fleet surrounds the place!"

"Woman, there isn't any fleet here."

"Och!" she exclaimed, "Then what was that hosting?"

"It was assembled," he replied, "to break your curse on your son, and to get arms for him. And he did get arms, no thanks to you."

"I swear to God," she said, "you are a wicked man. Many a boy could have lost his life over the uprising you caused in this cantref today. But I will put a curse on him," she said, "that he will never get a wife from any race that's on this earth now."

"Well," he said, "you have always been a wicked woman, and no one should maintain you. But he shall have a wife, just as he got a name and arms."

They came to Math son of Mathonwy, complaining most

persistently about Aranrhod, and related how he had caused him to be armed.

"Well," said Math," we two shall seek by means of our magic and our enchantment, to charm a wife for him out of flowers."

At that time he had a man's physique and was the most handsome fellow anyone ever saw. So they took the flowers of oak, broom, and meadow sweet, and from these they created the fairest and most beautiful maiden anyone ever saw. And they baptized her in the way they did then, and named her Blodeuedd. At the feast they slept together.

"It is not easy," said Gwydion, "for a man without territory of his own to support himself."

"Well," said Math, "I will give him the one best cantref a young man can have."

"Which is that, Lord?" he asked.

"Cantref Dinoding," he replied. That place is now called Eifynydd and Ardudwy.

The place where he kept his court in that cantref is called Mur Castell, in the upper part of Ardudwy. And he dwelt there and ruled that land; everyone was pleased with him and his governance. One day he travelled to Caer Dathl, to visit Math son of Mathonwy. On the day that he went to Caer Dathl, she was going for a walk in the court. She heard a hunting horn, and after the sound of the horn, there was a weary stag going past, with dogs and hunters chasing it. Behind the dogs and the hunters came a crowd of men on foot.

"Lad," she said, "go down and find out what that crowd is."

The boy went, and asked who they were.

"It's Gronw Pebyr, the man who is Lord of Penllyn," they told him.

He relayed that to her, while Gronw kept after the stag. They overtook the stag and slew it at the river Cynfael. He was busy skinning the stag and baiting his hounds until night overtook him. And as the day declined and night drew near, he came past the gate of the court.

"God knows," she said, "unless we invite him in, he will satirize us for letting him go off to another land at this hour."

"God knows, Lady," they replied, "the most proper thing is to invite him."

Messengers went up to him, then, to invite him. He accepted

the invitation gladly, and came to the court; she came forth to welcome him and greet him.

He removed his gear and they went to sit down. What Blodeuedd did was to look at him, and as she gazed, her entire being was filled with love of him. And he noticed her, too, and the same feeling was awakened in him as awakened in her. He could not conceal being in love with her, and he told her; she rejoiced exceedingly, and that night they talked of the love and affection they felt for one another. Nor did they put off past that night embracing each other; they slept together the same night.

The next day he meant to depart.

"God knows," she said, "you won't leave me tonight?"

That night they stayed together again. The same night they conspired together about what ruse they could devise to remain together.

"There is but one advice for you," he said, "find out from him how his death may be encompassed, as if you were concerned about him."

The next day he meant to depart.

"God knows, I don't advise you to leave me today."

"Well, since you don't advise it, I won't go," he said. "I do say, though, that there is a danger that the chieftain whose court this is may come home."

"Yes," she said, "tomorrow I will let you go."

The next day he sought to go and she did not prevent him.

"Well," he said, "remember what I told you, and talk diligently with him; do it as if out of the tenacity of your love for him, and pursue with him how his death might come about."

That night he came home, and they spent the time conversing and in song and revelry; that night they went to bed together. He spoke to her, and spoke a second time, but he got no response.

"What has happened to you?" he said. "Are you well?"

"I am thinking," she replied, "something you would never guess: in fact, I am worrying about your death—in case you should go before me."

'Well," he said, "God reward your concern. But unless God strikes me dead, it will not be easy to kill me."

"For God's sake—and for mine—will you explain to me how you could be killed? For my memory is better for being wary than yours."

"I will gladly," he answered. "It is not easy to kill me with a cast. One would have to spend a year making the spear that was thrown at me, working on it only when people were at prayers on Sunday."

"Are you safe from that?"

"No doubt I am," he said. "I cannot be killed in a house, nor outside; neither on a horse nor on foot."

"Well," she said, "how can you be killed?"

"I will tell you," he replied. "You make a bath for me on a river bank, and construct a roof-frame above the tub; after that, roof it so as to make it a good shelter. Then bring along a billy-goat and station him beside the tub; I put my one foot on the billy's back and the other on the edge of the tub. Whoever should hit me in that position will kill me."

"Well," she said, "thank God for that! That can be avoided easily."

No sooner did she get that information than she sent it to Gronw Pebyr. Gronw labored over the spear, and a year from that very day it was ready. On the same day he let her know that.

"Lord," she said, "I'm wondering how that which you told me before could be. Will you show me how you would stand on the edge of the tub and the billy's back if I make the bath?"

"Yes," he said.

She sent word to Gronw, and asked him to be in the shadow of the hill that is now called Bryn Cyfergyr (Hill of the Battle); on the shore of the Cynfael it was. She had all the goats she could find in the cantref gathered together and brought to the far side of the river, facing Bryn Cyfergyr.

Next day, she said, "Lord, I have had the frame arranged, as well as the bath, and they're all ready."

"Well," he said, "let's go look at them, gladly."

They came to look at the bath.

"Will you get into the bath, Lord?" she asked.

"I will, gladly," he replied.

He got into the bath and washed.

"Lord," she said, "here are the animals you said were called billy-goats."

"Well," he said, "have one of them caught and brought here."

It was done. He rose then from the bath, put on his trousers, and placed one foot on the edge of the tub and the other on the billy's back. Gronw rose up from the hill called Bryn Cyfergyr, knelt on one knee, and cast the poison spear at him. It struck him in the side, so that the shaft stuck out of him but the head remained inside. He uttered a horrible scream then, and took flight in the shape of an eagle until they lost sight of him. As quickly as he disappeared, they went to the court, and that night they slept together. The next day Gronw arose and took possession of Ardudwy. After taking possession of the land, he ruled it until both Ardudwy and Penllyn were in his power.

The news went to Math son of Mathonwy. Math became anxious and depressed, and Gwydion even more so.

"Lord," said Gwydion, "I will never rest until I have news of my nephew."

"Yes," said Math, "and may God strengthen you."

He set forth then, and began to walk; he traversed Gwynedd and all of Powys, and after wandering everywhere, he came to Arfon, to a peasant's house in Maenawr Bennardd. He went inside and stayed there that night. The head of the household and his family came in, and lastly the swineherd.

The man said to the swineherd, "Lad, has the sow come in tonight?"

"Yes," he replied, "she has just come to the pigs."

"Where does that sow go?" asked Gwydion.

"When the pen is opened each day, she goes out. She isn't observed closely and we don't know where she goes, any more than if she went into the earth."

"For my sake," said Gwydion, "will you not open the pen until I am on the other side of the pen with you?"

"All right, gladly," he replied.

They went to sleep that night.

When the swineherd saw the light of day, he awakened Gwydion, who rose, dressed, and came with him to the pen. The swineherd opened it. As soon as he did, here she came, bounding out. She set a brisk pace, and Gwydion pursued her. She went upstream, travelling in the brook now called Nantlleu; there she paused and fed.

Then Gwydion came under the tree, and looked to see what the sow was feeding on; he saw her eating rotten flesh and maggots. What he did then was to look at the top of the tree. When he did, he saw an eagle there. When the eagle would stir, the lice and rotten flesh would slake off him, and the sow would eat that. Then it occurred to him that the eagle was Lleu, and he sang the *englyn*:

> There's an oak that grows between two lakes,
> Gloomy is the air and the glen;
> If I speak no lie,
> This comes from Lleu's flowers.

At that point the eagle let himself slip down until he was in the middle of the tree. What Gwydion did was to sing another *englyn*:

> There's an oak that grows on a high plain;
> Rain wets it not, nor does it melt;
> It nourished a score of torments.
> In its top is Lleu Llaw Gyffes.

Then he slipped down farther until he was on the lowest branch of the tree. He sang this *englyn* to him then:

> There's an oak that grows along a slope;
> Stately prince in his temple.
> If I speak no lie,
> Lleu will come to my lap.

And at that he landed on Gwydion's knee. Gwydion struck him with his magician's rod, so that he was changed into his own shape. But never had anyone seen a more wretched appearance in a man than his; he was mere skin and bone. He took him to Caer Dathl, then, and all the good doctors that could be found in Gwynedd were brought to him. Before the year was out, he was completely healed.

"Lord," he said to Math son of Mathonwy, "the time has come for me to exact justice upon the man who caused me such affliction."

"God knows, he will not be able to maintain himself, owing you redress."

"Well," said the other, "the sooner I get justice the better."

They mustered Gwynedd then, and marched on Ardudwy.

Gwydion marched in front and assaulted Mur Castell. What Blodeuedd did when she heard them coming was to take her maidens and head for the mountain and the court that was there, across the Cynfael river. Because they were afraid, they could only proceed by looking backwards, so they were unaware until they fell into the lake; all drowned except she alone.

Gwydion overtook her then, and said to her, "I won't kill you, I'll do worse: I'll let you go in the form of a bird. And because of the shame you brought upon Lleu Llaw Gyffes, you shall not dare show your face ever in the light of day for fear of the other birds. There shall be enmity between you and all the rest of the birds. It shall be natural for them to persecute you and dishonor you whereever they find you. You shall not lose your name, however, you shall always be called Blodeuwedd." What *blodeuwedd* is, is "owl" in the language of the present day. And from that cause the owl is hated by birds; the owl is still called "flower-face" (*blodeu-wedd*).

As for Gronw Pebyr, he went to Penllyn and sent a message from there asking Lleu Llaw Gyffes if he wanted land or territory, gold or silver in retribution.

"No, I confess to God," he said. "Here is the least I will accept from him: let him go to the place I was when I was hit by the spear and me be where he was, and let me cast a spear at him. That is the least I will accept."

That was told to Gronw Pebyr.

"Well," he said, "I must do that. My loyal nobles, my retinue and my foster-brothers, is there one of you who would take the blow for me?"

"Certainly not," they said.

Because of their refusal to suffer taking a blow on behalf of their lord, they have been called from that day to this, one of the three unloyal retinues.

"Well," he said, "I will take it."

Then those two came to the shore of Cynfael river. Gronw Pebyr stood where Lleu Llaw Gyffes had when he was struck, and Lleu stood in the other's place.

Then Gronw Pebyr said to Lleu, "Lord, since I did what I did to you through the maliciousness of a woman, I beg of you for God's sake let me put the stone I see there on the bank between me and the blow."

"God knows," said Lleu, "I won't refuse you that."

"Well," said the other, "God reward you."

Then Gronw picked up the stone and put it between him and the blow. Lleu cast the spear at him, and it pierced through the stone and through him so that it broke his back. And Gronw Pebyr died, and the stone is there still on the bank of the Cynfael in Ardudwy, with the hole through it. Because of that it is called Gronw's Stone.

Lleu Llaw Gyffes took possession of his land again and ruled successfully. According to the lore, he was lord over Gwynedd after that.

Thus ends this branch of the Mabinogi.

Lludd and Lleuelys

In his *History of Welsh Literature,* Thomas Parry concludes that "the merits of Lludd and Llefelys [sic] in regard to structure and style are small" (p. 80). However true his judgment may be, and however small the charms and grace of the tale may be, it is at least as important as the other stories gathered here, for it preserves the framework of a myth known to Irish tradition and apparently common to Indo-European culture. The tale tells how the Isle of Britain was besieged by three plagues, and how its king, Lludd, with the aid of his brother's counsel, overcame the plagues. The meaning of the story is most clearly perceived by reference to the thories of the great French scholar, Georges Dumézil. Professor Dumézil has amassed a staggering amount of evidence in support of his theory that Indo-European society was based upon a tripartite ideology that includes the functions of sovereignty (priests, law-givers, magicians), force (the warrior), and fecundity. Dumézil believes that this tripartition was so ingrained in Indo-European society that even after it had ceased to play a significant part in public life and religion it continued to be operative, so that even in a tale as relatively recent as "Lludd and Lleuelys" we may find the structure of an ancient ideology (he discusses the tale in *Mythe et Épopée* I, Paris, 1968, pp. 613–623).

The Irish tale to which our story bears a striking resemblance is "The Second Battle of Mag Tuiredh." There, the king of the Túatha Dé Danann, Nuadha, has been wounded: his arm has been cut off by the leading warrior of the Fir Bolg. The Physicians fashion a silver arm for him, and from that time he is known as Nuadha Airgetlám 'Silver-hand or -arm.' Under their new king, Bres, who is part Fomorian, the Túatha Dé Danann are tyrannized by the Fomorians, their champions reduced to menial chores, and the poets find no hospitality at the king's court. In effect, the reign of Bres is characterized by negation of the three functions; the sovereign is a tyrant, warriors lose their might, fertility is contravened by surrendering of crops and produce in tribute, and the king lacks generosity. At this point Lugh enters, and eventually he leads the Túatha Dé Danann to victorious battle against the Fomorians.

In "Lludd and Lleuelys" the realm of Lludd has been weakened in each of the three functions: the Coraniaid effectively tyrannize the people by virtue of their magical auditory powers, a scream is raised over the island annually, the effect of which is to diminish the strength of men, and food not consumed on the first night of feasting in the king's courts disappears, even though it be a year's provisions. Lludd calls on his brother, Lleuelys, who offers advice that rids the land of the plagues.

The name Lludd turns up in the tale of "Culhwch and Olwen" with the epithet *Llawereint* 'Silver-hand,' and it is generally agreed that the name Lludd was originally Nudd, the initial being changed by process of assimilation. *Nudd Llawereint would be the exact equivalent of the Irish name Nuadha Airgetlám (disregarding the fact that the elements in the compound "silver-hand" are reversed in the latter). Lleuelys has as its first syllable *lleu-*, the Welsh form of a name that in Irish is Lugh. In other words, both Irish and Welsh preserved versions of a Celtic myth in which the kingdom of a god Nodons (Irish Nuadha, Welsh Nudd→Lludd) was rescued from plagues that sought to undermine the three functions by the wisdom of a god Lugus (Irish Lugh, Welsh Lleu-). The Indo-European considerations go even further, as Dumézil has shown, and he adduces evidence from Indo-Iranian and Scandinavian, as well as from ancient Irish laws, to show that the three plagues that menace human society are an archaic formulation.

As we have seen, myth provides the sub-structure of the four branches, while the interests of the redactor (and his audience, no doubt) lie in the super-structure; at times the sub-structure and the super-structure are in conflict and the mythic content sometimes interferes with the literary design of the work. We may assume that the tales survived mainly because the characters were so interesting; they were subjected to various treatment that marked their translation from the world of gods to that of mortals, and eventually it was the psychological orientation of the redactors and story-tellers that determined characterization. Yet the mythic elements remained. In the case of "Lludd and Lleuelys," the characters have little to recommend them to a modern audience, but a tale of magic such as this is could not have failed to appeal to the same medieval audiences who delighted in the marvels of the other tales in this collection. Furthermore, however we may reconstruct the original form of his name, Lludd was widely known as the eponym of the city of London (Caer Lludd), thanks to the popularity of Geoffrey of Monmouth's *History of the Kings of Britain* and the numerous Welsh translations of it.

Beli Mawr son of Mynogan had three sons: Lludd, Caswallawn, and Ninniaw; according to the lore about him, Lleuelys was a fourth son. After Beli died, the kingdom of the Ise of Britain fell into the hands of Lludd, his eldest son, and Lludd ruled it successfully. He refurbished the walls of London, and surmounted them with countless towers. After that he ordered the citizens to build houses of such quality that no kingdom would have houses as splendid as were in London.

And besides that, he was a good warrior and generous, and he gave food and drink freely to all who sought it, and although he had many forts and cities, he loved this one more than any other, and dwelt there most of the year. For that reason it was called Caer Lludd, and finally Caer Llundein. After the foreign people came it was called Llundein or Londres.

Lludd loved Lleuelys best of all his brothers, for he was a wise and prudent man. When Lleuelys heard that the king of France had died leaving no heir save a daughter, and that he had left his realm in her hands, he came to his brother Lludd seeking counsel and encouragement from him. And not only for personal advantage, but to try to add honor, dignity, and merit to their race, if he could go to the kingdom of France to seek that woman for his wife. His brother agreed with him immediately, and he was pleased with that counsel. Without delay ships were made ready and filled with armed horsemen, and they set out for France. As soon as they disembarked, they sent messengers to announce to the nobles of France the nature of the business they had come to attempt. And by joint counsel of the nobles of France and her princes, the maiden was given to Lleuelys, and the realm's crown along with her. After that, he ruled the land wisely, prudently, and in good fortune, as long as he lived.

After some time had passed, three oppressions came upon the isle of Britain, such that none of the islands had ever seen before. The first of these was the advent of a people called the Coraniaid; so great was their knowledge that there was no utterance over the face of the land—however low it was spoken—that, if the wind met it, they didn't know. For that reason, one could do them no harm.

The second oppression was a cry that resounded every Mayday eve above every hearth in Britain; it went through the hearts of men and terrified them so much that men lost their color and their strength, women miscarried, sons and daughters lost their senses and all animals, forests, earth and waters were left barren.

The third oppression was that despite how extensive the preparations and provisions were that were readied in the king's courts, even though it be a year's provision of food and drink, nothing was ever had of it except what could be consumed on the very first night.

The first oppression was evident and clear enough, but no one knew the meaning of the other two oppressions. There was greater hope, therefore, of deliverance from the first than from the second or third.

Lludd, the king, grew anxious and worried then, for he didn't know how he could get relief from those oppressions. He summoned all the nobles of his realm, and sought advice from them concerning what they could do against those oppressions. With the unanimous counsel of the nobles, Lludd son of Beli determined to go to his brother Lleuelys, king of France, for he was a man of great and wise counsel, from whom to seek advice. And they prepared a fleet—secretly and quietly, lest that people or anyone else know the meaning of their business except the king and his counselors. When they had been prepared, Lludd and those whom he had selected went to their ships and began to plough the seas toward France.

When news of that came to Lleuelys—since he did not know the reason for his brother's fleet—he came from the other side to meet him, with an enormous fleet. When Lludd saw that, he left all his ships out at sea except one, and in that he went to meet his brother. The other did the same. After they came together, each put his arms around the other's neck, and they greeted each other with brotherly affection. When Lludd had told his brother the purpose of his mission, Lleuelys said that he knew the meaning of his arrival in those lands. Then they conspired to conduct their business differently, in order that the wind might not carry their speech, lest the Coraniaid know what they said. So Lleuelys had a long brass horn made, and they talked through that. But whatever speech one of them uttered through the horn, only adverse, contrary speech was heard by the other. When Lleuelys saw that, and that a demon was obstructing them and creating turmoil in the horn, he had wine poured into the horn to cleanse it. By virtue of the wine, the demon was driven out.

When their speech was unobstructed, Lleuelys told his brother that he would give him some vermin, and that he should let some of them live to breed, in case by chance that sort of oppression came again. The others he should take and break up in water. That, he affirmed, would be good to destroy the race of Coraniaid, as follows: after he came home to his realm, he should summon all the people together—his people and the Coraniaid people in the same assembly, with the pretext of making peace between them. When they were all together, he should take that charged water and sprinkle it on everyone universally. And he affirmed that that water would poison the Coraniaid people, but that it would neither kill nor injure any of his own people.

"The second oppression in your realm," he said, "is a dragon. A dragon of foreign blood is fighting with him and seeking to overthrow him. Because of that, your dragon utters a horrible scream. This is how you shall be instructed regarding that: after you return home, have the length and width of the island measured. Where you discover the exact center, have that place dug up. Then, have a vatful of the best mead that can be made put into that hole, with a cover of silk brocade over the top of the vat. And then you yourself stand watch, and you will see the dragons fighting in the shape of horrible animals. Finally, they will assume the form of dragons in the air. Last of all, after they cease their violent and fierce battle, being tired, they will fall in the shape of two young pigs onto the coverlet. They will sink the sheet with them and draw it down to the bottom of the vat; they will drink all the mead, and after that they will sleep. Then immediately wrap the cover around them. In the strongest place you can find in your kingdom, deposit them in a stone chest, and hide it in the ground. And as long as they remain in that secure place, no oppression shall visit the isle of Britain from another place."

"The cause of the third oppression," he said, "is a powerful magician who carries off your food, your drink, and your provisions, and by his sorcery and his magic he puts everyone to sleep. And so you yourself must stand guard over your banquets and your feasts. And lest he induce sleep in you, have a vat of cold water at hand, and when sleep weighs you down, get into the vat."

Lludd returned to his country then, and without delay summoned every single one of his own people and the Coraniaid. He broke the vermin up in the water, as Lleuelys had taught him, and sprinkled it generally over everyone. All the Coraniaid folk were destroyed instantly without injury to any of the Britons.

Some time after that, Lludd had the island measured in length and breadth; the middle point was found to be in Oxford. There he had the earth dug up, and in that hole he put a vat full of the best mead that could be made, with a silk veil over the surface. He himself stood watch that night. As he was thus, he could see the dragons fighting. When they grew weary and exhausted, they fell onto the screen and dragged it down with them to the bottom of the vat. After they drank the mead they slept; as they slept, Lludd wrapped the veil about them. In the safest place he could find in Eryri, he secluded them in a stone chest. After that the place was called Dinas Emrys; before that it was known as Dinas Ffaraon Dandde. He was one of three stewards whose hearts broke from sorrow.

Thus was stopped the tempestuous scream that was in the realm.

When that was done, Lludd the king had a feast of great magnitude prepared. When it was ready, he put a vat full of cold water beside him and he personally stood guard. And as he stood there fully armed, about the third watch of the night, he heard much magnificent music and songs of different kinds, and drowsiness driving him to sleep. What he did then—lest his plan be thwarted and he be overcome by sleep—was to leap into the water frequently. At last a man of enormous stature, armed with powerful, heavy weapons, came in carrying a basket. As was his custom, he put all the preparations and the provisions of food and drink into the basket and started out with it. Nothing astounded Lludd more than such a quantity as that fitting into that basket. Thereupon, Lludd the King set out after him, and shouted; "Stop! Stop!" he said, "though you have committed many outrages and have been responsible for many losses before this, you'll do it no more—unless your prowess proves you stronger than I or more valiant."

Immediately, he set the basket on the floor and waited for him. They fought ferociously, until sparks flew from their weapons. Finally, Lludd took hold of him, and fate took care that the victory fell to Lludd, casting the tyrant to the ground beneath him. When he had conquered him through force and violence, the fellow sought protection from him.

"How could I give you protection," said the King, "after how much loss and injury you have perpetrated against me?"

"All the losses I have ever caused you," said the other, "I will restore to you, as well as I have carried them off, and I will not do the like from this moment on, but will be your faithful man henceforth."

And the King accepted that from him. Thus did Lludd ward off the three oppressions from the Isle of Britain. From then until the end of his life, Lludd ruled the Isle of Britain successfully and peacefully.

This tale is called the Adventure of Lludd and Lleuelys, and so it ends.

Culhwch and Olwen

"Culhwch and Olwen" is an important tale in many respects. It is one of our earliest sources for information about the native Arthur, a repository of lore about characters from Celtic tradition, many of whom are otherwise unknown, and a mine of legal idioms of Celtic provenance. It is part myth, part folklore, and its language ranges from simple lists and catalogs to exuberant and alliterative passages in a high rhetorical style. Some of its mythological implications have been discussed in the Introduction; I confine my remarks here to its form and style.

The tale ostensibly deals with the love of Culhwch for Olwen, the giant's daughter, and describes how, with the help of his cousin Arthur, the impossible tasks imposed by the giant were accomplished and Olwen won. But in fact, Culhwch is a flat character, and Olwen, although her description is one of the most elegant passages in the tale, has no development as a character at all. The story is really about Arthur, his wonder-working retinue, and a series of exploits performed by them, culminating in the pursuit of the great boar, Twrch Trwyth. This last ends virtually in a draw between Arthur and the boar, although the carnage on both sides is great.

That is the nucleus of the tale, but it has attracted other traditions that once were part of the lore concerning the Celtic swine god; no doubt the name Cul-hwch '-swine,-pig' was once a part of these traditions. Moreover, it became part of a tale type known universally as "the giant's daughter," and as folktale it has survived. The redactor who gave us the tale as we have it here appears to have set down his material rather indiscriminately, omitting nothing he had at hand. Parts of the story have little interest for him, but when it engages him fully, his language is brilliant and reflects a rhetorical virtuosity unequalled in these tales.

Until the departure of Culhwch for the court of Arthur, the prose does not have much to distinguish it. The passage that describes Culhwch atop his four-year-old steed, however, is a remarkable one. It reminds us very much of the descriptions of CúChulainn and his horses in the Irish tale, "The Wooing of Emer," with its strings of alliterating compounds. It is reminiscent of the "runs" of later Irish story-telling tradition, but it seems also to belong to the rhetorical tradition represented by the *areithiau* 'orations,' as Dr. Parry has noted (*History of Welsh Literature,* pp. 80, 131). Parry's point is well-taken, for the man who wrote this tale down was sure to be familiar with the work of the rhetoricians. The same familiarity is evidenced in Glewlwyd's recitation to Arthur, in which he declares that he has been with his chief throughout the world. A third *locus* for this high-flown and highly artificial rhetoric is the catalog of names. With a few exceptions, these names, together with their patronyms, epithets, and–to a lesser extent–descriptive chains, often form metrical units in which alliteration, rhyme (including assonance and consonance) and other paronymic types predominate. Some of these features may be seen in the translation, but for the total effect one must turn to the Welsh text. The rhythmic effect of this litany of heroes was apparently so mesmerizing that the author carried it to the point of absurdity. Here are some of the accoutrements of Bwlch, Cyfwlch and Sefwlch:

> tair gorwen gwen eu tair ysgwyd
> ('three resplendent whites were their three shields')
> tri gofan gwan eu tri gwayw
> ('three finely pointed piercers their three spears')

But when he gets to their three grandchildren, he is no longer fabricating for the sake of maintaining the rhythmic monotony, he is being downright silly; their names are Och ('Alas'), Garm ('Shout'), and Diaspad ('Cry'). Their three servants are Drwg ('Bad'), Gwaeth ('Worse'), and Gwaethaf Oll ('Worst of all'). It is as if the redactor took a perverse delight in sneaking in a perfectly ridiculous unit every now and then, so apt in rhythm that it was virtually indistinct from the authentic lore conveyed in the section.

Again, in his description of the beautiful Olwen, the author's language soars, and I am compelled to give the Welsh text here, too:

> Oedd melynach ei phen no blodau y banadyl
> ('Her hair was yellower than the flowers of broom')
> Oedd gwynnach ei chnawd no distrych y donn
> ('Her skin whiter than the foam of a wave')
> Oedd gwynnach ei phalfau a'i bysedd no chanawon godrwyth o blith man grayan ffynhon ffynhonus
> 'Her palms and fingers whiter than the blooms of the marsh trefoil amidst the sands of a gushing spring")

The literary sensitivities of the author or redactor of "Culhwch and Olwen" are not confined to these rhetorical flourishes. He has a good sense of the dramatic, as in the scene where Culhwch enters Arthur's court with great impetuosity and firmness of purpose. Cei (the Sir Kay of later romance) already displays here signs of jealously protecting courtly prerogative, a tendency that springs, perhaps, from the behavior required (in early Welsh law) of a porter, and that leads him to meanness and surliness, and finally foolishness in the later romances. His character is quite clearly defined, although like the other members of the court, including Arthur himself, Cei is still semi-divine, and his superhuman characteristics carefully detailed.

It is well to remember that despite its title, this story is essentially Arthurian and a collection of anecdotes about various heroes associated with the court of Arthur, a primitive court, to be sure, not at all like that we find in the later Arthurian romances of English, Continental, and even Welsh tradition. To that end, the reader would do well to proceed carefully through the long list of heroes upon whom Culhwch invokes his boon. This list tends to be tedious, but a careful reading will be repaid by the insights it gives into the nature of the early Arthurian milieu. Wherever possible, I have endeavored to translate the epithets that accompany personal names, hence "Osla Cyllellfawr big-knife," where 'big-knife' renders *cyllell-fawr* literally. This procedure makes the passage even more cumbersome than it is in the original text, and I have not been entirely consistent in carrying it out; my purpose has been only to give the reader some sense of the colorful and imaginative onomastics employed in this section.

Cilydd son of Celyddon Wledig desired a woman as well-born as himself. The woman he wanted was Goleuddydd daughter of Anlawdd Wledig. After his wedding feast with her, the country went to prayer to see whether they would have an heir. And through the country's prayers, they got a son. From the time she became pregnant she went mad and avoided civilized places. When her time came her senses returned to her. Where they did so was in a place where a swineherd was watching a herd of pigs, and the queen gave birth from fright of the swine. The swineherd took the boy and brought him to court. They baptized him and named him Culhwch, because he was found in a pig run. The boy was noble, however, and a cousin to Arthur. He was put out to fosterage.

After that, the boy's mother, Goleuddydd daughter of Anlawdd Wledig, became ill. What she did was to summon her spouse to her, and she said to him, "I shall die of this sickness, and you will want another wife. Women are dispersers of gifts these days, but you will be loathe to despoil your son. This is what I ask of you: do not seek a wife until you see a two-headed briar growing on my grave."

He promised her that. She summoned her tutor and asked him to trim her grave every year, so that nothing could grow on it. Then the queen died. What the king did was to send a boy every morning to see whether anything was growing on the grave. At the end of the seventh year, the tutor neglected to do what he had promised the queen. One day when the king was hunting, he paid a visit to the burial ground; he wanted to see the grave by which he might marry. He saw a briar, and as he did he took counsel where he might find a wife.

"I know a marriage that would suit you well," said one of his counsellors, "the wife of King Doged."

They decided to seek her.

They killed the king and carried his wife back home with them, and her daughter with her. Then they took possession of the king's land.

One day the noble lady went out to take a walk, and came upon the house of a toothless old hag who lived in the town.

"Old woman," said the queen, "for God's sake, tell me what I want to know: where are the children of the man who carried me off forcibly?"

"He has no children," said the hag.

"Woe is me," said the queen, "coming to an impotent man."

"You mustn't say that," said the hag, "for it is prophesied that he shall have offspring, and by you he shall have it since he has not had it. Do not grieve, either, for he has one son."

The noble lady went home happy.

"Why do you conceal your children from me?" she asked her mate.

"I won't conceal him any longer," said the king.

Messengers were sent for the boy and he came to the court.

"It would be well for you to get married, boy," said his stepmother to the boy, "and I have a daughter fit for any nobleman in the world."

"It's not time for me to marry yet," he replied.

"I put a curse on you," she said, "that your flesh shall not touch woman's till you get Olwen daughter of Ysbaddaden Chief-giant!"

The boy blushed at that, and love for the girl entered his every limb, though he had never seen her.

"My boy," said his father, "why do you blush? What troubles you?"

"My step-mother has cursed me that I shall never have a wife until I get Olwen daughter of Ysbaddaden Chief-giant."

"It's easy for you to achieve that, son," his father told him. "Go to Arthur, who is your cousin, to have your hair trimmed, and request that from him as your gift."

The boy went off on a four-year-old steed with a gleaming grey head, sturdy-legged, hollow-hoofed, a tubular gold bridle around his head, and a precious golden saddle upon his back. He had two sharp silver-mounted spears in his hand. A sword in his hand twice the length of a man's forearm from ridge to edge: it would bring blood from the wind, would be quicker than the quickest dewdrop drops when June's dew is wettest. On his hip a gold-hilted sword, edged in gold, with a gold-chased cross on it, colored with the brilliance of the heavens and inlaid with ivory. Before him, a pair of spotted white-breasted hunting hounds, with thick reddish-gold neck torques on each from shoulder-top to ear. The one on the left would bound to the right, and the one on the right would bound to the left, and thus like two terns they played about him. The steed's four hooves would hurl four clods into the air above his head—like four swallows, now up, now down. A purple four-cornered mantle about him, with a reddish-gold apple mounted at each corner, each apple worth one hundred cows. The valuable gold in his buskins and stirrups from the top of his knee to the tip of his toe was worth three hundred cows. Such was the ease of the steed's motion under him making toward Arthur's court that not even the tip of a hair on him stirred.

"Is there a porter?" asked the boy.

"There is, and as for you—you may lose your head for asking. I am porter to Arthur every year on the calends of January. And my lieutenants for the rest of the year, none other than Huandaw and Gogigwr and Llaesgenym and Penpingion, who goes about on his head to save his feet, not upright and not downright but like a rolling stone on the floor of the court."

"Open the gate."

"No."

"Why won't you open it?"

"Knife has gone into food, drink into horns, and there is thronging in the Hall of Arthur. None save the son of a rightful territorial king, or a craftsman who comes with a craft is allowed in. There's food for your dogs, grain for your horse, and hot wholesome chops and brimming cupfuls of wine for you. Entertaining songs and refection for fifty awaits you yonder in the hostel there, where distant travellers and sons of other lands who do not insist on the rights of Arthur's court eat. You'll be as well off there as Arthur is at the court: a woman to sleep with you, and songs to entertain you. Tomorrow, in the morning when the gates are opened to the multitude that has come here today, it shall be opened to you first, and you can seat yourself anywhere you choose in Arthur's Hall from the uppermost part to the very bottom."

"I want none of that," said the boy. "If you open the door, fine, if not, I will satirize your lord and give you a bad name. And I will raise three shouts at the entrance of this gate that will be as audible to the top of Pengwaedd in Cornwall as at the bottom of Dinsol in the North, and in Esgeir Oerfel, the accursed ridge, in Ireland. All the women in the court that are pregnant will abort, and those that are not, their wombs will be consigned to sterility so that from this day forth they shall never conceive."

Glewlwyd Gafaelfawr replied, "Whatever cry you may raise for the rights and privileges of Arthur's court, you shall not be allowed in until I go to speak with Arthur first."

Glewlwyd came into the hall and Arthur said to him, "Have you news from the gate?"

"Two parts of my life have gone," he replied, "and two parts of your own.

I was once in Caer Se and Asse,
    in Sach and Salach,
    in Lotor and Ffotor,
I was in Great India and Little India.
I was once in the battle of the two Ynyrs
    when the twelve hostages were taken from Llychlyn.
I was once in Europe.

I was once in Africa and the islands of Corsica,
 in Caer Brythwch and Brythach and Nerthach.
I was once there where you killed the retinue
 of Gleis son of Merin,
 when you killed Black Mil son of Dugum.
I was once there where you conquered Greece in the East.
I was once in Caer Oeth and Anoeth
 in Caer Nefenhir of the nine natures.

Fair lords we saw there, but never have I seen a man as noble as he who stands at the gate this moment."

Arthur said, "If you came in walking, go back on the double. An injunction on those who look to the light and who open and close their eyes; let some serve him from solid gold horns, others sizzling hot chops until he has plenty of food and drink. 'Tis a deplorable thing to leave such a man as you tell of out in the wind and rain."

"By God, my friend," said Cei, "if you took my advice you would not break the customs of the court for him."

"Not so, fair Cei. We are nobles as long as anyone seeks us out; the greater the favor we bestow, the greater shall be our nobility, our fame, and our honor."

Glewlwyd went out to the gate and opened it for him. Although everyone used to dismount at the mounting block on entering the gate, he did not: he came in on the steed.

"Hail, Chief of the nobles of this island," said Culhwch, "may the lower end of your house be no worse than the uppermost part. Let this greeting go equally to your warriors, your retinue, and your battlechiefs. May none be deprived of it; as it is a complete greeting I give to you, so let your protection, your warranty, and your renown be full in this island."

"Be it God's truth, chieftain! And greetings to you, too. Sit between two of these warriors, and you shall have entertaining song and the privileges of a crown-prince so long as you are here. And when I divide my goods among the guests and distant travelers, 'tis in your hand that I shall begin."

"I did not come here to wheedle food and drink," said the lad, "but if I get my gift, I shall repay it and praise it; if I don't, I shall satirize you to the farthest corners your fame has reached."

"Though you do not reside here," said Arthur, "you shall

have what your head and tongue may claim, as long as the wind dries, the rain wets, the sun moves, as far as land and sea reach—except my ship and my mantle, Caledfwlch my sword, Rhongomiant my spear, Wynebgwrthucher my shield, Carnwennan my knife, and Gwenhwyfar my wife. God's truth on it: you shall have it gladly: demand what you will."

"I demand that my hair be trimmed."

"You shall have it." And Arthur took a gold comb and shears with silver handles and he combed his head. Then he asked who he was.

"My heart inclines toward you: I know we are of the same blood. Tell me who you are."

"I will," said the lad. "I am Culhwch son of Cilydd son of Celyddon Wledig by Goleuddydd daughter of Anlawdd Wledig who is my mother."

"True," said Arthur, "you are my cousin. Claim what you will and you shall have whatever your head and tongue may claim."

"God's truth about that and the truth of your kingdom."

"You shall have it gladly."

"I request that you get for me Olwen daughter of Ysbaddaden Chief-giant. And I invoke her in the name of your warriors."

He invoked his gift from him in the name of Cei and Bedwyr, Greidawl Gallddofydd tamer of enemies, Gwythyr son of Greidawl, Greid son of Eri, Cynddylig Cyfarwydd the guide, Tathal Twyll Golau whose treachery was patent, Maelwys son of Baeddan, Cnychwr son of Nes, Cubert son of Daere, Fergos son of Roch, Lluber Beuthach, Corfil Berfach, Gwyn son of Esni, Gwyn son of Nwyfre, Gwyn son of Nudd, Edern son of Nudd, Cadwy son of Geraint, Fflewdwr Fflam Wledig the blazing lord, Rhuawn Bebyr son of Dorath, Bradwen son of Moren Mynawg the king, and Moren Mynawg the king himself.

Dalldaf son of Cimin Cof of the memory, the son of Alun Dyfed, the son of Saidi, the son of Gwrion, Uchdryd Ardwyad Cad protector in battle, Cynwas Cwryfagyl the clumsy, Gwrhyr Gwarthegfras rich in cattle, Isberyr Ewingath cat-claws, Gallgoid Gofyniad the claimant. Duach, Brathach, and Nerthach, sons of Gwawrddur Cyrfach the hunchback—these men came from the borderlands of Hell; Cilydd Canastyr hundred-grips, Canastyr Canllaw hundred-hands, Cors Cant Ewin hundred-claws, Esgeir

Gulhwch Gonyn Cawn with the stinging stalks, Drwst Dwrnhaearn the iron-fisted warrior, Glewlwyd Gafaelfawr of the mighty grip, Llwch Llawwynnawg of the furious hand, Anwas Adeiniawg swift as a bird, Sinnoch son of Seithfed, Wadu son of Seithfed, Naw son of Seithfed, Gwenwynwyn son of Naw son of Seithfed, Bedyw son of Seithfed, Gofrwy son of Echel Morddwyd Twll of the pierced thigh, Echel Morddwyd Twll himself, Mael son of Roycol, Dadweir Dallben the blind, Garwyli son of Gwythawg Gwyr, and Gwythawg Gwyr himself.

Gormant son of Ricca, Menw son of Teirgwaedd, Digon son of Alar, Selyf son of Sinoid, Gusg son of Achen, Nerth son of Cadarn, Drudwas son of Tryffin, Twrch son of Peryf, Twrch son of Anwas, Iona king of France, Sel son of Selgi, Teregud son of Iaen, Sulien son of Iaen, Bradwen son of Iaen, Moren son of Iaen, Siawn son of Iaen, and Cradawg son of Iaen—they were men of Caer Dathl, related to Arthur on his father's side.

Dirmyg son of Caw, Iustig son of Caw, Edmyg son of Caw, Angawdd son of Caw, Gofan son of Caw, Celin son of Caw, Conyn son of Caw, Mabsant son of Caw, Gwyngad son of Caw, Llwybyr son of Caw, Coch son of Caw, Meilig son of Caw, Cynwal son of Caw, Ardwyad son of Caw, Ergyriad son of Caw, Neb son of Caw, Gildas son of Caw, Calchas son of Caw, and Hueil son of Caw who never sought a lord's protection.

Samson Finsych the dry-lipped, Taliesin chief of poets, Manawydan son of Llŷr, Llary son of Casnar Wledig, Sperin son of Fflergant king of Brittany, Sarannon son of Glythfyr, Llawr son of Erw, Anynnawg son of Menw son of Teirgwaedd, Gwyn son of Nwyfre, Fflam son of Nwyfre, Geraint son of Erbin, Ermid son of Erbin, Dywel son of Erbin, Gwyn son of Ermid, Cyndrwyn son of Ermid, Hyfaidd Unllen who had but one mantle, Eiddin Fawrfrydig the high-minded, Rheiddwn Arwy ,and Gormant son of Ricca—Arthur's brother through his mother, his father the chief elder of Cornwall.

Llawnrodded Farfawg the bearded, Noddawl Farf Twrch boar's beard, Berth son of Cado, Rheiddwn son of Beli, Isgofan Hael the generous, Ysgafn son of Banon, and Morfran son of Tegid—no one wounded him at the battle of Camlan because of his ugliness. Everyone thought he was an attendant demon; he had hair on him like a stag. Sanddef Pryd Angel angel-face—no one wounded him at the battle of Camlan because of his beauty. Everyone supposed he was an attendant angel. Cynwyl Sant the saint—one of three men who escaped from the battle of Camlan; he left Arthur last, on Hengroen his horse.

Uchdryd son of Erim, Eus son of Erim; Henwas Adeiniawg the swift son of Erim, Henbedestyr son of Erim, Sgilti Ysgafndroed the lightfooted son of Erim—three things characterized these three men: no one was ever found who could keep up with Henbedestyr, either on horseback or afoot; no four-legged animal could ever keep up with Henwas the swift as far as a furlong, much less any farther than that; when he set about travelling on his master's business, he never sought a road as long as he knew where he was going. But when he would be in a forest, he would travel along the tree-tops; when there was a mountain, he would go along the tips of reeds, and throughout his life, no stalk ever bent beneath his step, much less break, and that because of his lightness.

Teithi Hen the ancient son of Gwynnan, whose kingdom the sea inundated; he barely escaped and came to Arthur. From the time he came here, his knife had this peculiarity: no haft would ever remain on it. Because of that he became sick and enfeebled while he was alive, and then died of it.

Carnedyr son of Gofynion Hen the ancient, Gwenwynwyn son of Naw—Arthur's foremost champion, Llygadrudd Emys the red-eyed stallion, and Gwrfoddw Hen the ancient—uncles of Arthur, his mother's brothers. Culfanawyd son of Gwrion, Llenlleawg the Irishman from the headland of Gamon, Dyfnwal Moel the bald, Dunard king of the North, Teyrnon Twrf Liant, Tegfan Gloff the lame, Tegyr Talgellawg the cup-bearer, Gwrddywal son of Efrei, Morgant Hael the generous, Gwystl son of Nwython, Rhun son of Nwython, Llwydeu son of Nwython, Gwydre son of Llwydeu by Gwenabwy daughter of Caw. His uncle Hueil wounded him, and because of that injury there was enmity between Arthur and Hueil.

Drem son of Dremidydd, who could see from Celliwig in Cornwall to the top of Blathaon in Britain when the gnat would thrive in the morning sun. Eidoel son of Ner, Gwlyddyn the builder who made Ehangwen, Arthur's hall. Cynyr Ceinfarfawg fair-beard—Cei was said to be his son. He told his wife, "if there is any of me in your son, woman, his heart shall ever be cold; nor shall there be any warmth in his hands. If he's my son, he shall have another characteristic, he shall be unyielding. Another peculiarity shall be that when he carries a load either big or small, it shall never be seen, either from the front or the back. And no one shall endure water and fire as well as he. Another characteristic is that there shall never be a server or officer like him."

Henwas and Henwyneb and Hengydymdeith, Gallgoig another—though he came to a town of three hundred houses, if he needed anything he would let no one sleep while he was there. Berwyn son of Cyrenyr, Paris king of France—for whom the citadel of Paris was named. Osla Cyllellfawr great-knife, who used to carry the short and wide Bronllafn; when Arthur and his men would come to the edge of a river, they would seek a narrow crossing over the water, and the knife in its sheath would be placed over the water; that would be bridge enough for all the armies of the three isles of Britain, their three adjacent islands, and their goods.

Gwyddawg son of Menestyr, who killed Cei; Arthur slew him and his brothers in revenge for Cei. Garanwyn son of Cei, Amren son of Bedwyr, Eli, Myr, Rheu Rhwydd Dyrys swift and cunning, Rhun Rhuddwern the red alder, Eli and Trachmyr—Arthur's chief huntsmen, Llwydeu son of Cel Coed, Huabwy son of Gwrion, and Gwyn Godyfron. Gweir Dathar Gweinidog the servant, Gweir son of Cadellin Tal Ariant the burser, Gweir Gwrhyd Enwir malicious in battle, and Gweir Gwyn Paladr bright spear—uncles of Arthur, his mother's brothers, sons of Llwch Llawwynnawg of the furious arm from beyond the Tyrrhenian sea. Llenlleawg the Irishman—but renowned in Britain, Cas son of Saidi, Gwrfan Gwallt Afwyn who had unruly hair, Gwilenhin king of France, Gwitard son of Aodh king of Ireland, Garselid the Irishman, Panawr Penbagad leader of the host, Adlendor son of Naw, Gwyn Hywar the modest, steward of Cornwall and Devon; he was one of nine who planned the battle of Camlan.

Celi, Cuel, Gilla Goeshydd stag-legs—he could clear three-hundred acres at a single leap; he was the chief leaper of Ireland. Sol and Gwadn Osol the sturdy and Gwadn Oddaith the fiery—Sol could stand for a day on one leg; if Gwadn Osol stood on the tallest mountain in the world, it would become a level plain under his feet; Gwadn Oddaith: as great as the hot mass when it is withdrawn by the tongs was the flashing fire of his soles when they encountered something hard. He used to clear the way for Arthur in battle.

Hir Erwm and Hir Atrwm—on the day they came to a feast three cantrefs they would take for their needs; they would feast till noon, drink till they went to sleep at night; then they would devour the heads of animals from hunger, as if they had never eaten food before. When they went to a feast they left neither fat nor lean, hot nor cold, neither sour nor sweet, fresh nor salted, neither boiled nor raw.

Huarwar son of Halwn, who claimed as gift from Arthur his utter satisfaction. It was one of the three mighty plagues of Cornwall and Devon when they got him his fill; he never smiled except when he was full. Gwarae Gwallt Eurin golden-hair, the two pups of the bitch Rhymhi, Gwyddrud, Gwydden Astrus the abstruse, and Sugyn son of Sugnedydd, who would suck up an estuary in which there were three hundred ships until there was nothing but a dry beach; he had a red breast-pain.

Cacamwri, Arthur's servant—show him the desired barn, and though there be the work of thirty plows in it, he would thrash away with an iron flail until it was no better for the staves and planks and crossbeams than for the fine oats on the barn floor. Llwng, Dygyflwng, Anoeth Feiddawg the bold, Hir Eiddyl and Hir Amren—two tall servants of Arthur. Gwefyl son of Gwastad—on days when he was sad, he would let his lower lip sag down to his navel, while the other would be a cowl for his head.

Uchdryd Farf Draws the beard flinger—he would fling his red, well-sprouted beard across the fifty rafters that were in Arthur's hall. Elidyr Cyfarwydd the guide, Ysgyrdaf and Ysgudydd—two servants of Gwenhwyfar; their feet as they went about their business were as fleet as their thoughts. Brys son of Brysethach from the edge of the black fernland of Britain, Gruddlwyn Gor the dwarf, Bwlch and Cyfwlch and Sefwlch sons of Cleddyf Cyfwlch grandsons of Cleddyf Difwlch—three resplendant whites were their three shields, three finely pointed piercers their three spears, three sharp carvers their three swords; Glas, Glessig, and Gleissad their three dogs; Coll, Cuall, and Cafall their three horses; Hwyr Ddyddwg, Drwg Ddyddwg, and Llwyr Ddyddwg their three wives; Och, Garm, and Diaspad their three grandchildren; Lluched, Neued, and Eisiwed, their three daughters; Drwg, Gwaeth, and Gwaethaf Oll their three maidservants.

Eheubryd daughter of Cyfwlch, Gorasgwrn daughter of Nerth, Gwaeddan daughter of Cynfelyn Ceudod–she was a half-wit. Dwn Diysig Unben–the valorous chieftain, Eiladar son of Pen Llarcan, and Cynedyr Wyllt the wild one son of Hetwn Tal Ariant the burser. Sawyl Pen Uchel the overlord, Gwalchmai son of Gwyar, Gwalhafed son of Gwyar, Gwrhyr Gwastad Ieithoedd interpreter of tongues–he knew all languages, Cethrwm the priest, Clust son of Clustfeinad–though he were buried seven fathoms in the earth, he could hear an ant fifty miles away stirring in its hill in the morning.

Medyr son of Medredydd–from Celliwig in Cornwall he could hit a wren that was sitting atop Esgeir Oerfel the accursed ridge in Ireland, right through its legs. Gwiawn Llygad Cath cat's eye–he could hit a gnat in the corner of its eye without injuring the eye itself. Ol son of Olwydd–seven years before he was born his father's pigs were stolen; when he had grown into manhood, he traced the pigs, and brought them home in seven herds. Bedwini the bishop, who used to bless the food and drink of Arthur's court for the daughters of the gold-torqued ones of this Island.

The leading ladies of this Island besides Gwenhwyfar: Gwenhwyach her sister, Rathyen the only daughter of Clememyl, Celemon daughter of Cei, Tangwen daughter of Gweir Dathar Gweinidog the servant, Gwen Alarch the swan daughter of Cynwal Canhwch of the hundred hogs, Eurneid daughter of Clydno Eidin, Eneuawg daughter of Bedwyr, Enrhydreg daughter of Tuduathar, Gwenwledyr daughter of Gwaredur Cyrfach the hunchback, Erdudfyl daughter of Tryffin, Eurolwen daughter of Gwdolwyn Gor the dwarf, Teleri daughter of Peul, Indeg daughter of Garwy Hir the tall, Morfudd daughter of Urien Rheged, and Gwenlliant the fair–the high-minded maiden.

Creiddylad daughter of Lludd Llaw Ereint the silver-handed, the most majestic maiden there ever was in the three islands of Britain and their three adjacent islands; it is for her that Gwythyr son of Greidawl and Gwyn son of Nudd fight every May-day and shall do so until doomsday. Ellylw daughter of Neol Cyncroc–her life spanned three generations. Essyllt Fynwen of the white neck and Essyllt Fyngul of the slender neck. Culhwch son of

Cilydd invoked his gift in the name of all these.

"Well, chieftain," said Arthur, "I have never heard of the maiden of whom you speak, nor of her parents. I will gladly send messengers to seek her. Give me time to try to find her."

"Gladly," replied the lad, "I'll give you from tonight until a year from tomorrow night."

Then Arthur sent messengers to every part of his realm to look for that maiden. At the end of the year they returned to Arthur, without having had any more news or information about Olwen than they had the first day.

"Each has received his gift," said Culhwch, "and I am still without; I will go and take your reputation with me."

"You are too hasty with Arthur," said Cei. "Travel with us either until you are satisfied that the maiden does not exist or until we find her; we shall not forsake you." Then Cei arose.

Cei had these gifts: he could hold his breath under water for nine nights and nine days; a wound inflicted by Cei no doctor could heal; victorious was Cei; he could be as tall as the tallest tree in the forest when it pleased him. He had another peculiarity: when it would be raining hardest, whatever he held in his hand would be dry for a fist-length all around because of the greatness of his passion; and when his companions were coldest he would be fuel to kindle their fire.

Arthur summoned Bedwyr, who never stood in awe of any mission Cei went on. There was this about him: none was so fair as he in this island except Arthur and Drych son of Cibddar. And this too: though he were one-handed, three armed men in the same field as he would not draw blood before him. Another gift of his was that his spear held one wound and nine counter-thrusts.

Then Arthur summoned Cynddilig Cyfarwydd the guide: "go on this mission for me with the chieftain." He was as good a guide in lands he had never seen as he was in his own country.

He summoned Gwrhyr Gwastad Ieithoedd, interpreter of tongues, for he knew all languages.

He summoned Gwalchmai mab Gwyar, for he never returned home without his mission accomplished; he was the best on foot and the best on horse (he was Arthur's nephew—his sister's son—and his cousin).

Arthur summoned Menw son of Teirgwaedd, for should

they come to a pagan land, he could create an illusion so that none could see them, but they could see everyone.

They went forth until they came to a big, open plain; there they saw a fort, the most splendid in the world. They travelled all that day, but when they supposed they were nearing the fort, they were no closer than before. And they travelled a second and a third day, and with difficulty they got there and reached the vicinity of the fort. There they saw a vast, boundless flock of sheep and a skin-clad herdsman on top of a mound tending them, with a curly-haired mastiff bigger than a stallion of nine winters beside him. It was the custom of this shepherd that he never lost a lamb—much less a full-grown animal; no troop ever ventured past him that he did not wound or slay, and his breath could burn the dead wood and tufts that were on that plain right down to the bare ground.

"Go consult yonder fellow," said Cei to Gwrhyr Gwastad Ieithoedd.

"Cei," he replied, "I have only promised to go as far as you yourself go; let us proceed together."

"Don't worry about going there," said Menw son of Teirgwaedd, "I will put an enchantment on the dog so that he can harm no one."

They came to where the herdsman was.

"How magnificent you are, Herdsman!"

"You cannot be more magnificent than I. By God—since you are chief—no blemish mars me save my possessions."

"Whose sheep do you guard, and whose fort it this?"

"Throughout the world people know that this is the fort of Ysbaddaden Chief-giant."

"And you, who are you?"

"Custennin son of Mynwyedig am I, and as for my possessions, Ysbaddaden Chief-giant ruined me. Who are you?"

"We are messengers of Arthur, here to ask for Olwen."

"Ah, men, may God protect you! Don't do that for anything! No one has ever come to make that request who has gone away alive."

The herdsman rose up, and as he did so, Culhwch gave him a gold ring. He tried to put it on, but it wouldn't fit, so he put it onto the finger of his glove, and strode home. He gave the glove to his spouse, and she took the ring from the glove.

"Where did you get this ring, husband?" she asked. "You don't often make such a find."

"I went to the sea to seek sea-food, and behold! I saw a corpse coming in on the tide's crest; never had I seen a body as fair as that, and on its finger I found this ring."

"Husband, since the sea does not tolerate handsome corpses, show that body to me."

"Wife, you shall see whose body it is presently."

"Who is that?" asked the woman.

"Culhwch son of Cilydd son of Celyddon Wledig by Goleuddydd daughter of Anlawdd Wledig, his mother, come to ask for Olwen."

She had two thoughts about that: she was glad that her nephew—her sister's son—had come to her, but she was sad, because she had never seen anyone depart with his life who had come on that quest.

They made for the gate of Custennin the Herdsman's fort, and she heard the sound of their approach. She ran joyfully to meet them. Cei seized some wood from the woodpile to protect himself, and when she came to them and tried to throw her arms about their necks, he stuck a log between her two hands. She squeezed the log until it was a twisted mass.

"Had it been me that you squeezed like that," said Cei, "no one would ever have to embrace me again; that was a vicious hug!"

They came into the house and were served. After a while when everyone was milling about, the woman opened a locker at one end of the fire-place and a yellow curly-haired youth rose from it.

" 'Tis a great pity to conceal such a lad as this," said Gwrhyr, "I know it can be no fault of his that he is so treated."

"This one is all I have left," said the woman. "Ysbaddaden Chief-giant has slain twenty-three of my sons, and I have no more hope for this one than for the others."

"Let him remain with me," said Cei, "and neither of us will be slain unless we both are."

They began to eat then, and the woman said, "On what business have you come here?"

"We have come to seek Olwen for this lad."

"For God's sake," said the woman, "since no one from the fort has seen you yet, go back."

"God knows, we will not until we have seen the maiden. Will she come to a place where she may be seen?"

"She comes here every Saturday to wash her head. In the vessel in which she washes, she leaves all her rings, and neither she nor her messenger ever comes for them."

"Will she come here if sent for?"

"God knows I will not harm my sweet charge, nor will I deceive those who trust me. But if you give your pledge that you will do her no harm, I will send for her."

They gave it, and she was sent for. She came in wearing a flaming-red silk robe with a reddish-gold torque studded with precious stones and red gems about her neck. Her hair was yellower than the flowers of the broom; her skin whiter than the foam of a wave, her palms and fingers whiter than the blooms of the marsh trefoil amidst the sands of a gushing spring. Neither the eye of a mewed hawk nor the eye of a thrice-mewed falcon was brighter than her own. Her breasts were whiter than a swan's; her cheeks redder than fox-glove: whoever saw her was filled with love of her. Four white clovers would spring up in her track wherever she went. Because of that she was called Olwen (White-track).

She came into the house and sat down beside Culhwch on the chief seat. When he saw her he knew her: "Maiden," said Culhwch, "it is you I have loved. Come with me, lest they accuse us of wrong-doing."

"I can't do that. My father has extracted a pledge from me that I will never go without his counsel, for he can live only until I go with a husband. But I will give you some advice, if you will take it: go to my father to ask my hand, whatever he may ask of you, promise to get it and you shall have me. If you hesitate about anything, however, you shall not have me and you will be lucky to escape with your life."

"I shall promise it all, and I shall get it," he replied.

She went to her room, and they all rose after her, and went to the fort. They killed the nine porters at the nine gates without a single man crying out, and the nine mastiffs without a single sound. They then proceeded to the hall.

"Greetings, Ysbaddaden Chief-giant, from God and man," they said.

"You—where are you going?"

"We go to seek Olwen your daughter for Culhwch son of Cilydd."

"Where are my good-for-nothing servants and my wretched attendants?" he said. "Raise the forks under my eyelids so that I may see my prospective son-in-law."

They did that.

"Come here tomorrow," he said, "and I will give you some sort of answer."

They rose, and Ysbaddaden seized one of the three poisoned stone spears beside him and hurled it after them. Bedwyr caught it, hurled it back, and pierced Ysbaddaden Chief-giant precisely through the middle of the knee-cap.

"Damned and barbarous son-in-law! All the worse shall I walk the hillside; the poison iron has stung me like the bite of a horse-fly. Damn the smith who forged it and the anvil on which it was hammered, it is so painful!"

They feasted that night in Custennin's house, and the next day, majestically, with fine combs set in their hair they came to the hall.

"Ysbaddaden Chief-giant," they said, "give us your daughter in exchange for her marriage gift and her gift to you, and her two kinswomen. If you do not, you shall die for it."

"She and her four great-grandmothers and her four great-grandfathers are yet alive. I must take counsel with them."

"Do that," they replied, "and we shall go eat."

As they rose to depart, he seized the second stone spear that was beside him and hurled it after them. Menw son of Teirgwaedd caught it and threw it back; it struck square in the middle of his breast and came out the small of his back.

"Damned and barbarous son-in-law! Like the bite of a sieve-headed leech has the hard iron stung me. Damn the furnace in which it was forged! When I go up a hill I will suffer chest pains, stomach ache, and even indigestion!"

They went to their food, and the third day came to court again.

"Don't shoot at us again, Ysbaddaden Chief-giant, seek not death and disfigurement!"

"Where are my servants! Prop up my eyelids with the forks so that I may look at my prospective son-in-law; they have fallen down over my eyeballs."

They did that, and as they did, he took the third poisoned stone spear and hurled it toward them. Culhwch caught it and hurled it back as he had longed to do; it pierced him through his eyeball so that it came out through the nape of his neck.

"Damned and barbarous son-in-law! As long as I live my vision shall be the worse; when I walk against the wind, my eyes will weep, and every moon shall cause me headache and giddiness. Damn the furnace in which it was forged, the poison iron has bit into me like a mad dog!"

They went to their food. Next day they came to the court, and said, "Don't shoot at us, and don't bring down deformity, death, and destruction on yourself—even more if you like. Give us your daughter!"

"Where's the one is said to seek my daughter?" asked Ysbaddaden.

" 'Tis I who seek her," replied Culhwch son of Cilydd.

"Come here, that I may visit with you."

A chair was placed below, opposite him.

"It's you who seeks my daughter, is it?" asked Ysbaddaden.

"It is."

"I want your pledge that you will not be less than honest with me."

"You have it."

"When I receive from you what I demand, then you shall have my daughter."

"Ask what you will," replied Culhwch.

"I will. Do you see that large uncleared field yonder?"

"I do."

"I want all the growth removed, and I want it burnt to the ground so that charred wood and ashes may be its fertilizer. Then I want it plowed and sown, and its crop mature by dew-time the next morning, so that its yield will furnish the food and drink for your wedding-feast guests—yours and the girl's. And all that I want done in one day."

"It is easy for me to accomplish that, though you may not think so."

"Though you accomplish that, here is something you won't

accomplish: the only husbandman who can farm land or prepare it is Amaethon son of Dôn, so wild is it; he will not assist you willingly, and you will not be able to force him."

"It is easy for me to accomplish that, though you may not think so."

"Though you accomplish that, here is something you won't accomplish: getting Gofannon son of Dôn, to come to the field to keep the ploughshares sharp; he performs his craft willingly only for a rightful king, and you won't be able to force him."

"It is easy for me to accomplish that, though you may not think so."

"Though you accomplish that, here is something you won't accomplish: the two oxen of Gwlwlydd Wineu, yoked together, to plough that wild land finely. He does not give them of his own free will, nor can you force him."

"It is easy for me to accomplish that, though you may not think so."

"Though you accomplish that, here is something you won't accomplish: I want the Melyn Gwanwyn and the Speckled Ox yoked together."

"It is easy for me to accomplish that, though you may not think so."

"Though you accomplish that, here is something you won't accomplish: the two oxen of Bannog—one from the far side of Bannog Mountain, one from this side—and yoke them to the same plough; they are Ninniaw and Peibiaw whom God shifted into oxen for their sins."

"It is easy for me to accomplish that, though you may not think so."

"Though you accomplish that, here is something you won't accomplish: do you see that red tilled slope yonder?"

"I do."

"When I first encountered the mother of that maiden, nine lots of linseed had been sown in it, but neither black nor white has come of it yet; I still have that measure. I want to have it sown in that new land there so that it may provide the white linen veil on my daughter's head at your wedding feast."

"It is easy for me to accomplish that, though you may not think so."

"Though you accomplish that, here is something you won't accomplish: honey that is nine-times sweeter than the honey of the first swarm out of the hive—without a drone, without bees—to provide choice liquors for the feast."

"It is easy for me to accomplish that, though you may not think so."

"Though you accomplish that, here is something you won't accomplish: the cup of Llwyr son of Llwyrion, which holds the best liquors, for there is no container in the world that can hold that strong drink except one. You will not get it willingly from him, nor will you be able to force him."

"It is easy for me to accomplish that, though you may not think so."

"Though you accomplish that, here is something you won't accomplish: the hamper of Gwyddneu Garanhir; if the whole world should come—three nines at a time—each would get all the food he wanted. I want to eat from that hamper the night my daughter sleeps with you. He will give it to no one willingly, nor can you force him to give it."

"It is easy for me to accomplish that, though you may not think so."

"Though you accomplish that, here is something you won't accomplish: the horn of Gwlgawd of Gododdin to pour for us that night. He will not give it willingly, and you will not be able to force him."

"It is easy for me to accomplish that, though you may not think so."

"Though you accomplish that, here is something you won't accomplish: the harp of Teirtu to entertain me on that night. It plays itself and when one wants it to be silent, it is. He will not give it willingly, nor can you force him to give it."

"It is easy for me to accomplish that, though you may not think so."

"Though you accomplish that, here is something you won't accomplish: the birds of Rhiannon—the ones that rouse the dead and make the living sleep—to entertain me that night."

"It is easy for me to accomplish that, though you may not think so."

"Though you accomplish that, here is something you won't

accomplish: the cauldron of Diwrnach the Irishman, steward of Odgar son of Aodh, king of Ireland, to cook the food for your wedding feast."

"It is easy for me to accomplish that, though you may not think so."

"Though you accomplish that, here is something you won't accomplish: I must wash my head and shave my beard, and I want the tusk of Ysgithrwyn Chief-boar to shave with. And it will do me no good unless it is pulled from his head with him alive."

"It is easy for me to accomplish that, though you may not think so."

"Though you accomplish that, here is something you won't accomplish: there is no one in the world who can pull it free from his head but Odgar son of Aodh, king of Ireland."

"It is easy for me to accomplish that, though you may not think so."

"Though you accomplish that, here is something you won't accomplish: I will not entrust the keeping of the tusk to anyone but Cadw of Britain. The sixty cantrefs of Britain are under his care, and he does not leave his kingdom willingly, nor will you be able to force him."

"It is easy for me to accomplish that, though you may not think so."

"Though you accomplish that, here is something you won't accomplish: in order to shave my hairs, I must stretch them out, and they will never stretch out without the blood of the pitch-black witch, daughter of the bright-white witch from the Valley of Grief in Hell's back country."

"It is easy for me to accomplish that, though you may not think so."

"Though you accomplish that, here is something you won't accomplish: the blood is of no use unless I receive it warm. There is no vessel in the world that can keep a liquid warm except the containers of Gwyddolwyn the Dwarf: they can keep warm any liquid put in them in the East until it is brought to the West. He will not give them willingly, nor can you force him."

"It is easy for me to accomplish that, though you may not think so."

"Though you accomplish that, here is something you won't

accomplish: some will want milk; there's no way of getting milk for everyone until the vessels of Rhinnon Rough-beard are got. No liquid has ever soured in them. He will not give them willingly, nor can you force him to give them."

"It is easy for me to accomplish that, though you may not think so."

"Though you accomplish that, here is something you won't accomplish: because of its coarseness, there are no comb and shears in the world that can dress my hair except the comb and shears that are between the ears of Twrch Trwyth son of Taredd Wledig. He will not give them willingly, nor can you force him to give them."

"It is easy for me to accomplish that, though you may not think so."

"Though you accomplish that, here is something you won't accomplish: Twrch Trwyth will not be hunted until you get Drudwyn, the pup of Greid son of Eri."

"It is easy for me to accomplish that, though you may not think so."

"Though you accomplish that, here is something you won't accomplish: there is no leash in the world that can hold him except the leash of Cors Cant Ewin hundred-claws."

"It is easy for me to accomplish that, though you may not think so."

"Though you accomplish that, here is something you won't accomplish: there is no collar in the world that can hold the leash except the collar of Canastyr Canllaw hundred-hands."

"It is easy for me to accomplish that, though you may not think so."

"Though you accomplish that, here is something you won't accomplish: the chain of Cilydd Canastyr hundred-grips to hold the collar and leash."

"It is easy for me to accomplish that, though you may not think so."

"Though you accomplish that, here is something you won't accomplish: there is no huntsman in the world who can hunt with that dog but Mabon son of Modron, who was stolen from his mother when only three nights old. No one knows where he is, nor whether he is alive or dead."

"It is easy for me to accomplish that, though you may not think so."

"Though you accomplish that, here is something you won't accomplish: White Brown-mane, the horse of Gweddw—swift as a wave—under Mabon son of Modron, to hunt Twrch Trwyth. He will not give it willingly, nor can you force him to give it."

"It is easy for me to accomplish that, though you may not think so."

"Though you accomplish that, here is something you won't accomplish: Mabon will never be found nor his whereabouts known until you get Eidoel son of Aer his chief kinsman, for he will be relentless in seeking him; they are first cousins."

"It is easy for me to accomplish that, though you may not think so."

"Though you accomplish that, here is something you won't accomplish: Garselid the Irishman is the chief huntsman of Ireland, and Twrch Trwyth will never be hunted without him."

"It is easy for me to accomplish that, though you may not think so."

"Though you accomplish that, here is something you won't accomplish: a leash made from the beard of Dillus the bearded, for there is nothing else that can hold those two pups. And it will be of no use to you unless the hairs are plucked with wooden tweezers —and he alive; no one who tries that escapes alive. And they will be of no use to you if he is dead, for they will be brittle."

"It is easy for me to accomplish that, though you may not think so."

"Though you accomplish that, here is something you won't accomplish: there is no huntsman in the world who can hold those two pups except Cynedyr Wyllt the wild son of Hetwn Clafyrywg the scab. He's nine times wilder than the wildest beast in the mountains; you will never get him, nor will you have my daughter."

"It is easy for me to accomplish that, though you may not think so."

"Though you accomplish that, here is something you won't accomplish: Twrch Trwyth will not be hunted until you get Gwyn son of Nudd in whom God has put the ferocity of the fiends of Annwfn lest the world be destroyed; he will not be spared thence."

"It is easy for me to accomplish that, though you may not think so."

"Though you accomplish that, here is something you won't accomplish: Gwyn will not succeed in hunting Twrch Trwyth with any horse but black Du, the horse of Moro Oerfeddawg."

"It is easy for me to accomplish that, though you may not think so."

"Though you accomplish that, here is something you won't accomplish: Twrch Trwyth will never be hunted until Gwilenhin, king of France comes. He is loathe to leave his kingdom and he will never come here."

"It is easy for me to accomplish that, though you may not think so."

"Though you accomplish that, here is something you won't accomplish: Twrch Trwyth will never be hunted until you get the son of Alun Dyfed; he is an expert master of hounds."

"It is easy for me to accomplish that, though you may not think so."

"Though you accomplish that, here is something you won't accomplish: Twrch Trwyth will never be hunted until you get Aned and Aethlem; they are as swift as the wind, and they have never been unleashed against an animal they did not kill."

"It is easy for me to accomplish that, though you may not think so."

"Though you accomplish that, here is something you won't accomplish: Arthur and his huntsmen to hunt Twrch Trwyth; he is a powerful man, but he will not accompany you. This is why: he owes homage to me."

"It is easy for me to accomplish that, though you may not think so."

"Though you accomplish that, here is something you won't accomplish: Twrch Trwyth cannot ever be hunted until you get Bwlch, Cyfwlch, and Sefwlch, sons of Cilydd Cyfwlch, grandsons of Cleddyf Difwlch: three resplendant whites are their three shields, three finely pointed piercers their three spears, three sharp carvers their three swords; Glas, Glessig, and Gleissad their three dogs; Coll, Cuall, and Cafall their three horses; Hwyr Ddyddwg, Drwg Ddyddwg, and Llwyr Ddyddwg their three wives; Och, Garm, and Diaspad their three witches; Lluched, Neued, and Eisiwed, their three daughters; Drwg, Gwaeth, and Gwaethaf Oll, their three maidservants. The three men sound their horns and all the others set about screaming until no one could care whether the sky fell in on the earth."

"It is easy for me to accomplish that, though you may not think so."

"Though you accomplish that, here is something you won't accomplish: the sword of Wrnach the Giant; he can never be slain except with that. He gives it to no one either for money or as a gift, and you cannot force him."

"It is easy for me to accomplish that, though you may not think so."

"You shall stay awake without sleeping a single night seeking those things, but you shall not get them, nor shall you win my daughter."

"I will get horses and riders, and my noble kinsman Arthur will get me all those things; I will win your daughter and you will lose your life."

"Go forth, now; you will not be responsible for either food or clothing for my daughter. Seek those things, and when you have obtained them, you shall have my daughter."

They travelled that day until evening, and until they saw a stone and mortar fort, the greatest of forts in the world. And then, they saw a dark man, bigger than three men of this world, coming out of the fort. They spoke to him.

"Where do you come from?"

"From the fort you see there."

"Whose fort is it?"

"You're a strange company of men! There isn't anyone in the world who doesn't know whose fort this is–it belongs to Wrnach the Giant!"

"How do you treat guests and distant travellers who alight at this fort?"

"Ha! May God protect you, chieftain: no guest has ever left here alive. None is allowed in except he who comes with a craft."

They made for the gate.

"Is there a porter?" asked Gwrhyr Gwastad Ieithoedd the interpreter.

"There is, and you may lose your head if you summon him."

"Open the gate."

"No!"

"Why won't you open it?"

"Knife has gone into food, drink into horns, and there is thronging in the hall of Wrnach; it shall not be opened except for a craftsman who comes with a craft."

"Porter," said Cei, "I have a craft."

"What craft do you have?"

"I am the best sword-burnisher in the world."

"I'll go tell Wrnach the Giant that and bring you an answer." The porter went in.

"Have you news of the gate?" said Wrnach the Giant.

"Yes. There is a band of men at the gate, and they want to come in."

"Did you ask if they practiced a craft?"

"I did, and one of them said he could burnish swords."

"I was needing that; for some time I have been seeking someone who could cleanse my sword, but I haven't found him. Let that man in, since he has a craft."

The porter went back and opened the door. Cei went in alone and saluted Wrnach the Giant. A chair was brought for him.

"Well, now," said Wrnach, "is it true what they say about you, that you can burnish swords?"

"I can," said Cei.

The sword was brought to him, and Cei took a fragment of whetstone from under his arm.

"Which do you prefer for it, white haft or purple haft?"

"Whatever would please you, if it was your own you were working."

He polished one half of the blade for him; and handed it to him.

"Does that please you?"

"If it were all like that I would like it better than anything in my domain. It is a remarkable thing that a man as good as you is without companions."

"Well, Sir, I do have a companion, although he cannot do this craft."

"Who is that?"

"Let the porter go out, and I will tell you of his wonders. The head of his spear comes off its shaft and draws blood from the wind; then it returns to the shaft."

The gate was opened and Bedwyr came in.

"Bedwyr is very talented," said Cei, "though he can't do this craft."

And there was considerable consultation by the men outside concerning Cei and Bedwyr's entrance and the young man who went with them—Custennin the Shepherd's only son. What he and his companions with him did—as though it were nothing for them—was to cross the three court yards until they came into the fort. The companions of the son of Custennin said to him:

"You did it! You're the best!"

And from then on he was called Goreu ('best') son of Custennin. They spread out to their lodgings so that they could kill their hostelers without the giant knowing.

Cei finished restoring the sword, and handed it to Wrnach the Giant, as if to see if the work satisfied him.

"The work is good, and I am satisfied," said the giant.

"Your scabbard has sullied the sword," said Cei. "Give it to me to remove its wooden side-pieces and I will have new ones made for it."

And he took the scabbard from him, and the sword in the other hand. He stood over the giant as if he were going to put the sword in the scabbard. He aimed up at the giant's head, and with a violent blow struck the head from him. They pulled down the fort and carried off what they wanted of treasures. At the end of a year from that day they came to the court of Arthur, and with them the sword of Wrnach the Giant. They told Arthur how they had fared.

"Of all these wonders," said Arthur, "which is it most appropriate to seek first?"

"It is most appropriate," they replied, "to seek Mabon son of Modron, but he cannot be found until we first find Eidoel son of Aer, his kinsman."

Arthur and the soldiers of the Isle of Britain arose to go seek Eidoel. They travelled until they reached the fore-court of Glini's fort where Eidoel was imprisoned; Glini stood atop the fort, and said to Arthur:

"What do you want from me, since you do not leave me in peace on this rock? I have no good of it, and no pleasure, no wheat, no oats, even if you didn't seek to do me wrong."

"I have not come here to harm you," said Arthur, "but to seek your prisoner."

"I will give the prisoner to you, but I had not intended to give him to anybody. And you shall have my strength and support besides."

"Lord," said his men to Arthur, "go home. You can't go with your host to seek such insignificant things as these."

"Gwrhyr Gwastad Ieithoedd interpreter of tongues, it is right for you to go on this quest," said Arthur. "You know all tongues, and can translate the language of birds and animals. Eidoel, it is right for you to go on this mission to seek your cousin, along with my own men. Cei and Bedwyr, it is my hope that you succeed in the quest you undertake; do it for me."

They went forth until they came to the Blackbird of Cilgwri.

"For God's sake," said Gwrhyr, "do you know anything about Mabon son of Modron, who was stolen from between his mother and the wall when only three nights old?"

"When I first came here," replied the Blackbird, "a smith's anvil was here, and I was a young bird. No work was done on it except while my beak rested upon it each evening; today there is not so much as a nut-sized piece that isn't worn away, and God's revenge on me if I have heard anything of the man you want. But what is right and just for me to do for Arthur's messengers, I will do: there is a species of animal that God shaped before me, and I will guide you there."

They came to where the Stag of Rhedynfre was.

"Stag of Rhedynfre, we messengers of Arthur have come here to you because we know of no animal older than you. Tell us, do you know anything about Mabon son of Modron, who was taken from his mother when only three nights old?"

"When I first came here," replied the Stag, "there was only one antler on either side of my head, and the only tree here was an oak sapling. That grew into an oak of a hundred branches, and finally tumbled down, so that today nothing of it remains but a red stump. From that time to this I have been here, and I have heard nothing of the one you want. However, I will be a guide for you, since you are Arthur's messengers, to where there is a creature God shaped before me."

They came to where the Owl of Cwm Cawlwyd was.

"Owl of Cwm Cawlwyd, we are Arthur's messengers. Do you know anything of Mabon son of Modron, who was taken from his mother when only three nights old?"

"If I knew I would tell. When I first came here this great valley you see was a wooded glen and a race of men came and laid it waste. A second forest grew in it, and this is the third; as for me, my wings are mere stumps. From that time to this I have heard nothing of the man you want. However, I will be a guide for Arthur's messengers, until you come to the oldest animal in this world, and the one who has wandered farthest, the Eagle of Gwernabwy."

"Eagle of Gwernabwy," said Gwrhyr, "we, Arthur's messengers, have come to you to ask if you know anything about Mabon son of Modron, who was taken from his mother when only three nights old."

"I came here," said the Eagle, "a long time ago. And when I first came here, I had a stone. From the top of that stone I could peck the stars each night; now it is but the size of a fist in height. From that time to this I have been here and have heard nothing of the man you want—except for one flight I took to seek food at Llyn Llyw. When I got there I sunk my claws into a salmon, thinking that there would be my food for a good while. But he pulled me down to the depths, so that I barely escaped from him. What I did, I and all my kinsmen, was to go attack him and try to destroy him. He sent messengers to make peace with me, and he himself came to me to remove fifty tridents from his back. Unless he knows something of this thing you seek, I don't know who does. But I will guide you to where he is."

They came to the place, and the Eagle spoke.

"Salmon of Llyn Llyw, I have come to you with messengers of Arthur to ask if you know anything about Mabon son of Modron, who was taken from his mother when only three nights old."

"As much as I know, I will tell you. With every tide I go up along the river until I come alongside the wall of Caer Loyw. There I have found grieving the likes of which I have never seen. And so that you may believe me, let one of you here climb on my two shoulders."

It was Cei and Gwrhyr Gwastad Ieithoedd the interpreter who got on the Salmon's shoulders. They travelled on until they came to the wall that enclosed the prisoner, and they could hear lamenting and groaning on the other side of it.

"What man cries out in this stone building?" asked Gwrhyr.

"Ah, Sirs! There is reason for the one here to cry out! 'Tis Mabon son of Modron who is imprisoned here, and no one has been so painfully incarcerated in such a prison as I have been, neither the prison of Lludd Llawereint silver-hand, nor that of Greid son of Eri."

"Do you have hope of securing your release by gold or worldly riches, or is it by fighting and battle?"

"However much of me is rescued will be rescued by fighting."

They returned from there and came to where Arthur was. They told him where Mabon son of Modron was in prison. Arthur summoned soldiers of this island and went to Caer Loyw where Mabon was in prison. Cei and Bedwyr went on the shoulders of the fish, and while Arthur's men were attacking the fort, Cei demolished the wall and took the prisoner on his back—fighting with the men as before. Arthur returned, and Mabon with him, freed.

"Which of the marvels is it most appropriate for us to seek first?" asked Arthur.

"The most appropriate is to seek the two whelps of the bitch Rhymhi."

"Do we know where she is?" asked Arthur.

"She's at Aber Deu Gleddyf," said one of them.

Arthur came to the house of Tringad in Aber Cleddyf and said to him, "Have you heard about her here? What shape has she taken?"

"The shape of a wolf-bitch, and she travels about with her two whelps. She has killed stock of mine many times, and she is down in Aber Cleddyf in a cave."

What Arthur did was to go by sea in his ship, Prydwen, to hunt the bitch; the others went by land, and thus did they surround her and her whelps. And God disenchanted them for Arthur, and restored them to their own shapes. Arthur's host dispersed then, by ones and by twos.

One day as Gwythyr son of Greidawl was travelling over a mountain, he heard crying and woeful wailing, and they were terrible to hear. He dashed off in their direction, and as he arrived, he unsheathed his sword and cut the ant-hill he saw there to the ground; in that way he saved its inhabitants from a fire.

"Take God's blessing and ours with you," they said to him, "and whatever man cannot help you with, we will come to do for you."

It was they who afterwards brought the nine lots of linseed that Ysbaddaden Chief-giant had demanded of Culhwch, complete in measure and lacking nothing but a single linseed—and a lame ant brought that before nightfall.

Once, when Cei and Bedwyr were sitting atop Pumlumon on Gwylathyr Cairn in the greatest wind in the world, they looked around them and saw a great quantity of smoke far away toward the South, undisturbed by the wind.

"By God, my friend," exclaimed Cei, "look there! The fire of a champion!"

They hurried off toward the smoke, and drew near to where they could watch from a little way off, where Dillus Farfawg the bearded was roasting a wild boar. He, moreover, was the greatest warrior who had ever avoided Arthur.

"Do you know him?" Bedwyr asked Cei.

"Yes," replied Cei. "This is Dillus Farfawg the bearded. There is no leash in the world that can hold Drudwyn, the whelp of Greid son of Eri except a leash made from the beard of the fellow you see there. But it will be of no use unless the hairs are plucked with wooden tweezers while he is yet alive, for they'll be brittle when he's dead."

"What is our plan for doing that?" asked Bedwyr.

"We will let him eat his full of the meat," said Cei, "and after that, he will go to sleep."

While he was doing just that, they were making wooden tweezers. When Cei was certain that he was asleep, he dug the biggest pit in the world under his feet. Then he struck him an enormous blow, and stuffed him into the pit, until they had plucked his beard completely with the wooden tweezers. Then they killed him outright. From there they set out for Celliwig in Cornwall, together with the leash from the beard of Dillus Farfawg the bearded, and Cei gave it to Arthur. Thereupon, Arthur sang this *englyn*:

A leash was made by Cei
From the beard of Dillus son of Eurei;
If he were hale, 'tis you he'd slay!

And Cei became so indignant at that, that the warriors of this Island could barely make peace between him and Arthur. And yet from that time on neither Arthur's need nor the killing of his men could induce Cei to join in battle with him.

"Which of the wonders is it most appropriate for us to seek now?" asked Arthur.

"It is most appropriate for us to seek Drudwyn, the whelp of Greid son of Eri."

A little while before that, Creiddylad daughter of Lludd Llawereint, went off with Gwythyr son of Greidawl. But before he could sleep with her, Gwyn son of Nudd, came and took her by force. Gwythyr son of Greidawl gathered a host and came to attack Gwyn son of Nudd. Gwyn won the battle and took Greid son of Eri, Glinneu son of Taran, Gwrgwst Lledlwm and Dyfnarth, his son. And he took Oben son of Nethawg, and Nwython, and Cyledyr Wyllt the wild, his son. He killed Nwython, cut out his heart, and forced Cyledyr to eat his father's heart; because of that Cyledyr went mad.

Arthur heard about that and came to the North. He summoned Gwyn son of Nudd to him, released his nobles from his prison, and made peace between Gwyn son of Nudd, and Gwythyr son of Greidawl. This is the peace that was concluded: to leave the maiden unmolested by either party in her father's house, and a battle between Gwyn and Gwythyr every May first, forever, until Judgment Day, from that day forth. The one that conquered on Judgment Day would get the maiden.

After settling the matter in that way between those two nobles, Arthur got the brown-maned horse of Gweddw and the leash of Cors Cant Ewin hundred-claws. Then Arthur went over to Brittany accompanied by Mabon son of Mellt, and Gware Gwallt Eurin golden-hair to seek the two dogs of Glythfyr Lydaweg. After he got them, Arthur went into the West of Ireland to find Gwrgi Seferi and Odgar son of Aodh, king of Ireland, as well. From there Arthur went to the North and seized Cyledyr Wyllt the wild.

Then he pursued Ysgithrwyn Chief-boar. Mabon son of Mellt came holding the two dogs of Glythfyr Lydaweg and Drudwyn, the whelp of Greid son of Eri; and Arthur himself went on the chase holding his dog Cafall. Caw of Britain mounted Llamrei, Arthur's mare, and took up the challenge. Then Caw armed himself with a small axe, fiercely and vigorously set upon the boar, split its head in two, and took the tusk. It was not the dogs that Ysbaddaden had demanded of Culhwch that killed the boar, but Cafall, Arthur's own dog.

After Ysgithrwyn Chief-boar had been killed, Arthur and his retinue went to Celliwig in Cornwall. From there he sent Menw son of Teirgwaedd into Ireland to see if the treasures were between the ears of Twrch Trwyth, for it would be beneath his own dignity to fight him unless he had the treasures. That he was there was certain; he had already destroyed a third of Ireland.

Menw went to seek them; where he found them was at Esgeir Oerfel the accursed ridge in Ireland. He turned himself into a bird, swooped down on top of their lair, and tried to make off with one of his treasures; but all he got was one bristle. The boar rose up ferociously then, and shook himself so that some of the poison caught up with him; after that Menw was never without blemish.

After that, Arthur sent a messenger to Odgar son of Aodh, king of Ireland, to request the cauldron of Diwrnach the Irishman, his steward. Odgar asked him to give it.

"God knows," said Diwrnach, "were he the better for getting a single glimpse of it he would not get even that."

The messenger returned from Ireland with a "no," so Arthur set out with a light force and sailed to Ireland in Prydwen his ship. They made for Diwrnach the Irishman's house. Odgar's retinue noted their size. After they had eaten and drunk their ration, Arthur asked for the cauldron. Diwrnach replied that if he were to give it to anybody, he would have given it at the request of Odgar, king of Ireland. When they were told "no," Bedwyr stood up, took hold of the cauldron, and placed it on the back of Hygwydd, Arthur's servant. The latter was a brother by the same mother to Cacamwri, servant of Arthur. This was his regular job: to carry Arthur's cauldron, and to build a fire under it.

Llenlleawg the Irishman seized Caledfwlch and let it go out in a circle: it killed Diwrnach and his entire retinue. The hosts of

Ireland came to fight them, and when they had been driven off completely, Arthur and his men took the cauldron—full of Irish treasures—and entered the ship before their very eyes. They disembarked at the house of Llwydeu son of Cel Coed at Porth Cerddin in Dyfed. And "Cauldron's Measure" is there.

And then Arthur assembled all the warriors there were in the three Islands of Britain and their three adjacent islands, and in France, Brittany, Normandy, and the Summer Land; he assembled choice foot-soldiers and renowned horses, and all those multitudes went to Ireland.

There was mighty fear and terror in Ireland at his coming, and after Arthur disembarked, the saints of Ireland came to seek protection from him. He gave protection to them, and they in turn gave their blessing to him. The men of Ireland approached Arthur with a tribute of food.

Then Arthur came to Esgeir Oerfel in Ireland, where Twrch Trwyth and his seven piglets were. Dogs were set upon him from every direction, and the Irish battled him the whole day until evening; despite that, a fifth of Ireland was destroyed by him. The next day, Arthur's retinue fought with him; they won no advantage of him, only misery. On the third day Arthur himself battled the boar; nine nights and nine days they fought, and he killed but a single piglet of that brood.

Arthur's men asked what significance the boar had. He replied that he had been a king, but God changed him into a swine for his sins. Arthur sent Gwrhyr Gwastad Ieithoedd the interpreter to seek parley with him. Gwrhyr went in the shape of a bird, and alighted above the lair of Twrch Trwyth and his seven piglets.

"For the sake of him who put you in this form," said Gwrhyr, "if you can speak, I ask that one of you come down to parley with Arthur."

Grugyn Gwrych Ereint silver-bristles flatly refused. His bristles were all like wings of silver; the way he would course through the forest and across the field you could see how the bristles glittered. This was his answer:

"By Him who put us in this form, no! We will say nothing to Arthur. God has brought us enough grief putting us in this form without you coming to attack us. I say to you that Arthur will have to fight for the comb and the razor and the shears that are between Twrch Trwyth's two ears. Until you have taken his life," he concluded, "you will not get those treasures. Tomorrow morning we set out from here for Arthur's country, and the most destruction we can possibly do, we shall do there."

The next morning they sailed for Wales. Arthur and his hosts, his horses and his dogs came in Prydwen, keeping an eye out for them. Twrch Trwyth came ashore at Porth Clais in Dyfed; Arthur came as far as Mynyw that night.

The next day, Arthur was told that they had gone past. He caught up with the boar killing the cattle of Cynwas Cwryfagyl the clumsy, having killed all the men and beasts there were in Deu Gleddyf before Arthur arrived. As soon as Arthur came Twrch Trwyth set out for Presseleu. Arthur followed with the hosts of the World and sent his men to the hunt: Eli and Trachmyr, and Drudwyn, the whelp of Greid son of Eri, in his own hand. Gwarthegydd son of Caw on another flank with the two hounds of Glythfyr Lydaweg in his hand, and Bedwyr, holding Cafall, Arthur's dog. He ranged his warriors about the Nyfer. The three sons of Cleddyf Difwlch came, men who had won renown slaying Ysgithrwyn Chief-boar.

They set out then from Glyn Nyfer and came to Cwm Cerwyn, and there he put up resistance. He killed four of Arthur's warriors: Gwarthegydd son of Caw, Tarawg Allt-Clwyd, Rheiddwn son of Eli Adfer, and Isgofan Hael the generous. After that slaughter, he gave battle again immediately, and he killed Gwydre son of Arthur, Garselid the Irishman, Glew son of Ysgawd, and Ysgafn son of Banon, and he too was wounded.

The next morning at break of day some of the men overtook him, and he killed Huandaw, Gogigwr, and Penpingion, three servants of Glewlwyd Gafaelfawr mighty-grip, so that God knew not a servant in the world in his possession except Llaesgenym himself—and no one was the better for him. At the same time he killed many men of the country including Gwlyddyn Saer, Arthur's chief architect. Arthur overtook him again in Pelumiawg, and there the boar killed Madawg son of Teithion, Gwyn son of Tringad son of Nefedd, and Eiriawn Penlloran. From there he went to Abertywi and he made a stand there. That is where he killed Cynlas son of Cynan and Gwilenhin, king of France. From there he went to Glyn Ystu, and there the men and hounds lost him.

Arthur summoned Gwyn son of Nudd, and asked him if he had any information about Twrch Trwyth. He replied that he hadn't. Then all the huntsmen began to hunt the swine as far as Dyffryn Llychwr, where Grugyn Gwallt [*recte* Gwrych] Ereint silver-bristles and Llwydawg Gofyniad the claimant rushed out upon them. Such was the slaughter of huntsmen that not one of them escaped alive except one man. What Arthur did then was to bring his hosts to where Grugyn and Llwydawg were, and let loose upon them all the hounds that had been required by Ysbaddaden. As soon as they had the boars at bay, Twrch Trwyth came and rescued them. From the time they had come across the Irish Sea until then, he had not seen them. Then the men and dogs came upon him, and he took flight as far as Amanw Mountain. There one of the piglets was slain, and mortal battle was joined. Twrch Llawin was killed and then another of his pigs by the name of Gwys. From there they fled to Amanw Valley, and there boar and sow alike were killed; none of his brood was left alive save Grugyn Gwallt [*sic*] Ereint silver-bristles and Llwydawg Gofyniad the claimant.

From there they went to Llwch Ewin, where Arthur overtook him. He gave battle there, and slew Echel Morddwyd Twll of the pierced thigh, Arwyli son of Gwyddawg Gwyr and many men and hounds besides. From there they went to Llwch Tawy.

Grugyn Gwallt [*sic*] Ereint silver-bristles left then, and made for Din Tywi. From there he went to Ceredigion with Eli and Trachmyr and a host of others besides in pursuit. He went as far as Garth Grugyn where he was killed among them, and he killed Rhuddfyw Rhys and many others besides.

Llwydawg Gofyniad the claimant went as far as Ystrad Yw, where the men of Brittany encountered him. It was there he slew Hir Peisawg long-coat, king of Brittany, and Llygadrudd Emys red-eyed stallion, and Gwrfoddw, uncles of Arthur, his mother's brothers. And then he, Llwydawg, was slain.

Twrch Trwyth went along between the Tawy and Ewyas. Arthur gathered the men of Cornwall and Devon to oppose him at the estuary of the Severn.

"Twrch Trwyth has killed many of my men," said Arthur to the warriors of this Island, "and by the might of my men he shall not go into Cornwall while I am alive! I will chase him no more, but engage him in mortal combat; you do what you will."

This is what he decided to do: send an army of mounted horsemen accompanied by all the hounds of the Island as far as the Ewyas, turn in from there to the Severn, and ambush him there with all the experienced warriors in this Island, and drive him by sheer force into the Severn. Mabon son of Modron, mounted on White Brown-mane, Gweddw's horse, went with him to the Severn, and Goreu son of Custennin and Menw son of Teirgwaedd between Llyn Lliwan and Aber Gwy. Arthur and the champions of Britain fell upon him; Osla Cyllellfawr great-knife drew near, and Manawydan son of Llŷr, Cacamwri, Arthur's servant, and Gwyngelli closed in for the kill. They seized him first by the feet and dunked him in the Severn until he was submerged. Mabon son of Modron spurred on his horse on the one side and snatched the razor from him. On the other side, Cyledyr Wyllt the wild charged into the Severn on another steed and carried off the shears. But before the comb could be grabbed, he got his feet on dry land, and from the time he reached land, neither hound, man, nor horse could keep up with him until he came to Cornwall.

But whatever misery was got seeking those treasures, worse still was got trying to save the two men from drowning. As Cacamwri was being pulled up, two mill-stones pulled him back to the depths; as Osla Cyllellfawr great-knife was running after Twrch, his knife fell out of the scabbard and was lost, and after that the scabbard filled with water. As he was being pulled up, it, in turn, pulled him back to the depths.

From there, Arthur and his hosts went forth until they overtook him in Cornwall. The misery they got from him before was but play to the misery they got trying to get the comb; but from misery to misery the comb was taken from him. Thereupon he was chased out of Cornwall, and they drove him to the sea. No one ever knew after that where he went, and Aned and Aethlem with him. After that Arthur went to Celliwig in Cornwall to bathe and throw off his weariness.

"Is there any one of the marvels that remains unachieved?" asked Arthur.

"Yes," replied one of the men, "the blood of the pitch-black witch, daughter of the bright-white witch from the Valley of Grief in Hell's back country."

Arthur set out for the North, and came to the witch's cave. Gwyn son of Nudd and Gwythyr son of Greidawl advised that Cacamwri and his brother Hygwydd be sent to fight the witch. As they entered the cave, the witch seized them, and grabbed Hygwydd by the hair, throwing him to the ground. Then Cacamwri grabbed her by her hair and pulled her off Hygwydd, but she turned on Cacamwri and thrashed the two of them, disarmed them and drove them out pushing and shoving.

Arthur grew angry at seeing the two fellows nearly killed, and tried to assault the cave.

"It is not right, nor are we pleased to see you wrestling with a witch," Gwyn and Gwythyr told him, "let tall Amren and tall Eiddil go into the cave."

They went, and if the first two had met disaster, worse still was the fate of these two, until God knows how any of the four of them could have left that place had they not been put on Llamrei, Arthur's mare. Then Arthur made for the entrance to the cave; from there he threw Carnwennan his knife at the witch and cut her in half until she was twin tubs. Caw of Britain took the witch's blood and kept it with him.

And then Culhwch set out for the court with Goreu son of Custennin and those that wished ill to Ysbaddaden Chief-giant, and with them the wonders; Caw of Britain came to shave his beard—and his flesh and skin down to the bone, and his two ears.

"Have you been shaved, man?" asked Culhwch.

"I have," he replied.

"Is your daughter mine now?"

"She is," he replied, "but don't thank me for that, thank Arthur, who brought it about for you. If I'd had my way you never would have got her. Now the time has come to end my life."

Thereupon Goreu son of Custennin seized him by the hair, dragged him to the cairn, cut off his head and stuck it on the courtyard post. Culhwch took possession of the fort and his kingdom, and that night slept with Olwen; as long as he lived she was his only wife. And Arthur's troops disbanded, each into his own land.

Thus did Culhwch obtain Olwen daughter of Ysbaddaden Chief-giant.

The Tale of Gwion Bach and The Tale of Taliesin

The two tales that follow require but a single head-note, for they are virtually one story. Strangely enough, many of the manuscripts that record the Taliesin material have only what is called here "The Tale of Gwion Bach," that is, the part of the story that tells how Gwion Bach came to acquire the magical drops of poetic inspiration, how he was pursued and swallowed by the witch Ceridwen, and reborn as Taliesin. The remainder of the story tells how Taliesin, as a young lad of thirteen, came to the court of Maelgwn, King of Gwynedd, confused the king's bards, and rescued his master Elphin, whose misfortunes are delightfully recounted in Thomas Love Peacock's novel, *The Misfortunes of Elphin.* It is easy to understand how these two sections of the saga of Taliesin drifted apart; the first section deals with a witch, a magical brew, shape-shifting, and is set in the days of the legendary king, Arthur. Its wonder and magic remind us of "Culhwch and Olwen." The second part, however, has few of those qualities. There is some magic there, to be sure, but the setting is historical, and a good deal of attention is paid to customs and manners of the court. It is peopled with bards and heralds, nobles and ladies, and is motivated by economic misfortune and the consequences of unbridled pride and boasting. While the two parts are chronologically consecutive, they are worlds apart in setting and, perhaps, in audience.

There can be little doubt that the tale of Taliesin is very old, and yet none of it turns up in any Welsh manuscript before the sixteenth century. The earliest recorded version appears to be that found in a manuscript written by Elis Gruffydd sometime in the middle of that century. Gruffydd was in fact compiling a "Chronicle of the World," but at the same time he was preserving bits of lore from his own Welsh tradition, and inserting them into his chronicle in the appropriate places. The Taliesin tale is fit into the events of the sixth century, in the days of the legendary Arthur and the historical Maelgwn Gwynedd. Gruffydd implies that he knew the story from oral and written sources, but he is not content to simply copy out the story, or record a version he knew; he comments on his text frequently, sometimes referring in a self-conscious way to the story or "the opinion of the people," sometimes objecting to the impiety of the story or its irrationality, or doubting its veracity with such comments as, "if the story can be believed" and "indeed, in my opinion it is very difficult for anyone to believe that this tale is true." The total effect is very different from anything found in the other tales in this collection. In those, the scribe is simply recording aspects of a tradition that is an integral part of his own heritage. Gruffydd is at a distance from the tradition; as a man of letters and somewhat cosmopolitan figure who knew French and English, and perhaps Latin, as well as his native Welsh, and who had travelled extensively, his attitude is less parochial than that of the scribes of the fourteenth century who gave us faithful copies of the *mabinogi* and other tales. Gruffydd acts partly as judge and editor of his material.

And yet, it is a well-developed story that Gruffydd records, and the characters are full of life for the most part. Morfran is so ugly he is nicknamed Afagddu (alternatively Y Fagddu), after the pitch-black night, but like most sons and daughters, however cheated by nature, he has a loving mother. The story does not say she was "loving," but it does say that it saddened her to think that he would have trouble getting on in the world because of his ugliness. Fortunately for him, she was a witch, and after consulting her book on the Virgilian arts, she brews a brew from which three distilled drops will make him so full of knowledge and prohpecy that he shall never want for patronage and respect if not love and admiration. And though the story at this point is "illogical and contrary to faith and piety," Gruffydd gives us a fine picture of the gathering of herbs, and the occupations of her two assistants, Gwion Bach and his nameless and blind companion. Apparently exhausted from her year-long activities, Ceridwen is asleep at the crucial moment, and the three distilled drops impart their wisdom to Gwion Bach; Morfran, about whom we hear no more in this story, remains ignorant as well as ugly. (In "Culhwch and Olwen" we discover that he was at the battle of Camlan. He went unwounded there because of his ugliness; he had hair on him like a stag, and everyone thought he was an attendant demon; above, p. 127). The rest of this part of the story perhaps embarrassed Gruffydd too much to give all the details, for in almost every other version of the story known to me, the transformations undergone by Ceridwen and Gwion as she pursued him are specified: he turns into a hare, she pursues in the shape of a greyhound; he escapes into the water in the shape of a fish, she continues the chase as an otter; he takes to the air as a bird, she flies after him as a hawk; at last, he descends into the barn where there is a stack of winnowed wheat and turns himself into one of the grains.

But when the story does not violate reason or faith, Gruffydd allows the tale to unfold unimpeded. It concentrates on the character of Elphin, the hopeless spendthrift who has ingratiated himself with the courtiers at Maelgwn's court by spreading his father's money around. Alas for poor Elphin, his father falls on hard times. With the help of his cronies, the son manages to get one last gift from Gwyddno, namely, the miraculous Hallowe'en catch of fish from Gwyddno's weir. Imagine Elphin's dismay when instead of finding the expected ten (a hundred in other versions) pounds worth of fish, he finds nothing but a hide-covered basket. His lamentations and dejection are so great that the baby Taliesin, who has arrived in this unlikely conveyance, offers a poetic consolation as they make their way back to Elphin's court (though "this is far from reason and sense").

The story changes course here, and we lose sight of Elphin's former companions. He has a wife now, and she is entrusted with the rearing of the child Taliesin. From this point on Elphin's fortunes increase; he becomes wealthier, though we are not told under what circumstances, and he finds greater "favor and acceptance with the king." But when he boasts in Maelgwn's court that his wife is more chaste than the king's wife, and his bard more skilful, Elphin is thrown into prison. The king calls on his son Rhun to test the chastity and continence of Elphin's wife, for the story has it that Rhun was the most successful seducer of his time. Taliesin knows of this plan by divination, and Rhun is tricked into believing he has come away with a sure trophy of the incontinence of Elphin's wife. Gruffydd seems to have enjoyed this part of the story, and it is very carefully developed. The ruse works well, and Maelgwn is in high spirts as he summons Elphin before him to taunt him with what he supposes is the finger of Elphin's wife with Elphin's own ring upon it. But calmly, and with a perceptivity that would win the approval of Sherlock Holmes, the prisoner demonstrates that the finger cannot have been cut from his wife's hand, her faithlessness has not been proved ,and Rhun has been duped. The king's pride is outraged by the event, and he consigns Elphin to prison once again.

Young Taliesin's success in the court of Maelgwn at the expense of the company of bards is equally entertaining. By sympathetic magic he causes the dignified bards to stand before the king and make bumbling sounds more befitting babes and idiots. The king's response after several warnings is suited to the preposterous behavior of the bards, and poor Heinin Fardd, the chief poet, suffers the indignity of a blow to the head from a serving platter. None of this part of the tale has much to do with the mythological traditions of the archetypal poet, as does the first part, but it is a good satire against the pomposity and idolatry of official court poets.

The poems in the tale present a special problem. They were not considered an integral part of the tale, and many manuscripts omit them entirely. Elsewhere, we find the poems, but without the prose or separated from it. Even where the poems are integrated with the text, there is little agreement on their order from one manuscript to the next. The poems identify their speaker as personified wisdom and contain prophecies that are sometimes relevant to the tale. The tale, on the other hand, describes how wisdom was acquired by the archetypal poet and how he established his supremacy over all other poets.

The Tale of Gwion Bach

In the days when Arthur began to rule, there was a nobleman living in the land now called Penllyn. His name was Tegid Foel, and his patrimony—according to the story—was the body of water that is known today as Llyn Tegid.

And the story says that he had a wife, and that she was named Ceridwen. She was a magician, says the text, and learned in the three arts: magic, enchantment, and divination. The text also says that Tegid and Ceridwen had a son whose looks, shape and carriage were extraordinarily odious. They named him Morfran, "Great-crow," but in the end they called him Afagddu, "Utter darkness," on account of his gloomy appearance. Because of his wretched looks his mother grew very sad in her heart, for she saw clearly that there was neither manner nor means for her son to win acceptance amongst the nobility unless he possessed qualities different from his looks. And so to encompass this matter, she turned her thoughts to the contemplation of her arts to see how best she could make him full of the spirit of prophecy and a great prognosticator of the world to come.

After laboring long in her arts, she discovered that there was a way of achieving such knowledge by the special properties of the earth's herbs and by human effort and cunning. This was the method: choose and gather certain kinds of the earth's herbs on certain days and hours, put them all in a cauldron of water, and set the cauldron on the fire. It had to be kindled continually in order to boil the cauldron day and night for a year and a day. In that time, she would see ultimately that three drops containing all the virtues of the multitude of herbs would spring forth; on whatever man those three drops fell, she would see that he would be extraordinarily learned in various arts and full of the spirit of prophecy. Furthermore, she would see that all the juice of those herbs except the three aforementioned drops would be as powerful a poison as there could be in the world, and that it would shatter the cauldron and spill the poison across the land.

(Indeed, this tale is illogical and contrary to faith and piety; but as before:) the text of the story shows clearly that she collected great numbers of the earth's herbs, that she put them into a cauldron of water, and put it on the fire. The story says that she engaged an old blind man to stir the cauldron and tend it, but it says nothing of his name any more than it says who the author of this tale was. However, it does name the lad who was leading this man: Gwion Bach, whom Ceridwen set to stoke the fire under the cauldron. In this way, each kept to his own job, kindling the fire, tending the cauldron, and stirring it, with Ceridwen keeping it full of water and herbs till the end of a year and a day. At that time Ceridwen took hold of Morfran, her son, and stationed him close to the cauldron to receive the drops when their hour to spring forth from the pot arrived. Then Ceridwen set her haunches down to rest.

She was asleep at the moment the three marvellous drops sprung from the cauldron, and they fell upon Gwion Bach, who had shoved Morfran out of the way. Thereupon the cauldron uttered a cry and, from the strength of the poison, shattered. Then Ceridwen woke from her sleep, like one crazed, and saw Gwion. He was filled with wisdom, and could perceive that her mood was so poisonous that she would utterly destroy him as soon as she discovered how he had deprived her son of the marvellous drops. So he took to his heels and fled. But as soon as Ceridwen recovered from her madness, she examined her son, who told her the full account of how Gwion drove him away from where she had stationed him.

She rushed out of the house in a frenzy in pursuit of Gwion Bach, and the story says that she saw him fleeing swiftly in the form of a hare. She turned herself into a black greyhound and pursued him from one place to another. Finally, after a long pursuit in various shapes, she pressed him so hard that he was forced to flee into a barn where there was a great pile of winnowed wheat. There he turned himself into one of the grains; what Ceridwen did then was to change herself into a tufted black hen, and the story says that in this form she swallowed Gwion into her belly.

She carried him there for nine months, at which time she got deliverance of him. But when she gazed upon him after he had come into the world, she could not in her heart do him any physical harm herself, nor could she bear to see anyone else do it. In the end she had the prince put into a coracle or hide-covered basket, which she had fitted snugly all around him; then she caused it to be cast into the lake—according to some books, but some say he was put into a river, others that she had him put into the sea—where he was found a long time afterwards, as the present work will show when the time comes.

[Here follows a religious poem (*Odl Ddwyfol*) attributed to Taliesin; 23 stanzas beginning '*Gwae . . .* ', followed by 5 beginning '*man . . .*' and a final stanza.]

The Tale of Taliesin

In the days when Maelgwn Gwynedd was holding court in Castell Deganwy, there was a holy man named Cybi living in Môn. Also in that time there lived a wealthy squire near Caer Deganwy, and the story says he was called Gwyddno Garanhir (he was a lord). The text says that he had a weir on the shore of the Conway adjacent to the sea, in which was caught as much as ten pounds worth of salmon every eve of All Hallows. The tale also says that Gwyddno had a son called Elphin son of Gwyddno, who was in service in the court of King Maelgwn. The text says that he was a noble and generous man, much loved among his companions, but that he was an incorrigible spendthrift—as are the majority of courtiers. As long as Gwyddno's wealth lasted, Elphin did not lack for money to spend among his friends. But as Gwyddno's riches began to dwindle, he stopped lavishing money on his son. The latter regretfully informed his friends that he was no longer able to maintain a social life and keep company with them in the manner he had been accustomed to in the past, because his father had fallen on hard times. But as before, he asked some of the men of the court to request the fish from the weir as a gift to him on the next All Hallow's eve; they did that and Gwyddno granted their petition.

And so when the day and the time arrived, Elphin took some servants with him, and came to set up and watch the weir, which he tended from high tide until the ebb.

When Elphin and his people came within the arms of the weir, they saw there neither head nor tail of a single young salmon; its sides were usually full of such on that night. But the story says that on this occasion he saw nothing but some dark hulk within the enclosure. On account of that, he lowered his head and began to protest his ill-fortune, saying as he turned homeward that his misery and misfortune were greater than those of any man in the world. Then it occurred to him to turn around and see what the thing in the weir was. Immediately, he found a coracle or hide-covered basket, wrapped from above as well as from below. Without delay, he took his knife and cut a slit in the hide, revealing a human forehead.

As soon as Elphin saw the forehead, he said, "behold the radiant forehead (i.e., *tal iesin*)!" To those words the child replied from the coracle, "Tal-iesin he is!" People suppose that this was the spirit of Gwion Bach, who had been in the womb of Ceridwen; after she was delivered of him, she had cast him into fresh water or into the sea, as the present work shows above. He had been in the pouch, floating about in the sea, from the beginning of Arthur's time until about the beginning of Maelgwn's time—and that was approximately forty years.

Indeed, this is far from reason and sense. But as before, I will keep to the story, which says that Elphin took the bundle and placed it in a basket upon one of the horses. Thereupon, Taliesin sang the stanzas known as *Dehuddiant Elphin*, or, "Elphin's Consolation," saying as follows:

Fair Elphin, cease your weeping!
Despair brings no profit.
No catch in Gwyddno's weir
Was ever as good as tonight's.
Let no one revile what is his.
Man sees not what nurtures him;
Gwyddno's prayers shall not be in vain.
God breaks not his promises.

Fair Elphin, dry your cheeks!
It does not become you to be sad.
Though you think you got no gain
Undue grief will bring you nothing—
Nor will doubting the miracles of the Lord.
Though I am small, I am gifted.
From the sea and the mountain, from rivers' depths
God sends bounty to the blessed.

Elphin of the cheerful disposition—
Meek is your mind—
You must not lament so heavily.
Better God than gloomy foreboding.
Though I am frail and little
And wet with the spume of Dylan's sea,
I shall earn in a day of contention
Riches better than three score for you.

Elphin of the remarkable qualities.
Grieve not for your catch.
Though I am frail here in my bunting,
There are wonders on my tongue.
You must not fear greatly
While I am watching over you.
By remembering the name of the Trinity
None can overcome you.

Together with various other stanzas which he sang to cheer Elphin along the path from there toward home, where Elphin turned over his catch to his wife. She raised him lovingly and dearly.

From that moment on, Elphin's wealth increased more and more each succeeding day, as well as his favor and acceptance with the king. Some while after this, at the feast of Christmas, the king was holding open court at Deganwy Castle, and all his lords—both spiritual and temporal—were there, with a multitude of knights and squires. Their conversation grew, as they queried one another, saying:

"Is there in the entire world a man as powerful as Maelgwn? Or one to whom the heavenly father has given as many spiritual gifts as God has given him: beauty, shape, nobility, and strength, besides all the powers of the soul?" And with these gifts, they proclaimed that the Father had given him an excellent gift, one that surpassed all of the others, namely, the beauty, appearance, demeanor, wisdom, and faithfulness of his queen. In these virtues, she excelled all the ladies and daughters of the nobility in the entire land. Beside that, they asked themselves: "whose men are more valiant? Whose horses and hounds are swifter and fairer? Whose bards more proficient and wiser than Maelgwn's?"

At that time poets were received with great esteem among the eminent ones of the realm. And in those days, none of whom we now call "heralds" were appointed to that office, unless they were learned men, and not only in the proper service of kings and princes, but steeped and skilled in pedigrees, arms, the deeds of kings and princes of foreign kingdoms as well as the ancestors of this kingdom, especially in the history of the chief nobility. Furthermore, each of these bards had to have their responses readily prepared in various languages, such as Latin, French, Welsh, and English, and in addition, be a great historian and good chronicler, be skilled in the composition of poetry and ready to compose metrical stanzas in each of these languages. On this feast, there was in the court of Maelgwn no less than twenty-four of these; chief among them was the one called Heinin Fardd the Poet.

And so after everyone had spoken in praise of the king and his blessings, Elphin happened to say this: "Indeed, no one can compete with a king except another king; but, truly, were he not a king, I would surely say that I had a wife as chaste as any lady in the kingdom. Furthermore, I have a bard who is more proficient than all the king's bards."

Some time later, the king's companions told him the extent of Elphin's boast, and the king commanded that he be put into a secure prison until he could get confirmation of his wife's chastity and his poet's knowledge. And after putting Elphin in one of the castle towers with a heavy chain on his feet (some people say that it was a silver chain that was put upon him, because he was of the king's blood), the story says that the king sent his son Rhun to test the continence of Elphin's wife. It says that Rhun was one of the lustiest men in the world, and that neither woman nor maiden with whom he had spent a diverting moment came away with her reputation intact.

As Rhun was hastening toward Elphin's residence, fully intending to despoil Elphin's wife, Taliesin was explaining to her how the king had thrown his master into prison and how Rhun was hurrying there with the intention of corrupting her virtue. Because of that he had his mistress dress one of the scullery maids in her own garb. The lady did this cheerfully and unstintingly, adorning the maid's fingers with the finest rings that she and her husband possessed. In this guise, Taliesin had his mistress seat the girl in her own chamber to sup at her own table and in her own place; Taliesin had made the girl look like his mistress, his mistress like the girl.

As they sat most handsomely at their supper in the manner described above, Rhun appeared suddenly at the court of Elphin. He was received cheerfully, for all the servants knew him well. They escorted him without delay to their mistress's chamber. The girl disguised as the mistress rose from her supper and greeted him pleasantly, then sat back down to her meal, and Rhun with her. He began to beguile the girl with seductive talk, while she preserved the mien of her mistress.

The story says that the maiden got so inebriated that she fell asleep. It says that Rhun had put a powder in her drink that made her sleep so heavily—if the tale can be believed—that she didn't even feel him cutting off her little finger, around which was Elphin's signet ring that he had sent to his wife as a token a short time before. In this way he did his will with the maiden, and afterwards, he took the finger—with the ring on it—to the king as proof. He told him that he had violated her chastity, explaining how he had cut off her finger as he left, without her awakening.

The king took great delight in this news, and, because of it, summoned his council, to whom he explained the whole affair from one end to the other. Then he had Elphin brought from the prison to taunt him for his boast, and said to him as follows:

"It should be clear to you, Elphin, and beyond doubt, that it is nothing but foolishness for any man in the world to trust his wife in the matter of chastity any farther than he can see her. And so that you may harbor no doubts that your wife broke her marriage vows last night, here is her finger as evidence for you, with your own signet ring on it; the one who lay with her cut it off her hand while she slept. So that there is no way that you can argue that she did not violate her fidelity."

To this Elphin replied, "with your permission, honorable king, indeed, there is no way I can deny my ring, for a number of people know it. But, indeed, I do deny vehemently that the finger encircled by my ring was ever on my wife's hand, for one sees there three peculiar things not one of which ever characterized a single finger of my wife's hands. The first of these is that—with your grace's permission—wherever my wife is at this moment, whether she is sitting, standing, or lying down, this ring will not even fit her thumb! And you can easily see that it was difficult to force the ring over the knuckle of the little finger of the hand from which it was cut. The second thing is that my wife has never gone a single Saturday since I have known her without paring her nails before going to bed. And you can see clearly that the nail of this finger has not been cut for a month. And the third thing, indeed, is that the hand from which this finger was cut kneaded rye dough within the past three days, and I assure you, your graciousness, that my wife has not kneaded rye dough since she became my wife."

The story says that the king became more outraged at Elphin for standing so firmly against him in the matter of his wife's fidelity. As a result, the king ordered him to be imprisoned again, saying that he would not gain release from there until he proved true his boast about the wisdom of his bard as well as about the fidelity of his wife.

Those two, meanwhile, were in Elphin's palace, taking their ease. Then Taliesin related to his mistress how Elphin was in prison on account of them. But he exhorted her to be of good cheer, explaining to her how he would go to the court of Maelgwn to free his master. She asked him how he could set his master free, and he replied as follows:

I shall set out on foot,
Come to the gate,
And make for the hall.
I shall sing my song
And proclaim my verse,
And the lord's bards I shall inhibit:
Before the chief one
I shall make demands,
And I shall overcome them.

And when the contention comes
In the presence of the chieftains,
And a summons to the minstrels
For precise and harmonious songs
In the court of the scions of nobles,
Companion to Gwion,
There are some who assumed the appearance
Of anguish and great pains.

They shall fall silent by rough words,
If it grows ever worse, like Arthur, Chief of givers,
With his blades long and red
From the blood of nobles;
The king's battle against his enemies,
Whose gentles' blood flows
From the battle of the woods in the distant North.

May there be neither blessing nor beauty
On Maelgwn Gwynedd,
But let the wrong be avenged–
And the violence and the arrogance–finally,
For the act of Rhun his offspring:
Let his lands be desolate,
Let his life be short,
Let the punishment last long
on Maelgwn Gwynedd.

And after that he took leave of his mistress, and came at last to the court of Maelgwn Gwynedd. The latter, in his royal dignity, was going to sit in his hall at supper, as kings and princes were accustomed to do on every high feast in those days.

And as soon as Taliesin came into the hall, he saw a place for himself to sit in an inconspicuous corner, beside the place where the poets and minstrels had to pass to pay their respects and duty to the king—as is still customary in proclaiming largess in the courts on high holidays, except that they are proclaimed now in French. And so the time came for the bards or the heralds to come and proclaim the *largesse*, power, and might of the king. They came past the spot where Taliesin sat hunched over in the corner, and as they went by, he puckered his lips and with his finger made a sound like *blerum blerum.* Those going past paid no attention to him, but continued on until they stood before the king. They performed their customary curtsy as they were obliged to do; not a single word came from their mouths, but they puckered up, made faces at the king, and made the *blerum blerum* sound on their lips with their fingers as they had seen the lad do it earlier. The sight astonished the king, and he wondered to himself whether they had had too much to drink. So he ordered one of the lords who was administering to his table to go to them and ask them to summon their wits and reflect upon where they were standing and what they were obliged to do. The lord complied.

But they did not stop their nonsense directly, so he sent to them again, and a third time, ordering them to leave the hall; finally, the king asked one of the squires to clout their chief, the one called Heinin Fardd. The squire seized a platter and struck him over the head with it until he fell back on his rump. From that spot, he rose up onto his knees whence he begged the king's mercy and leave to show him that it was neither of the two failings on them—neither lack of intelligence nor drunkenness—but due to some spirit that was inside the hall. And then Heinin said as follows: "O glorious king! Let it be known to your grace, that it is not from the pickling effect of a surfeit of spirits that we stand here dumb, unable to speak properly, like drunkards, but because of a spirit, who sits in the corner yonder, in the guise of a little man."

Whereupon, the king ordered a squire to fetch him. He went to the corner where Taliesin sat, and brought him thence before the king, who asked him what sort of thing he was and whence he came. He answered the king in verse, and spoke as follows:

Official chief-poet
    to Elphin am I,
And my native abode
    is the land of the Cherubim.

Then the king asked him what he was called, and he answered him saying this:

Johannes the prophet
    called me Merlin,
But now all kings
    call me Taliesin.

Then the king asked him where he had been, and thereupon he recited his history to the king, as follows here in this work:

I was with my lord
    in the heavens
When Lucifer fell
    into the depths of hell;
I carried a banner
    before Alexander;
I know the stars' names
    from the North to the South
I was in the fort of Gwydion,
    in the Tetragramaton;
I was in the canon
    when Absalon was killed;
I brought seed down
    to the vale of Hebron;
I was in the court of Dôn
    before the birth of Gwydion;
I was patriarch
    to Elijah and Enoch;
I was head keeper
    on the work of Nimrod's tower;
I was atop the cross
    of the merciful son of God;
I was three times
    in the prison of Arianrhod;

I was in the ark
    with Noah and Alpha;
I witnessed the destruction
    of Sodom and Gomorrah;
I was in Africa
    before the building of Rome;
I came here
    to the survivors of Troy.

And I was with my lord
    in the manger of oxen and asses;
I upheld Moses
    through the water of Jordan;
I was in the sky
    with Mary Magdalen;
I got poetic inspiration
    from the cauldron of Ceridwen;
I was poet-harper
    to Lleon Llychlyn;
I was in Gwynfryn
    in the court of Cynfelyn;
In stock and fetters
    a day and a year.

I was revealed
    in the land of the Trinity;
And I was moved
    through the entire universe;
And I shall remain till doomsday,
    upon the face of the earth.
And no one knows what my flesh is—
    whether meat or fish.

And I was nearly nine months
    in the womb of the witch Ceridwen;
I was formerly Gwion Bach,
    but now I am Taliesin.

And the story says that this song amazed the king and his court greatly. Then he sang a song to explain to the king and his people why he had come there and what he was attempting to do, as the following poem sets forth.

Provincial bards! I am contending!
To refrain I am unable.
I shall proclaim in prophetic song
To those that will listen.
And I seek that loss
That I suffer:
Elphin, from the punishment
Of Caer Deganwy.

And from him, my lord will pull
The binding chain.
The Chair of Caer Deganwy—
Mighty is my pride—
Three hundred songs and more
Are the songs I shall sing;
No bard that knows them not
Shall merit spear
Nor stone nor ring,
Nor remain about me.

Elphin son of Gwyddno
Suffers torment now,
'Neath thirteen locks
For praising his master-bard.

And I am Taliesin,
Chief-poet of the West,
And I shall release Elphin
From the gilded fetters.

After this, as the text shows, he sang a song of succour, and they say that instantly a tempestuous wind arose, until the king and his people felt that the castle would fall upon them. Because of that, the king had Elphin fetched from prison in a hurry, and brought to the side of Taliesin. He is said to have sung a song at that moment that resulted in the opening of the fetters from around his feet—indeed, in my opinion, it is very difficult for anyone to believe that this tale is true. But I will continue the story with as many of the poems by him as I have seen written down.

Following this, he sang the verses called "Interrogation of the Bards," which follows herewith.

What being first
    Made Alpha?
    What is the fairest refined language
    Designed by the Lord?

What food? What drink?
    Whose raiment prudent?
    Who endured rejection
    From a deceitful land?

Why is a stone hard?
    Why is a thorn sharp?
    Who is hard as a stone,
    And as salty as salt?

Why is the nose like a ridge?
    Why is the wheel round?
    Why does the tongue articulate
    More than any one organ?

Then he sang a series of verses called "The Rebuke of the Bards," and it begins like this:

If you are a fierce bard
Of spirited poetic-inspiration,
Be not testy
In your king's court,
Unless you know the name for *rimin,*
And the name for *ramin,*
And the name for *rimiad,*
And the name for *ramiad,*
And the name of your forefather
Before his baptism.

And the name of the firmament,
And the name of the element,
And the name of your language,
And the name of your district.

Company of poets above,
Company of poets below;
My darling is below

'Neath the fetters of Aranrhod.
You certainly do not know
The meaning of what my lips sing,
Nor the true distinction
Between the true and the false.
Bards of limited horizons,
Why do you not flee?
The bard who cannot shut me up
Shall have no quiet
Till he come to rest
Beneath a gravelly grave.
And those who listen to me,
Let God listen to them.

And after this follows the verses called "The Satire on the Bards."

Minstrels of malfeasance make
Impious lyrics; in their praise
They sing vain and evanescent song,
Ever exercising lies.
They mock guileless men
They corrupt married women,
They despoil Mary's chaste maidens.
Their lives and times they waste in vain,
They scorn the frail and the guileless,
They drink by night, sleep by day,
Idly, lazily, making their way.
They despise the Church
Lurch toward the taverns;
In harmony with thieves and lechers,
They seek out courts and feasts,
Extol every idiotic utterance,
Praise every deadly sin.
They lead every manner of base life,
Roam every village, town, and land.
The distresses of death concern them not,
Never do they give lodging or alms.
Excessive food they consume.
They rehearse neither the psalms nor prayer,
Pay neither tithes nor offerings to God,
Worship not on Holy Days nor the Lord's day,
Fast on neither Holy Days nor ember days.
Birds fly,

Fish swim,
Bees gather honey,
Vermin crawl;
Everything bustles
To earn its keep
Except minstrels and thieves, the lazy and worthless.

I do not revile your minstrelsy,
For God gave that to ward off evil blasphemy;
But he who practices it in perfidy
Reviles Jesus and his worship.

After Taliesin had freed his master from prison, verified the chastity of his mistress, and silenced the bards so that none of them dared say a single word, he asked Elphin to wager the king that he had a horse faster and swifter than all the king's horses. Elphin did that.

On the day, time, and place determined—the place known today as Morfa Rhianedd—the king arrived with his people and twenty-four of the swiftest horses he owned. Then, after a long while, the course was set, and a place for the horses to run. Taliesin came there with twenty-four sticks of holly, burnt black. He had the lad who was riding his master's horse put them under his belt, instructing him to let all the king's horses go ahead of him, and as he caught up with each of them in turn, to take one of the rods and whip the horse across his rump, and then throw it to the ground. Then take another rod and do in the same manner to each of the horses as he overtook them. And he instructed the rider to observe carefully the spot where his horse finished, and throw down his cap on that spot.

The lad accomplished all of this, both the whipping of each of the king's horses as well as throwing down his cap in the place where the horse finished. Taliesin brought his master there after his horse won the race, and he and Elphin set men to work to dig a hole. When they had dug the earth to a certain depth, they found a huge cauldron of gold, and therewith Taliesin said, "Elphin, here is payment and reward for you for having brought me from the weir and raising me from that day to this." In that very place there stands a pool of water, which from that day to this is called "Cauldon's Pool."

After that, the king had Taliesin brought before him, and asked for information concerning the origin of the human race. Forthwith, he sang the verses that follow here below, and that are known today as one of the four pillars of song. They begin as follows:

Here begin the prophecies of Taliesin.

The Lord made
In the midst of Glen Hebron
With his blessed hands,
  I know, the shape of Adam.

He made the beautiful;
In the court of paradise,
From a rib, he put together
  Fair woman.

Seven hours they
Tended the Orchard
Before Satan's strife,
  Most insistent suitor.

Thence they were driven
Through cold and chill
To lead their lives
  In this world.

To bear in affliction
Sons and daughters,
To get tribute
  From the land of Asia.

One hundred and eight
Was she fertile,
Bearing a mixed brood,
  Masculine and feminine.

And then, openly,
When she bore Abel
And Cain, unconcealable,
  Most unredeemable.

To Adam and his mate
Was given a digging shovel
To break the earth
　　To gain bread.

And shining white wheat
To sow, the instrument
To feed all men
　　Until the great feast.

Angels sent
From God Almighty
Brought the seed of growth
　　To Eve.

She hid
A tenth of the gift
So that not all did
　　The whole garden enclose.

But black rye was had
In place of the fine wheat,
Showing the evil
　　For stealing.

Because of that treacherous turn,
It is necessary, says Sattwrn,
For each to give his tithe
　　To God first.

From crimson red wine
Planted on a sunny day,
And the moon's night prevails
　　Over white wine.

From wheat of true privilege,
From red wine generous and privileged.
Is made the finely molded body
　　Of Christ son of Alpha.

From the wafer is the flesh.
From the wine is the flow of blood.

And the words of the Trinity
    Consecrated him.

Every sort of mystical book
Of Emmanuel's work
Rafael brought
    To give to Adam.

When he was in ferment,
Above his two jaws
Within the Jordan river
    Fasting.

Moses found,
To guard against great need,
The secret of the three
    Most famous rods.

Samson got
Within the tower of Babylon
All the magical arts
    Of Asia land.

I got, indeed,
In my bardic song,
All the magical arts
    Of Europe and Africa.

And I know whence she emanates
And her home and her hospitality,
Her fate and her destiny
    Till Doomsday.

Alas, God, how wretched,
Through excessive plaint,
Comes the prophecy
    To the race of Troy.

A coiled serpent,
Proud and merciless,
With golden wings
    Out of Germany.

It shall conquer
England and Scotland,
From the shore of the Scandinavian Sea
To the Severn.

Then shall the Britons be
Like prisoners,
With status of aliens,
To the Saxons.

Their lord they shall praise.
Their language preserve,
And their land they will lose—
Save wild Wales.

Until comes a certain period
After long servitude,
When shall be of equal duration
The two proud ones.

Then will the Britons gain
Their land and their crown,
And the foreigners
Will disappear.

And the words of the angels
On peace and war
Will be true
Concerning Britain.

And after this he proclaimed to the king various prophecies in verse, concerning the world that would come hereafter.

Appendix: Cad Goddeu

The following selection belongs to the so-called transformational poems of Taliesin. The persona is the shape-shifting archetypal poet whom we meet in the tales of Gwion Bach and Taliesin, and the subject matter, albeit interspersed with biblical and classical references, is Celtic mythology. The title means either "The Army of the Trees" or "The Battle of the Trees," the sense of which must remain obscure, at least for the present. Special powers are attributed to the trees enumerated in the poem, and it seems likely that these characteristics derive from traditions about sacred trees and sacred groves. The latter were well-attested among continental Celtic and Germanic tribes, and one cannot help but think specifically of the magical tree in the fourth branch, which rain does not wet nor fire destroy, the tree in whose branches the transformed Lleu languishes until he is delivered by Gwydion. In this context, Tomás Ó Broin has recently given us a remarkable insight into the Irish "Red-Branch" cycle of King Conchobar and his warriors (*Éigse*, XV, 1973, 103–113). Red-Branch has usually been taken to be a kenning for Conchobar's court, referring specifically to the roof-tree, and then, pars pro toto, to the entire structure. Ó Broin suggests, however, that this special designation may derive from great antiquity, that the Red-Branch may be the central tree in a sacred grove, and that the "Heroes of the Red-Branch" may have been a host that had some special and, no doubt, sacred connection with such a grove. The army or battle of the trees so obscurely recounted here may contain the detritus of British traditions about such sacred wood.

The poem is translated from the text in *The Book of Taliesin,* reproduced and edited by J. Gwenogvryn Evans, Llanbedrog, 1910, pp. 23.09–27.12. It should be stressed that the translation is very tentative, and is intended only to give readers a general idea of the nature of this type of poem from the Book of Taliesin and its similarity to the material found in the tale. It was worked out largely in a seminar at the University College of Wales in the Spring of 1974, with the generous and invaluable assistance of Professors Eric Hamp and R. Geraint

Gruffydd and Dr. Brynley Roberts. The infelicities and errors are, of course, my own; I have indicated ellipses where the text was hopelessly obscure to me.

I was in many shapes before I was released:
I was a slender, enchanted sword—I believe that it was done.
I was rain-drops in the air, I was stars' beam;
I was a word in letters, I was a book in origin;
I was lanterns of light for a year and a half;
I was a bridge that stretched over sixty estuaries;
I was a path, I was an eagle, I was a coracle in seas;
I was a bubble in beer, I was a drop in a shower;
I was a sword in hand, I was a shield in battle.
I was a string in a harp enchanted nine years, in the water as foam;
I was a spark in fire, I was wood in a bonfire;
I am not one who does not sing; I have sung since I was small.
I sang in the army of the trees' branches before the ruler of Britain.
I wounded swift horses, destroyed powerful fleets;
I wounded a great scaly animal: a hundred heads on him
And a fierce host beneath the base of his tongue,
And another host is on his necks.
A black, forked toad: a hundred claws on him.
An enchanted, crested snake in whose skin a hundred souls are punished.
I was in Caer Nefenhir where grass and trees attacked,
Poets sang, warriors rushed forth.
Gwydion raised his staff of enchantment,
Called upon the Lord, upon Christ, making pleas
So that he, the Lord who had made him, might deliver him.
The Lord replied in language and in the land:
"Transform stalwart trees into armies with him
and obstruct Peblig the powerful from giving battle."
When the trees were enchanted, in the hope of our purpose,
They hewed down trees with . . . . .
Three chieftains fell in grievous days' battles.
A maiden uttered a bitter sigh, grief broke forth;
Foremost in lineage, pre-eminent maiden. Life and wakefulness
Gain us no vantage in Mellun: men's blood up to our thighs.
The three greatest upheavals that have happened in the world:
And one comes to pass in the story of the flood,
And Christ's crucifying, and then Doomsday.
Alder, pre-eminent in lineage, attacked in the beginning;

Willow and rowan were late to the army;
Thorny plum was greedy for slaughter;
Powerful dogwood, resisting prince;
Rose-trees went against a host in wrath;
Rasberry bushes performed, did not make an enclosure
For the protection of life . . . . and honeysuckle
And ivy for its beauty; sea gorse for terror;
Cherries mocked; birch for high-mindedness–it was late that it armed,
Not because of cowardice, but because of greatness.
Goldenrod held a shape, foreigners over foreign waters;
Fir trees to the fore, ruler in battles;
Ash performed excellently before monarchs;
Elm because of its ferocity did not budge a foot:
It would strike in the middle, on the flanks, and in the end.
Hazel wood was deemed arms for the tumult;
Happy the privet, bull of battle, lord of the world
. . . . fir trees prospered;
Holly turned green, it was in battle;
Fine hawthorn delivered pain;
Attacking vines attacked in battle;
Destructive fern; broom before the host
Were plowed under. Gorse was not lucky,
But despite that it was turned into an army, fine fighting heather
Was changed into a host, pursuer of men.
Swift and mighty oak: before him trembled heaven and earth;
Fierce enemy of warriors, his name in wax tablets.
. . . . . . tree gave terror in combat;
He used to oppose, he opposed others from a hole;
Pear worked oppression in the battlefield,
Fearful drawing up of a flood of noble trees.
Chestnut, shame of the prince of fir trees.
Jet is black, mountains are rounded, trees are sharp;
Great seas are swifter since I heard the scream.
Tips of birch sprouted for us, immutable energy;
Tips of oak stained for us from *Gwarchan Maelderw*
Laughing from the hillside, a lord not . . . . . .
Not from a mother and father was I made;
As for creation, I was created from nine forms of elements:
From the fruit of fruits, from the fruit of God at the beginning;
From primroses and flowers of the hill, from the blooms of woods and trees;
From the essence of soils was I made,

From the bloom of nettles, from water of the ninth wave.
Math enchanted me before I was mobile;
Gwydion created me, great magic from the staff of enchantment;
From Eurwys and Euron, from Euron and Modron,
From five fifties of magicians and teachers like Math was I produced.
The lord produced me when he was quite inflamed;
The magician of magicians created me before the world—
When I had existence, there was expanse to the world.
Fair bard! Our custom is profit; I can put in song what the tongue can utter.
I passed time at dawn, I slept in purple;
I was in the rampart with Dylan Eil Mor,
In a cloak in the middle between kings,
In two lusty spears that came from heaven;
In Annwfn they will sharpen in the battle to which they will come;
Four-score hundred I pierced because of their lust—
They are neither older nor younger than me in their passion.
The passion of a hundred men is needed by each, I had that of nine hundred.
In an enchanted sword, renowned blood flowing in me
from a lord from his place of concealment;
from a drop was the warrior killed.
Peoples were made, re-made, and made again.
The brilliant one his name, the strong hand; like lightning he governed the host.
They scattered in sparks from the tame one on high.
I was a snake enchanted in a hill, I was a viper in a lake;
I was a star with a shaft; I was this hunting-shaft.
Not badly shall I prepare my cloak and cup.
Four twenties of smoke will come upon each.
Five fifties of bonds-maids the value of my knife;
Six yellowish-brown horses—a hundred times is better;
My pale-yellow horse is swift as a seagull;
I myself am not feeble between sea and shore.
I shall cause a field of blood, on it a hundred warriors;
Scaly and red my shield, gold is my shield-ring.
There was not born in Adwy anyone who attacked me
Except Goronwy from Doleu Edrywy.
Long and white are my fingers; long have I not been a shepherd;
I lived as a warrior before I was a man of letters;
I wandered, I encircled, I slept in a hundred islands, I dwelt in a hundred forts.

Druids, wise one, prophesy to Arthur;
There is what is before, they perceive what has been.
And one occurs in the story of the flood
And Christ's crucifying and then Doomsday.
Golden, gold-skinned, I shall deck myself in riches,
And I shall be in luxury because of the prophecy of Virgil.

Glossary

ABERFFRAW, chief seat of the kings of Gwynedd, though it is not mentioned in the fourth branch, which is set in that province. As an ancient site of kingship, however, it is appropriate that the host repaired there to celebrate Branwen's wedding feast (see Introduction).

ABER HENFELEN, rather more than an *aber* 'estuary'; Sir Ifor Williams suggests the sea between Wales and Cornwall.

ABERMENAI, the estuary of the Menai, which separates Anglesey (Môn) from the mainland of Wales.

ANNWFN, otherwise, Annwn; the Welsh name for the Otherworld, corresponding roughly to the *sídh* (pronounced as in *banshee* "woman of the *sídh*") of Irish tradition, where the Túatha Dé Danann dwelt. In later Christian sources, Annwfn is used for "Hell."

ARANRHOD, otherwise Arianrhod; daughter of Dôn, sister of Gilfaethwy and Gwydion, mother of Dylan Eil Ton and Lleu Llaw Gyffes.

ARAWN, King of Annwfn; he exchanges places with Pwyll so that the latter may defeat his enemy Hafgan.

ARBERTH, probably modern Narberth (see map).

BADGER-IN-THE-BAG, a rather grim game, derived it seems, from a method of capturing and subduing the fierce badger. The fourteenth-century Welsh poet, Dafydd ap Gwilym, warns his rival that if he should ever invade his territory, he would become "a badger-in-the-bag" (*Gwaith Dafydd ap Gwilym*, Cardiff, 1952, #152.46).

BEDWYR, son of Pedrawg, who together with Cei is named frequently in the early Welsh Arthurian sources.

BENDIGEIDFRAN, son of Llŷr, King of the Isle of the Mighty.

BLEIDDWN, offspring of Gilfaethwy and Gwydion when they were in the shape of wolf and bitch; the name means (wolf) cub.

BLODEUEDD, wife of Lleu Llaw Gyffes, conjured out of flowers by Math and Gwydion.

BRANWEN, daughter of Llŷr, wife of Matholwch, an Irish king.

CAER, a fort.

CAER SEINT, one of Bendigeidfran's assembly sites, located in Arfon, the region opposite the island of Anglesey (Môn).

CANTREF, an ancient division of land containing a hundred dwellings or hamlets.

CARADAWG, son of Bran, chief of the seven stewards left by Bendigeidfran when he went to Ireland; he died of grief when the invisible Caswallawn slew the other six.

CASWALLAWN, son of Beli, usurper who slew six of the seven left in the Isle of the Mighty when Bendigeidfran went to Ireland; he was crowned king in London. Later, Pryderi paid homage to him.

CEI, son of Cynyr, appears along with Bedwyr as Arthur's companions in the earliest Welsh sources. Cei's magical and supernatural qualities help establish the mythological milieu of the native Arthurian "court."

CEREDIGION, in English, Cardiganshire.

CERIDWEN, shape-shifting mother of Morfran (Y Fagddu), brewer of the cauldron of inspired wisdom.

CIGFA, daughter of Gwyn Gohoyw (*al. Gloyw*), wife of Pryderi.

CILYDD, son of Celyddon Wledig, father of Culhwch.

COMMOTE, "district" or "region," two or more of which comprised a CANTREF.

CORANIAID, a people of great knowledge who, like Math, could hear every sound carried on the wind; one of the three plagues that threatened the kingdom of Lludd. The name may be based on the word for 'dwarf,' and the race has been identified in a general way with the fairy folk.

CULHWCH, son of Cilydd, Arthur's first cousin.

CUSTENNIN, son of Mynwyedig, shepherd of Ysbaddaden, husband of Culhwch's mother's sister.

CYMIDEI CYMEINFOLL, wife of Llassar Llaes Gyfnewid; it was prophesied that she would give birth to a fully-armed warrior.

DEHEUBARTH, "South-part" of Wales.

DINAS EMRYS, the citadel of Ambrosius (= W. Emrys), where Lludd entombed the two dragons. According to Welsh tradition, the place was given to Merlin Ambrosius by Vortigern, who had attempted unsuccessfully to build his fort there. Merlin revealed that it was the fighting of the two dragons buried there that caused the ground to quake and the walls tumble.

DÔN, the Welsh name of a goddess known in Irish as Danu, mother of the Túatha Dé Danann.

DYFED, in southwest Wales, land of Pwyll and Pryderi.

DYLAN EIL TON, aquatic offspring of Aranrhod daughter of Dôn; he took to the sea at birth, was killed by his uncle, Gofannon.

EFNISIEN, malevolent son of Euroswydd, half-brother of Bendigeidfran, Manawydan, and Branwen.

ELPHIN, son of Gwyddno; he discovered the baby Taliesin in his father's fish-dam, reared him, and became his patron.

ENGLAND; the Welsh word is always *Lloegr*, which is counted in one tradition as one of the three realms of Britain (*Prydein*), the other two being Wales and Scotland (*Cymry*, later *Cymru*, and *Alban*); see Bromwich, *Trioedd*, p. cxxv.

ENGLYN, a metrical unit, consisting of three or four lines and a fixed number of syllables; *englynion* (pl.) were used frequently in gnomic and nature poems.

FOOT-HOLDER, one of the officers of the court of a king. Designated male in the Welsh laws, one of his duties was to "rub" the king.

GILFAETHWY, son of Dôn, brother of Gwydion; he raped Goewin, the king's foot-holder.

GLEWLWYD GAFAELFAWR, Arthur's porter; the second name means "mighty-grip."

GOEWIN, daughter of Pebin and Math's virgin foot-holder; she was raped by Gilfaethwy son of Dôn.

GOFANNON, uncle of Dylan; one of the children of Dôn. In Celtic mythology, he is a smith god, the equivalent of the Irish Goibhniu.

GOLEUDDYDD, daughter of Anlawdd Wledig, mother of Culhwch.

GRONW PEBYR, Lord o f Penllyn, who has an adulterous affair with Blodeuedd, and with her plots the death of Lleu Llaw Gyffes, her husband.

GWALCHMAI, son of Gwyar, the Gawain of English Arthurian romance. His name means either "Hawk of May" or "Hawk of/in the field."

GWALES, probably the island Grassholme, off the coast of Pembrokeshire in southwest Wales.

GWAWL, son of Clud, Pwyll's rival suitor for the hand of Rhiannon; it was on him that the game of "Badger-in-the-Bag" was first played.

GWERN, son of Branwen and Matholwch; he was thrown into the fire by Efnisien.

GWION BACH, "Little Gwion," a shape-shifter who acquired the wisdom intended for Morfran; after he was reborn of Ceridwen, he was named Taliesin.

GWRI GOLDEN-HAIR, the name given to Rhiannon's son by Teyrnon Twrf Liant and his wife; the name was later changed to Pryderi.

GWYDDNO GARANHIR, father of Elphin, owner of the magical fish-dam (weir). He is probably identical with Gwyddneu Garanhir, the owner of a magical food hamper whose contents were never exhausted. According to Welsh tradition, Gwyddno's kingdom was overrun by the sea.

GWYDION, son of Dôn, brother of Gilfaethwy; he and his uncle, King Math, were powerful magicians.

GWYN, son of Nudd, a figure connected closely with Annwfn; it is said that in him resided all the destructive power of the demons of Annwfn. He fought an annual battle on May-day to win the daughter of Lludd Llawereint.

GWYNFRYN, literally "White-mount," though Sir Ifor Williams notes that it is said to be the Tower of London. Originally, it must have been simply a sacred or holy (*gwyn*) mound (*-fryn*), a fitting place to conceal the talismanic head of Bendigeidfran.

HAFGAN, a king of Annwfn, foe of Arawn; he was mortally wounded by Pwyll.

HARLECH, site of the Otherworldly feast presided over by the head of Bendigeidfran, and one of the seats of his kingship.

HEBRON, a valley southwest of Jerusalem, the site of the creation, according to the poem on p. 178. It was an important site in biblical history, being the land of the patriarchs, where Abraham, Isaac, and others were buried. In it also stood the graves of Adam and Seth, or Adam and Abel, or even Adam and Eve.

HEILYN, son of Gwyn, one of the seven who escaped from Ireland; it was he who ended the eighty-year feast in Gwales by opening the forbidden door.

HEININ FARDD, chief poet in the court of Maelgwn Gwynedd, disgraced by Taliesin.

HENFFORDD = Hereford.

HONOR-PRICE, literally, "face-price"; compensation for insults depended upon the rank of the offended. The rod of silver and plate of gold are actually named in the Welsh laws as part of the compensation due a king of Aberffraw.

HYCHDWN (HIR), offspring of Gwydion and Gilfaethwy when they were in the shape of boar and sow; the name means (tall) piglet.

HYDDWN, offspring of Gilfaethwy and Gwydion when they were in the shape of stag and hind; the name means "little stag."

HYFAIDD HEN, father of Rhiannon.

HYFAIDD HIR, one of Bendigeidfran's messengers, and one of the seven left in the Isle of the Mighty as stewards when Bendigeidfran invaded Ireland; possibly a doublet of Hyfaidd Hen.

LLASSAR LLAES GYFNEWID, original possessor of the cauldron of regeneration, who, with his wife Cymidei Cymeinfoll, escaped death in Ireland and came to Britain. In "Manawydan," he is known for his craftsmanship.

LLEUELYS, son of Beli Mawr; he became king of France by marrying the dead king's daughter. Later, he delivered the kingdom of his brother Lludd from the three plagues.

LLEU LLAW GYFFES, son of Aranrhod, protégé of Gwydion. His name means "Lleu (cognate with Irish Lugh) of the Skilled Hand."

LLUDD, son of Beli Mawr; London was allegedly named for him (Caer Lludd, later Llundein). His kingdom was besieged by three plagues, but he rid them with the counsel of his brother Lleuelys.

LLWYD, son of Cil Coed, friend of Gwawl son of Clud; he avenged Gwawl's maltreatment in the game of "Badger-in-the-Bag" by enchanting the land of Dyfed. Later he released the enchantment and restored Rhiannon and Pryderi in exchange for his pregnant wife, who had been transformed into a mouse.

MABON, son of Modron, stolen from his mother when three nights old and imprisoned until Arthur freed him. The *mabinogi* may have originally told of his birth and exploits. His doublet occurs, perhaps, in the name Mabon son of Mellt ("lightning").

MAELGWN GWYNEDD, an historical sixth-century king of Gwynedd, denounced by the contemporary historian Gildas (*De Excidio Britanniae*) for being excessively fond of listening to his own praise sung by poets, a fact well supported by our story.

MANAWYDAN, son of Llŷr, husband of Rhiannon after the death of Pwyll.

MATH, son of Mathonwy, Lord of Gwynedd in northern Wales; he and his nephew Gwydion were powerful magicians.

MATHOLWCH, a king of Ireland; he wed Branwen daughter of Llŷr.

MAY-DAY, the beginning of Summer, one of the four great quarter days of Celtic tradition, the others being August 1 (in Ireland, the festival of Lughnasadh, commemorating the god Lugh), November 1, the beginning of Winter, the dark half of the year, and February 1. In Irish tradition, November 1 (*Samhain*) was the most auspicious of these quarter days; it was a day when the doors of the Otherworld stood open and there was free passage between it and the world of mortals. It was also a day on which magical and ominous events took place. In Welsh tradition, this significance seems to have been shifted to the other end of the year, May 1.

MERLIN, poet and prophet, known in Welsh as Myrddin, in later romance he became a celebrated magician.

MORFRAN, "Great-crow," hideous son of Ceridwen; he was also called Y Fagddu (alternatively, Afagddu), which means "utter darkness."

NISIEN, benevolent son of Euroswydd, half-brother of Bendigeidfran, Manawydan, and Branwen.

OLWEN, daughter of Ysbaddaden Chief-giant.

PENDARAN DYFED, fosterer of Pryderi son of Pwyll; it was he who decided that Gwri would be renamed Pryderi.

PORTER, an officer in the court of a king, who, along with the door-keepers, was responsible for the traffic into and out of the fort and the like. They must have been a surly lot, and must have challenged visitors often and peremptorily, for there were special fines levied against them for wrongly challenging one of the king's advisors.

PRYDERI, son of Pwyll and Rhiannon; he disappeared the night of his birth and was found by Teyrnon Twrf Liant and his wife, who called him Gwri Golden-hair.

PWYLL, Prince of Dyfed, Head of Annwfn; he was the father of Pryderi and husband of Rhiannon. His principal temporal residence was at Arberth.

RHIANNON, wife of Pwyll, mother of Pryderi, daughter of Hyfaidd Hen.

RHUN, son of Maelgwn Gwynedd; he was sent to seduce Elphin's wife, but was foiled by Taliesin.

TALIESIN, divine, or divinely inspired, poet, whose epiphany occurred in the fish-dam of Gwyddno Garanhir.

TEYRNON TWRF LIANT, Lord of Gwent Is Coed; he and his wife raised Gwri Golden-hair (later named Pryderi).

TWRCH TRWYTH, son of Taredd, said to have been turned into a boar by God in punishment for his sins, but probably a reflex of the divine boar of Celtic mythology, who was known on the Continent as Moccus.

YSBADDADEN, Chief-giant, father of Olwen.

A Guide to Pronunciation

The following guide is intended only to enable those readers who do not know Middle or Modern Welsh to gain some feeling for the sound of the names in these tales. It is not intended as an accurate phonological inventory of the language. Equivalences are given in terms of American-English unless otherwise stated.

Welsh vowels are pronounced as follows:

i short as in *it*
long as in *eat*

e short as in *let*
long as in *late*

a short as in *pot*
long as in *father*

o short as in *cope*
long as in *mower*

w short as in *roof*
long as in *tool*
(sometimes a consonant, as in *wedi* 'after,' and pronounced as in Engl. *watch*)

u short as in *ill*
long as in *eel*

y In final syllables and stressed monosyllables:
short as in *in*
long as in *screen*
(in nonfinal syylables and unstressed monosyllables pronounced like the colorless sound in *but*)
(Note that there does not appear to be much difference between the sounds represented by Welsh *i*, *u*, and *y*; these may be articulated almost identically by the beginner.)

The Welsh diphthongs are best left with only the comment that they may be closely approximated by producing the sounds of the individual components as above, for example, *aw* by combining closely the vowel sounds of *pot* and *roof*, the result being something like the dipthong in American-English *how*.

Generally speaking, the Welsh consonants are more heavily aspirated than their American-English counterparts.

- *b* as in *best* (but approaching, e.g. *pest*)
- *c* as in *cat*; never as in *cent*
- *ch* as in German *ach*, Scottish *loch*; never as in *Engl. church*
- *d* as in *den*.
- *dd* as in *then* (i.e., voiced, as opposed to *thin*; cf. *th* below)
- *f* as in *of* (the sound of *v*)
- *ff* as in *off*
- *g* as in *get*; never as in *gin*
- *ng* as in *sing* (not as in *finger*)
- *ngh* as above followed by *h* as in *heart*
- *gw* at the beginning of a word is sometimes *g* + the consonant *w*, *e.g.*, *gwaith* 'work,' sometimes *g* + the vowel *w*, *e.g.*, *gwr* 'man,' sometimes *g* + rounding, e.g., *gwlad* 'country' which is monosyllabic
- *h* as in *heart*
- *l* as in *lady*
- *ll* has no English equivalent; it is the voiceless counterpart of the *l* sound and may be approximated by producing the combination *tl* as a single sound
- *m* as in *man*
- *n* as in *not*
- *mh* and *nh* are heavily aspirated nasal sounds
- *p* as in *park*
- *ph* as in *phrase*
- *r* trilled, with the tip of the tongue
- *rh* has no English equivalent; it is the voiceless *r* and may be approximated by pronouncing it as if it were written *hr* (without, of course, trilling the *r*)
- *s* as in *sap*; never as in *his*
- *t* as in *top*
- *th* as in *thin* (cf. *dd*, above)

The accent stands on the penultimate syllable. The sign ^ is sometimes used to indicate long vowels.

Index of Proper Names